10/23

Adverse Possession

Adverse Possession

by

Louis N. Jones

CONQUEST
PUBLISHERS

Bladensburg, Maryland
www.conquestpublishers.com

Conquest Publishers
A division of Conquest Industries, LLC
P.O. Box 611
Bladensburg, MD 20710-0611
www.conquestpublishers.com

ISBN: 978-0-9883809-3-6 (eBook)
ISBN: 978-0-9883809-7-4 (paperback)

Published in the United States of America

Be still before the Lord and wait patiently for him;

do not fret when people succeed in their ways, when they carry out their wicked schemes.

Refrain from anger and turn from wrath; do not fret—it leads only to evil.

For those who are evil will be destroyed, but those who hope in the Lord will inherit the land..

Psalm 37:7-9 (NIV)

6609 Bynum Drive

Her birth name was Lieselotte Koch, but most people in the neighborhood called her Lottie K. That was to differentiate her from Miss Lottie Morris, who lived farther down the road, near the cul-de-sac abutting Kent Gardens Park with its skyscraping white pines and cedars. Lottie K did not have a problem with the shortening of her name. After all, these darned Americans wanted everything so simple. The only time she heard her full name was when her relatives came to visit from her native Dresden. Even her American husband, who passed five years ago, simply called her "Lot."

It was a Wednesday morning in February. The residents of McLean, Virginia awoke to clear blue skies and weather chilly enough to whiten the dew that had fallen overnight on cars and lawns. Lottie's normal routine would go unchanged. At 7 a.m., she awoke and immediately switched on the TV to watch Charlie Rose. The TV was a 25-inch flat screen her daughter gave her last year for her 65th birthday, and it allowed her to spend time with Charlie in lifelike high definition. She delighted telling friends she had such a crush on him. At her age, calling it a crush was hardly apropos. Nonetheless, it made her feel more youthful and alive to try to cling to some trappings of her childhood, though most of them had long passed on.

By 7:30 a.m., she was downstairs switching off the burglar alarm near the front door. A woman her age living alone could not be too careful, she thought, though Fairfax County police had not answered a burglary call on Bynum Drive in ten years. It did not bother her that her alarm code was the same as her ATM code, which was the same as her daughter's gate code at her home in Sterling, which was the same as the month and day of her daughter's birthday. The fewer numbers she had to remember, the better.

Sometime between 7:30 and 7:45, she slipped on her Cole Haan down coat, a rare extravagant purchase from the Nordstrom at nearby Tysons Corner Center mall. She stepped outside just in time to greet a few of the neighborhood kids as they dipped in the rear of their parents' BMWs and Lexuses and headed off to school. The moment they saw Lottie, with her flaxen hair tied back into a bun and her supermodel complexion, they yelled, "Hi, Miss K!," further shortening her name. She always would respond with a wave or, if they were close enough, she would say, "Morning. Have a good day at school."

Lottie could tell that the kid who delivered the *Sun Gazette* this morning was the lazy rascal who rarely got out of his car, but tossed the paper from his driver's side window. Because her house, like most of the houses in the neighborhood, had front lawns about the length of a basketball court, the paper usually landed somewhere in the middle of the driveway, or on the top of her car. When this happened, Lottie had to walk down the driveway to retrieve the paper. However, this morning the paper landed in the middle of the yard, which meant it would be damp from the dew. Lottie grunted as she walked in the yard to retrieve her paper, the icy dew crunching under her slippers. She really preferred the kid who would walk up the driveway and place the paper neatly inside the mailbox, which was on the wall just to the left of her front door.

Over the past two months, Lottie K had added one slight thing to her routine. She glanced quickly at the five-bedroom, split-level ranch-styled house directly across from hers on Bynum Drive to make sure everything was okay. She had grown quite fond of the owners, a young couple who had bought the house just over a year ago for $950,000. Shortly after moving in, Jesse and Jennifer Kane saw Lottie in her front yard pruning the wild hydrangeas framing the eastern edge of her driveway, and they came over and talked with her. They talked frequently in the coming days and weeks, and their talks sometimes lasted for more than an hour. Whenever Lottie's 10-year-old granddaughter, Kaitlyn, came to visit her from Sterling, the Kanes' two children, 8-year-old Ashley and 7-year-old Aiden, would entertain her in their spacious basement, play the latest video games, and enjoy marathon couch potato sessions with *Adventures in Odyssey*. The Kanes had even invited Lottie to their church a few times, although Lottie was Catholic, and the Kanes' worship style was the loud hallelujah, lifting of the hands, falling prostrate on the floor, twirling in the aisles kind. Lottie couldn't really get into their worship style, but found the Kanes to be genuine and loving people, and connected with them based on their mutual admiration for each other.

Consequently, Lottie agreed to keep an eye on the Kanes' home while they were away on a missionary trip to Haiti. In a neighborhood as quiet and uneventful as Bynum Drive, the responsibility amounted to nothing more than making sure the UPS man hadn't placed any unexpected packages on their front doorstep. She did not need to worry about mail, because the Kanes had their mail temporarily held at the post office. The Kanes had left Lottie with the key to the house in case there were any emergencies, and in the past two months, she only needed to use it once. Two weeks ago, during heavy rain, she went to check the basement to make sure the rain did not flood it, as the sump pump was renowned for being lazy and finicky.

This morning, Lottie's quick glance at 6609 Bynum Drive found nothing out of order, so she went back inside her home to prepare for work. Today was a work day, so she could not salivate over Charlie Rose another hour. Instead, she had to shower and get dressed for her part-time fill-in receptionist job at Woodmore Associates, PC. Attorney Neil Woodmore had allowed his regular receptionist to attend morning classes at Northern Virginia Community College on Wednesdays, so Lottie K earned a few extra bucks, besides her social security checks, by filling in. After a quick bowl of muesli, Lottie reemerged from her home, climbed into her green Nissan Sentra, and headed off to work.

Unbeknownst to Lottie, someone was watching her every move. From the moment she emerged from her house, to the moment two minutes later when she started her car and pulled out of her driveway, eyes were focused on her.

Eyes were watching through the window from inside the master bedroom of 6609 Bynum Drive.

Adverse Possession

Coming Home

Three days prior

Jesse and Jennifer Kane disembarked their flight at Fort Lauderdale-Hollywood International Airport at 9:17 a.m. Jesse could not stand planes, and could only tolerate one flight per day. Once they cleared customs, they picked up a Lincoln Navigator at the Avis car rental booth, loaded seven bags of luggage into it, and began the 12-hour trip up I-75 toward Knoxville, Tennessee. They had been in Haiti for more than two months, and were anxious to get to Jennifer's parents' house to reunite with their kids.

"Slow down a bit, honey," Jennifer said to her husband, watching as the roadside palm trees whizzed by so fast, she could barely count them.

"Sorry," Jesse said, braking gently until the vehicle speed gauge read 70. His voice was deep and smooth, like a balm. "I'm trying to get there before it gets too late. I don't want the kids waiting up."

"Well, they ain't seen their Ma and Pa since Thanksgiving,

so what's the harm in them staying up a little longer to see us?" Jennifer's southern twang was proud and prominent. "They ain't gon' be able to sleep anyway."

"I'm more concerned about your parents. By the time the weather girl shows up on the 10 o'clock news, they're passed out. It's like clockwork. I don't want the kids keeping them up."

"Well, I think all parties concerned would be better off if we got there safely, or at least without being pulled over by a Florida State trooper."

That was Jennifer, always the voice of reason. It was one reason Jesse married her. The others were her compassion, her soft-spokenness relative to his own, and her passionate faith in God. Jesse cited these reasons whenever Jennifer asked him the question, *Why did you marry me?* The question came occasionally, usually when Jennifer suffered one of her frequent bouts of insecurity. Why would Jesse, a preacher's kid and eventual heir to the throne of one of the East Coast's biggest Pentecostal churches, be interested in Jennifer, the daughter of a manufacturing plant worker and a stock clerk at Hackney's? With Jesse's pedigree, he could have married someone worldlier and more sophisticated than Jennifer. Despite Jesse's frequent displays of love for her, Jennifer felt that he was too good for her.

They had met 10 years earlier, during a Christian financial development conference led by Jesse's father, Rodereck Kane. The small church that held the conference was booked to capacity within days of the conference being announced on WKCR radio. Jennifer Trudeau was lucky to be able to get three tickets before the closing of registration. She had frequently listened to Rodereck Kane's national broadcasts, particularly his signature message of living in prosperity. His message resonated with her because she wanted that type of life for herself. Growing up with her parents in Knoxville, they were never quite poor, but were always a paycheck or two from being there. Her dad usually started work the same time her mother got home from work, so she saw her parents together only on weekends. Her parents barely earned enough to pay the mortgage on their three-bedroom rambler on Pelham Park Road. When they paid for groceries and other necessities, there was nothing left over for luxuries such as clothes shopping or a night out at the movies. It was a hardscrabble life that Jennifer had no interest in emulating.

Yet Jennifer so loved her parents that any opportunity she could find to get them out of the house for a night on the town, she would. Since the conference tickets were free, she invited her parents to attend with her. Neither of her parents had been to church much since the days her grandparents would drag them off on selected Sundays, and they had little interest in déjà vu. However, since their daughter went through the trouble to obtain the tickets, they agreed to attend.

The day of the conference, Jennifer and her parents arrived early and found seats near the front of the auditorium. The conference began with fiery worship and praise for about 30 minutes, then moved to a heartfelt greeting and welcome from the host pastors. About 45 minutes after the start of the program, Rodereck Kane took the stage. Tall and thin, but not skinny, he led the congregation in an exuberant praise to God. His hands were lifted, his eyes blue and earnest, his crow's feet barely visible under his makeup, his almost impossibly well-coifed jet-black hair glimmering in the glow of the overhead lights. His voice was strong, with just the right measure of bass to give it a commanding, authoritative vibe. When he launched into his presentation, talking about the spiritual aspects of money, the Trudeaus paid rapt attention.

Midway through his talk, he brought another minister to the stage. Jesse Kane was almost the mirror image of his father, but more muscular and chiseled, revealing he had spent more time in the gym than his father. Jesse Kane gave a testimony about how following his father's financial principles got him through bankruptcy in his early 20s, and needing to give up his first home. During his talk, he looked around the audience and made eye contact with several people, as his father had taught him to do to connect with his audience. When he made eye contact with Jennifer, he no longer looked at anyone else.

Jesse would describe it as divine providence that Jennifer Trudeau caught his eye. After all, she was cute, but not remarkably gorgeous. The ends of her blond hair brushed her shoulders, and a slight run of barely noticeable freckles ran from cheek to cheek. Her bangs hung like a valance above her dark brown eyes, and she wore no jewelry or makeup—not even lipstick. She was model slender, but not skinny, and she wore a simple cream-colored blouse and blue jeans. She bore a striking contrast to a few of the other women seated in the first two rows. These women were dressed to the nines, complete with short three-figure skirts, legs crossed and heels dangling from well-manicured feet, décolletages slightly restrained and respectable for church but still prominently on display. These women were on the prowl for financially secure single ministers who were lonely and looking for love, and Jesse seemed to fit the bill. Jesse was financially secure, and the director of evangelism and missions at his father's church, Harvest of Righteousness Fellowship of Manassas, Virginia. He was not lonely, but he *was* looking for love. That day, during the final leg of his several minute testimony, he could not keep his eyes off Jennifer, though she was the plainest looking woman at the front of the church.

The only thing Jennifer wondered was, "Why is he looking at me so much?"

She would find out when, after the service was over, Jesse scrambled his way past several well-wishers to catch up with Jennifer, who was about to leave with her parents. They would only chat for a couple of minutes, while her mother stood by watching, and her dad went to get the car. It was enough time for him to tell her that he wanted to get to know her a little better. She would say, nonchalantly, "I'm not interested." Nevertheless, it was okay. Jesse would not press. After all, if God had meant for the two of them to be together, God would make it happen.

Divine providence came again when Jennifer's mother, under the guise of having forgotten her cell phone, returned to the church, found Jesse greeting other guests, and gently interrupted him. Sammie Trudeau gave Jesse a piece of paper with Jennifer's cell number written on it, and said only, "Call her. She's a little shy, but she'll warm up to you." Then she left as abruptly as she arrived. Sammie was not normally in the business of playing matchmaker, but she knew a good catch when she saw one. At the time, she had been married to her husband for 22 years, having married a year after Jennifer was born. Their marriage had their fluctuations, but she knew that Harlan Trudeau was a good man, and she would not trade him for all the tea in China.

As Sammie suggested, Jesse called Jennifer, and Jennifer immediately bucked. Fifty things went through her mind. Why would this proper gentleman be interested in me? On what level can I relate to him? What do we have in common? She hoped he was not one of those rich men who liked to slum it in the ghetto, searching out chicks with no profile, pedigree, or connections, have their way with them, and then slip them a few bucks to keep quiet. That was something those rich men could not do to rich socialites, not without Wendy Williams talking about it on TV the next day.

Jennifer decided she would humor him. After all, once he got to know the real Jennifer, he would hightail it in the other direction. She would tell him about her life growing up right next to a trailer park. She would tell him about the time she smoked a joint in Bobby Simons' rusty Mustang in the Shoney's parking lot. She would mention that during a two-year period in her life after she graduated from Austin East High School, more guys spent the night on top of her than a Sealy Posturepedic. She fully expected that he would lose her number, like so many other "good" men that had approached her.

Nevertheless, Jesse would not budge. He continued to call her, night after night. Rather than focus on all the negative aspects of her life, he preferred to focus on her life since she accepted Christ. He wanted to talk about her goals, and her aspirations, and what God was doing with her. He spent many hours listening to her talk about her parents, her grandparents, her aunts, her uncles, her cousins. He wanted to talk about her life growing up as an only child, since he was also one. He even confessed a few sins of his own as a teenager growing up in suburban Virginia, including the time he passed out after winning a drinking game at a college party, and several occasions of lying. He also spoke candidly about his father's divorcing his mom when he was 18. The confessions removed his "golden boy" sheen, but humanized him in Jennifer's eyes.

After two years of dating, they were married in a small Baptist church in downtown Knoxville. It was a wedding attended mostly by the relatives of the bride and groom, along with a few select friends. Rodereck Kane officiated over the wedding, mostly to keep up appearances. Still, deep inside, he loathed his son's choice of a wife. He would have preferred Jesse to marry one of the bourgeois "well-bred" single women at his church. He did not care if Jesse married pretty or ugly, black or white, thin or fat, if she had a pedigree that was in keeping with a successful minister. With Jennifer's past involving drug use and promiscuity, she did not have a dog in that fight. Rodereck was glad that at least Jesse insisted that Jennifer get a blood test before they married.

They were riding past Valdosta, Georgia when Jesse's cell chirped out *Amazing Grace* at twice the normal beat. Jennifer grabbed his phone from the armrest compartment and checked the caller ID.

"Who is it?" Jesse asked, his attention never wavering from the road.

"Says unknown number," Jennifer replied. She pushed the answer button and held the phone to her ear. "Hello?"

She heard about five seconds of silence before she heard a

click. She again looked at the phone display and, confirming the call was disconnected, placed the phone on the seat beside her. "Probably one of your girlfriends callin' you," she said.

Jesse scoffed, knowing that Jennifer was only joking. He also knew that she had never completely let go of a slight belief that he was receiving clandestine telephone calls from other women. Nonetheless, he had to reassure her.

"Honey, I would never cheat on you. You know that," Jesse told her.

"Really?" Jennifer's voice was challenging. "How do I know that? How do *you* know that? Everyone that's ever cheated on their spouse at one time said, 'I will never cheat on you.' How do I know that statement is valid?"

"Would you feel better if I told you that, statistically, there's an 80 percent chance that I will cheat on you?" Jesse said, quoting a statistic that he read in some blog.

"No, but at least I know you were living in reality."

"And what is that reality? Believe that one day I will cheat on you?" Jesse said. "No. I don't like impure thoughts like that. I prefer to focus my mind on what I need to do, and that's be completely faithful to you, no matter what stats say."

"Well, I thought that since you're a chip off the old block … ."

That statement angered Jesse so much that he pulled off to the side of the road in front of a shopping mall. He firmly placed the car in park and looked at Jennifer intently.

"Jennifer, we've been around about this for years now." Jesse's glare was angry yet reassuring. "I adore my father, but I am not him. He made a choice. I don't have to make the same choice. There's no cheating DNA running around in my body.

If anything, the way my Pop hurt my Mom, I would rather do anything than subject you to that kind of experience."

Jennifer stared straight ahead. The *vroom* of cars whizzing by punctuated the silence.

"Jen?"

She turned to him, searching his eyes.

"I love you. I wish you would believe that."

"I do believe that," Jennifer said. "Growing up hard makes you skeptical, I guess." She grabbed the phone from her seat and placed it back into the armrest compartment. "I should never have answered your phone. I need to trust you."

"I don't mind you answering my phone." Jesse put the car in drive and edged back onto I-75. "That's only because I have nothing to hide."

"I know. I'm sorry." Jennifer leaned toward him and gently stroked his forearm. "Let me make it up to you. There's a Hampton Inn we just passed. Let's turn around."

Jesse smiled. "What about the kids?"

"I'll call Ma and tell her we're gonna stop at a hotel, and we'll be at their house tomorrow morning. We ain't have much time to spend together in Haiti, so this may be the last hurrah before we get the kids and head back home."

"Yeah." Jesse took the next exit so he could cloverleaf to the other side of the highway. "But I, for one, cannot wait to get back home. I look forward to sleeping in my own bed."

* * *

Jesse and Jennifer would leave the hotel early the next morning and arrive at Knoxville shortly after 1 p.m. A light snow had fallen in the town, enough to blanch most of the grassy areas, but not enough to stick to roads or hinder travel. When they pulled onto Pelham Park Road, most of the snow had melted under the midday sun and cast a waxy sheen on every hard surface in sight.

Harlan and Samantha Trudeau lived in the same white siding rambler they had purchased when Jennifer was born, only now they did not own it. The house had been placed into foreclosure shortly after Jennifer moved with her husband to Northern Virginia after their honeymoon. The Trudeaus were too prideful to tell their daughter and son-in-law about the foreclosure. However, Jennifer learned about it only after she came across the foreclosure papers during a routine visit to her parents. Jennifer confronted her parents about the foreclosure, and after several heated words, slammed doors, and pouty faces, she called Jesse for assistance. Jesse drove to Knoxville, met with the new owners, and found out that they only intended to use the home as an investment property. He negotiated a deal where Harvest of Righteousness would lease the home for 10 years, and the Trudeaus would pay rent to the church as sublets. Rodereck found out about the deal afterwards, and was angry that they had not consulted him beforehand. It caused a rift between him and his son that had never healed.

The house was, like most ramblers, a one-story rectangular box with a gabled roof and vinyl siding that was badly in need of a coat of paint. It was the only house on the block with a wire fence surrounding the yard. A small shed sat near the rear of the property; next to the driveway, an old transmission and two rusty shock absorbers were perched on both sides of the door. A small barbecue grill sat alongside the driveway side of the house, along with a water hose that had unraveled and curled among the bushes like a rattler poised to strike. Jesse pulled the Navigator into the gravel driveway of the house. They parked next to their Nissan Armada, which they had driven down from McLean to drop off the kids before their trip to Haiti.

Jennifer looked around and did not see her dad's Ford Ranger anywhere. This meant that he was either at work, or hanging out at the bar and grill next to the pier on Fort Loudon Lake. Since it was too early to hang out at the bar and grill, and since he rarely went anywhere else without Samantha, Jennifer guessed that he was at work.

The noise from the crunching of the gravel drew Ashley Kane's attention, and she peered out the living room window. When she saw that the driver of the huge SUV was her father, she turned quickly, her armpit-length pigtails slapping her neck. She bolted to the front door and flung it open, straining the door's weak hinges.

"Ashley!"

The voice was from Samantha, seated in the dining room directly next to the living room. Ashley stopped to explain, almost pleading with her cherubic face and doe eyes that appeared larger through the lens of her glasses.

"It's Ma and Pa. They're here!"

"Put on your jacket and toboggan first," Samantha said.

Ashley's announcement of the arrival of Jesse and Jennifer was the rare thing that could draw Aiden's attention from the bullets and gore video game he was playing. He dropped the controller and tore out of the bedroom. He was just in time to see Ashley grab her coat from the living room coat rack and Samantha approach the front door.

"Ma and Pa are back," Ashley told him. She waited for what seemed like forever for Aiden to slip on his coat. They ran out the front door, barely touched by the drops of melting snow falling across the front porch. They ran around to the passenger side of the Navigator, where Jennifer had just stepped out of the vehicle. They charged toward her with the urgency of a victory-starved linebacker.

Jennifer knelt to receive her children's hugs, kisses, and declarations of how much they missed her. She then sent the kids around to Jesse, who received his fair share of squeezes and moist cool lips. The family walked together to the front porch, where Samantha was waiting. Her grey-streaked blond hair hung disheveled on her shoulders, and her stout frame was draped in an open peacoat that she had bought for seven bucks from the Goodwill.

"Welcome home," Samantha said, hugging both her daughter and her son-in-law. "Harlan and I are so glad you made it home safely." Her southern, Alabama-bred accent was prominent.

"Glad to be home, Ma," Jesse said. It took him a while to get used to calling his mother-in-law "Ma." He had always reserved that name for his natural mother, Camille, whom he still spoke with weekly though she and his father were divorced. Calling another woman "Ma" felt strange to him. It was like calling another woman "honey" instead of his wife. It was only after his mother told him she had no issue with him calling Samantha "Ma" that Jesse eventually warmed up to it.

———

He had no such issues with calling Harlan "Pop," however. Harlan had given Jesse tons of advice about how to conduct himself in a marriage and relate to his wife. Their talks had drawn them closer together. Jesse felt that Harlan was acting more like a father to him than his natural father. He knew that Rodereck secretly hoped and predicted that the marriage would not work out. Jesse was determined to prove him wrong.

They sat around the dining room table and ate turkey and rye sandwiches for lunch, and then talked about Jesse and Jennifer's time in Haiti helping to build schools for orphaned children. Afterwards, Aiden, who was not one for crowds of more than three people, went back downstairs to finish playing his video game. Ashley could not resist the urge to be a tattletale.

"He's down there playing *Medal of Honor*," she said, loud enough for Aiden to hear.

"What's *Medal of Honor*?" Jesse asked, looking at Samantha.

"It's a war game," Ashley said before Samantha could speak up.

"I didn't know he was playing that," Samantha said, slightly flustered. "I reckon he got it from one of his friends in the neighborhood."

"I'll talk to him," Jennifer said, leaving the table and heading downstairs.

"Check the emails while you're at it," Jesse said to his wife. She acknowledged him with a nod and disappeared through the doorway leading to the basement.

Jesse looked at Samantha, who could tell what he was thinking.

Adverse Possession

"I do respect your wishes," Samantha told him before he could say anything. "I know you don't want your kids playing them violent video games. I really didn't know that's what he was playing."

Jesse nodded. He had no reason to believe that Samantha was lying or being neglectful. "I know. Jen will deal with it." He quickly changed the subject. "How's Pop?"

"Doing good," Samantha said. "He got a merit increase last month."

"That's great," said Jesse.

"Yeah. Maybe we can afford to move outta this dump at some point."

"How have you been doing with the rent?"

"Good. We keeping up. Doing everything you told us. I offered to go back to work at one point, but Harlan ain't wanna heard none of it. He likes me barefoot and not pregnant."

Jesse looked around to see where Ashley was, and saw that she had gone back to her bedroom. Jesse lowered his voice to almost a whisper. "And Pop's staying away from it?"

"He is, so far. I mean, I ain't gonna tell you he don't play the Powerball from time to time."

"But no illegal joints?"

"No. He's done with that. You know they raided one over on Asheville last month."

"And he's going to meetings?" said Jesse.

"He was going to meetings at the church on Old Rutledge, up the road a piece, but they closed the meeting down for some reason," Samantha said. "Now the closest one is all the way in Nashville. So, he ain't been to one in a while."

"Ma, he needs to go to meetings," Jesse said. "Since you

guys aren't going to church, at the very least, he needs that. Other than that, you have to start going to church. He can't do this on his own."

"He been doing okay, since they shut down the meeting a year ago," said Samantha. "He been fine."

"He's not fine, Ma. He's still playing the Powerball, and that's gambling. May be legalized, but it's still gambling. That spirit is still present … ."

Jesse cut off his statement when he heard the muffled thud of footsteps ascending the basement stairs. Neither Jennifer nor the kids knew anything about Harlan's addictive gambling. Samantha had urged Jesse to keep it that way, not wanting to diminish Harlan in the eyes of his daughter and grandchildren. Jesse agreed to keep the secret, but hoped that after a 12-year addiction, he would be completely healed by now. Harlan's addiction led to the foreclosure of their home. Jesse was afraid that if Harlan did not continue to address his problem, he would relapse, and the Trudeaus would still lose their home. He knew that his father was just waiting for the Trudeaus to slip up, so he could evict them without much moral scrutiny.

Jennifer peeked at Jesse from around the basement door. "Honey, have you been checking the emails?"

Jesse shook his head. "No. Not since a week ago."

"All of them are un-bolded. Like they've been read. Even those that came in earlier today."

"Maybe the kids were on the computer."

"They were, but they don't have access to our email. They don't have the password. We changed it when we were in Haiti. Remember?"

"Yeah," said Jesse. "Well, there's probably a glitch in the system, or something."

"Okay. I'll call Verizon tomorrow."

Jennifer went back downstairs.

Neither she nor Jesse had any clue that their email *glitch* was anything but.

Power Play

* * *

Rodereck Kane walked in the Harvest of Righteousness conference room at 7:07 p.m., a few minutes late. He found all six of his elders and all 12 of his deacons gathered around the oak veneer conference table. Some were sitting. Some were standing. All were talking, except two, who were studying iPads and cell phones. He greeted a few of them, and then ordered everyone to their seats. There were several whooshes of air as everyone sat in the plushy cushioned faux-leather chairs.

Rodereck liked to have meetings with his ministerial staff at least twice per week, once on Tuesday evenings, and again on Friday evenings. He had meetings frequently so that issues did not build up so much that he needed to have long, marathon meetings that he could not stand. He wanted to have his meetings quickly, and then be done. *Time is money*, he liked to say, and he did not like to waste either of them.

He started the meeting with a prayer, then an encouragement

from Scripture, as he did almost every meeting. Then he entertained issues and concerns from his clergy, listening attentively to each of them. Then, he either tabled the item for later follow-up or addressed it directly. He had little patience for argument or spontaneous debate, and he would shut it off when it happened. If there were disagreement, he would bring the disagreeing parties together and deal with them separately. This meeting was not the time for squabbles.

Midway through the meeting, it was time for Elder Jayson O'Reilly, chair of the Council of Trustees, to give his report. Elder O'Reilly was the official bean counter for the church, but his bald head, thin blond mustache, intense stare, and serious demeanor could have easily qualified him for security. He spent most of the meeting flipping through papers and jotting things down, and did not stop even as he gave his report.

"The lease will be expiring on our property in Tennessee in a couple of months," Elder O'Reilly explained. "The owners want to know if we would like to renew the lease for another five years."

Elder Marty Williams, who had only been on the leadership team for a year, asked, "Why do we lease a property in Tennessee?"

"It's my son's doing," Rodereck said, with no small amount of disgust. "His in-laws once owned the home, but it was foreclosed, so my son signed a 10-year lease with the new owners, and then sublet the house to his in-laws."

"And then basically subsidized their rent," Elder O'Reilly said. "We are paying 1,200 dollars a month in rent, but the Trudeaus are only paying us back 400 dollars per month."

"And we've been doing this for 10 years?" Elder Williams

asked.

"Yes," Elder O'Reilly answered. "And that's why it is my recommendation that we move on from this."

"You mean let the lease expire?" Elder Williams asked.

"Yes."

"What will that mean for the tenants?"

"It means they will have to leave," Rodereck said. "We've been doing this for 10 years. We've done our part. It's time to let the Trudeaus take personal responsibility." He gave Elder O'Reilly a nod for him to move on with the rest of his report.

"What if they are not in a position to move in two months?" Elder Williams persisted. "Are we just going to put them out?"

"They are free to negotiate a rental agreement with the owners and remain in the home," Rodereck said.

"That won't happen." Elder O'Reilly finally laid his papers down and looked around at everyone seated around the table. "Apparently the Trudeaus do not have very good credit. The owners feel that leasing to them directly would be a risk. Not to mention, word on the street is that Mr. Trudeau has a gambling problem."

"Haven't they been paying the rent on time to the church?" Elder Williams asked.

"Yes," Elder O'Reilly answered. "But we are only talking 400 dollars here. My 15-year-old grandson can probably pay that without a problem. But the Trudeaus bring home only 20K a year combined. Paying 1,200 dollars in rent may be an issue. Plus, the rent for them will likely be higher, because the owners are taking on a huge risk."

"I don't want to shoulder this any longer," Rodereck said. "The church has been paying rent on this house for ten years.

Adverse Possession

We've done all we can to help this couple. Elder O'Reilly, please send a letter to the owners letting them know we will not renew the lease. Then, contact our attorneys to find out what type of legal notice we have to give to the tenants in Tennessee."

"Shouldn't we at least talk to the Trudeaus first, see if they are able to leave?" Elder Williams said. His comment drew reluctant nods from most of the elders and deacons at the table. Most of them had previously chosen to remain silent, because they knew how divisive this issue had been between Rodereck and Jesse. They were more than content to let Elder Williams speak for them.

"I'm making a business decision as pastor of this church," Rodereck said, his annoyed stare directed at Elder Williams. "I don't consult with certain outsiders to help inform my decisions."

"What about them?" Elder Williams continued. "What about the Trudeaus? What if they become homeless? As a church, shouldn't we be concerned about that? According to you, this wasn't even your idea. Maybe we should talk to Jesse Kane and see what he thinks."

The mere mention of Jesse Kane caused some of the deacons and elders to moan and rear back in their seats.

"Elder Williams, let's get one thing straight. I don't need to consult my son on a matter that has this church spending 1,200 dollars a month and receiving zero benefit." Rodereck directed his glare away from Elder Williams to the rest of the group. "The Trudeaus have taken advantage of this church for too long. They're paying 400 dollars a month for a three-bedroom home. Of course they are going to milk that for all it's worth. They have no motivation to work on paying market rate rent. The hallmark of my ministry, and my financial empowerment seminars, is getting people to take personal responsibility. I have no intention of letting this church become a welfare system for people who don't recognize the need to better themselves."

Rodereck knew Elder Williams had a response, but did not look his way nor allow him a second to speak. He looked straight at Elder O'Reilly and said, "Is there anything else, elder?"

Elder Williams spoke up. "I'm not finished, pastor. I don't see a problem with going on a month-to-month basis with the owners and allowing the Trudeaus more time to get their act together. With their income, it's going to take more than two months to find affordable housing. And then, figure in security deposits, time off work. It just makes no sense, and these are your son's in-laws. I think this is a personal decision rather than a business decision."

Rodereck's response was immediate. "Elder Williams, you're dismissed."

Elder Williams looked around at the group. Most of them were looking down at the table. He stood and adjusted his blazer. "Am I dismissed from this meeting, or dismissed from the church?"

"Dismissed from this *meeting*," Rodereck said, not taking his eyes off Elder Williams. "We'll decide the *other* when cooler heads prevail."

Elder Williams shot a final disapproving glare at Rodereck, and then walked out of the room.

Rodereck surveyed the group. Their silence was not

a stunned silence. In fact, dismissing someone from his meetings was usual for Rodereck, especially when someone challenged his authority or dared to argue with him. Each of them had gotten the boot at one time or another. It would probably happen again.

Rodereck repeated his question to Elder O'Reilly. "Is there anything else?"

Elder O'Reilly looked down at his papers again. "Yes, there's the tithe and offering report … ."

* * *

After the meeting, Rodereck went back to his office. He tossed his notepad on his cherry wood desk, and sat in a recliner facing his office window, which allowed an overhead view of the parking lot in the rear of his church. He seethed as he watched his elders file to their cars. He had let Elder Williams get under his skin, and Rodereck had only appointed him to the leadership team a year ago. He would not let Elder Williams, or anyone else, challenge him like that. This was his church, and he strived to make certain his authority was well understood.

Rodereck knew a lot about challenging pastors, because that was how he became one. He had joined an independent charismatic church shortly after his four years in Virginia Tech majoring in business management. Upon joining the church, he decided that he wanted to be in ministry, and set plans in motion to become a leader of the church. In his spare time—when he was not working his full-time job at a tech company as a marketing director—he was contributing his business acumen and marketing skills to the church. He helped it grow from 50 members to almost 300 within three years. He so impressed the senior pastor, David Seagraves, that Seagraves promoted Rodereck to the position of deacon after two years in the church, and then a year later, to associate pastor. Rodereck continued to apply his skills, and saw the church grow by 50 more members over the next year, with less than half that lost due to attrition.

Rodereck had also developed skills as a capable and charismatic speaker, and his ambition was stratospheric. Members in the church liked him, and preferred his leadership and teaching over that of Pastor Seagraves.

Outwardly, Pastor Seagraves appeared to support his charge. Inwardly, he detested Rodereck's growing popularity and grew suspicious of several initiatives that he felt were designed to cement Rodereck's status as a more capable leader of the church. One initiative was to cozy up to state leaders to obtain state funding for a program to train unemployed residents in building maintenance and landscaping. He did not get the funding that year, and Rodereck blamed Pastor Seagraves, who refused to eliminate religious education from the program plan.

Nonetheless, Rodereck's popularity increased, and he was asked to be a guest speaker at a business development conference sponsored by a gigantic megachurch in the area. Rodereck accepted the invitation, and through it, met and became good friends with the senior pastor of the megachurch, Bishop Albert Woodmore. Through his friendship with the bishop, Rodereck expanded his network of friends and associates, one of whom was the woman who would become his wife. Camille Fairchild was in charge of the megachurch's business initiatives.

Rodereck and Camille would marry just six months after they met. They married at the megachurch, and the bishop officiated over the wedding, which angered Pastor Seagraves even more. Pastor Seagraves attended the wedding to keep up appearances, but he knew he had lost control of his ambitious charge.

Three months later, Rodereck started a nonprofit organization, with his wife, Bishop Woodmore, and himself as the initial incorporators. He called the organization Harvest of Righteousness, Inc. Through his and Bishop Woodmore's connections, they got an attorney, an accountant, and two owners of well-established building and maintenance companies to join his board. He applied for the state funding again. This time, he got it, to the tune of $100,000.

By this time, Rodereck no longer felt a need to continue to attend Pastor Seagraves' church. He attended Bishop Woodmore's church with his wife, and all but abandoned Pastor Seagraves.

At a Sunday service, a visiting pastor prophesied over Rodereck and told him that God was calling him to start his own church.

Rodereck took that as a sign from God that it was time to begin.

Using his savings and some financial support from Bishop Woodmore, Rodereck leased a vacant property in Manassas that once held a carpet store. He used volunteers to fix it up, and then announced the first service of Harvest of Righteousness.

Forty people showed, including twenty from Pastor

Seagraves' church. Rodereck knew that with the tithes and offerings from forty people, he could not make the $5,000 per month lease payments on the property.

He started using the same tactics he had used with Pastor Seagraves' church. He conducted surveys of the surrounding neighborhood to learn the residents' needs and what they were looking for in a church. He used those surveys to make changes to the structure of his church, and then drew the neighborhood in with special events such as health screenings, fun days for children, and free concerts. He shortened his services to two hours, in deference to the busy lifestyles of Washington area families. Within three months, his congregation had grown to 100 people.

Eventually he outgrew the old carpet store, so Rodereck leased a larger property farther up on Rixlew Lane. Word got back to Pastor Seagraves' church that Harvest of Righteousness was flourishing and would not be a fly-by-night operation. Several members of pastor Seagraves' church left and joined Rodereck's church. By this time, his average Sunday attendance was greater than 150 people, including a few well-heeled tithe givers who wrote checks weighty enough to pay the monthly lease with plenty to spare.

Rodereck had met his goal. He was a successful pastor. He felt so confident in his financial status that he and his wife had their first child, Jesse, named for the biblical character.

That was more than 30 years ago. He had not spoken to Pastor Seagraves since, and was not even sure if he was still alive. Still, Rodereck was a successful pastor with a growing church. He had achieved his goals, but that was the easy part.

The hard part was holding on to everything he had worked

hard to get. Many people, he surmised, wanted to get their hands on Harvest of Righteousness. Some people joined specifically for that purpose, but he knew who they were, because he knew himself. He could spot the telltale signs that warned him someone was going to try to make a move for the church.

He did not spot those signs in Elder Williams at first. That was what baffled him. Elder Williams did not have that type of ambition, and seemed reluctant to take on a ministerial role. But now, Rodereck was not so sure. He had to keep his eye on Elder Williams and make sure he was kept in his place. It was not Williams' place to second guess or question Rodereck. Nor was it anyone else's. Not even his son's.

This was his church, of which Rodereck was immensely proud. And he had every intention of keeping it that way.

Something Amiss

* * *

Jesse and Jennifer had planned to stay at the Trudeaus' for only an hour or so, enough time to have lunch and get the kids' luggage loaded in their SUV before they headed out for the nine-hour trip back to McLean. But Samantha pressed them to stay long enough to see Harlan when he got home. Since Harlan was scheduled to work until 3 p.m., and would likely not make it home until 4, Jesse knew they probably would not get on the road until at least 5 p.m., which was too late for his tastes. Jesse and Jennifer agreed to double the kids in one bedroom, and they would spend the night in the remaining bedroom and head out in the morning. Samantha was delighted at the decision, and headed out to the supermarket in the Kanes' SUV to buy groceries, intending to cook a fabulous dinner.

Jesse remembered the first night, 10 years ago, he had spent in the Trudeaus' home, and he absolutely hated it. When they were dating, maintaining a long distance relationship had not been easy for them. Given Jesse's responsibilities at the church, it was difficult for him to drive to Knoxville to see Jennifer, so he would often send her plane tickets to come to Virginia to see him during weekends.

When they got engaged, Jesse made his first trip to Knoxville since meeting Jennifer. Since one of Jesse's favorite vacation spots was a resort in West Virginia, they had decided to marry in Knoxville so they would be closer to the resort for their honeymoon. About three weeks before the wedding, Jesse drove to Knoxville so he could accompany Jennifer to the clerk's office to obtain a marriage license. He had booked a hotel room so he could spend the night, and then drive back to Virginia the next day. However, after their late night at the movies, Jennifer insisted he spend the night in the Trudeaus' spare bedroom so that she could cook him breakfast early the next morning. Not wanting to disappoint his wife, and detesting confrontation, he agreed, although everything inside him wanted to resist.

Though the Trudeaus' home was not sloppy or unclean, it was homely enough to test Jesse's posh sensibilities. He was used to sleeping on plush beds draped with high-thread-count Egyptian cotton sheets. Instead, he had to sleep on a thin mattress with sheets that were so hard and stiff they might as well have been tarps. It was also a 90-degree day in the middle of June, and the Trudeaus did not have air conditioning. The lone box fan in the window shook and clanked, but its noise paled in comparison to the neighbors. Their loud, often obscene nighttime backyard conversations floated across the air and landed on Jesse's delicate ears.

He thought God's sense of humor was fully in play when

Jennifer asked him the next morning, "How did you sleep?"

"Not too well," Jesse answered, explaining why. Jennifer apologized and promised that things would be better for his next stay. They were, in a sense. The only thing that had changed was that Harlan had replaced the box fan with another box fan, the $4.99 Goodwill price sticker still prominently on the front of the grill.

He had no idea that years later he would travel to Haiti and spend all of two months sleeping on an air mattress in a leaky tent with neither fans nor air conditioning. It was moments like this, besides marrying Jennifer, which helped to break Jesse free of his hoity-toity lifestyle. It caused him to connect better with people who were not as privileged as he was.

He was 22 years old—and his bachelor's degree in business administration was hot off the press—when his father appointed him to the role of director of evangelism and missions. The title was designed to make Jesse seem as if he were chief over a department of workers, but in fact it was just he and an extroverted man from the church who had a passion to convert non-believers to Jesus. Jesse had no sense of calling to the role. He merely accepted it because his father had asked him, and because his father had told him it was part of his grooming to succeed him as pastor one day.

But Jesse was not sure he ever wanted to be a pastor, and he felt increasingly uncomfortable with his role as director of evangelism and missions. His father had always presented evangelism as standing on a privilege pedestal and preaching down to people who needed Jesus. This condescending approach worked occasionally, and it brought some people to the church, but Jesse doubted its true effectiveness. The more

Adverse Possession

Jesse became exposed to non-believers, the more he realized that many of them would need more that just a sermon. He met and talked with rich people who were successful in the world's eyes, but were miserable and just a doctor's visit away from popping Xanax every day. Conversely, he met people filled with the joy of life, but barely had two nickels to rub together.

Jesse had learned in college that the more a product is exposed to a customer, the better its chance of selling. He knew this was true with people as well. Evangelism had to be more than one-shot deals at converting people. It was about more than passing out tracts on street corners and having open-air meetings. It had to be about building relationships that allowed him and his team to have consistent contact with those in need.

This was the fundamental difference between Jesse and his father. Rodereck wanted a ministry of evangelism that reached to the masses like Billy Graham. Jesse preferred to reach out to one person at a time. He found no issues with either approach, but felt he was better suited for one-on-one ministry. A part of his unhappiness with his role in evangelism was his father's failure to recognize that. He was *not* like his father, who was more comfortable in a room full of people and thrived when speaking and ministering to crowds. Jesse preferred a more personal approach.

Rodereck had warned Jesse that such close personal involvement with people could affect him spiritually. He would always quote Benjamin Franklin's Poor Richard's Almanac, "If you lie down with dogs, you get up with fleas." However, Jesse could never see the people he was ministering to as dogs. He felt that they were no better or worse than he was. Jesse knew that without Christ, he might be in the same position they were.

These newfound eyes led him to meeting Jennifer. Rodereck saw her as a dog, but Jesse saw her as a gem. The past 10 years, he had not regretted it. Not one day. Not one minute. Not even when he was forced to sleep in an uncomfortable room on a bed with more lumps than Samantha's homemade mashed potatoes.

While Samantha was out at the grocery store, Jennifer sent the kids to their rooms for a nap, and then settled on the living room couch for an hour of *Dr. Oz* before Samantha returned. While the two ladies were in the kitchen preparing dinner, Harlan walked in and was surprised to see Jesse standing in his living room.

"Hey, dude!" Harlan dropped the duffle bag he was carrying and walked over to Jesse. He embraced him briefly and, for Jesse, mercifully. Harlan's hugs were not limp and passé. His entire body went into it, and he hugged hard.

"How's it going?" Jesse asked, smiling.

"Well, I ain't rich like you. But other than that, everything's good." Harlan was a short man with male-pattern baldness and a beer belly. "I put on a few since I saw you last."

"I thought I was supposed to say that, not you," Jesse joked.

"Hey, I'm just beating you to the punch, is all."

Jennifer emerged from the kitchen and ran to her father. He embraced her the same as he embraced everyone, but Jennifer had become used to it. She liked his bear hugs, and often tried to get Jesse to emulate them.

Once Harlan had put his coat away and greeted his wife

and the kids, he invited Jesse down to the basement—his man cave—which was his favorite spot to talk and catch up. Pennants from the University of Tennessee baseball team and the Tennessee Titans hung on the faux oak paneled walls, along with photos of Harlan at various work events. Harlan especially prized the photograph of him posed with Titans quarterback Matt Hasselbeck. The photo was a conversation piece, and cemented Harlan's reputation as a rabid football fan with his family and friends. Harlan could not bring himself to admit that the photograph was presented to him on his birthday by a tech savvy co-worker who had Photoshopped his body onto an existing photo of Hasselbeck.

Harlan went to a small refrigerator in a corner of the basement, pushed aside four Pabst Blue Ribbons, and pulled out colas for both him and Jesse. As a sign of respect for his son-in-law, he never drank beer when Jesse was visiting.

"So, how were things in Haiti?" Harlan asked, reclining on a futon couch.

"Got a lot done," Jesse said. "Built a couple of schools. Met a lot of good people. Established some real relationships. For once in my life, I feel that I have done something that mattered. Those schools are going to give a lot of those kids down there a fighting chance."

"Good thing y'all doing," Harlan said. "You plannin' a go back?"

"Maybe when the kids are older ... ," Jesse said, his eyes cutting to the left of Harlan. A chime from the computer momentarily distracted him. Glancing at the computer, he noticed that Jennifer had left their email account logged in and a new message was coming through.

Jesse continued. "We struggled with keeping the kids out of their schools for two months, but this was a once-in-lifetime opportunity. We're grateful that their teachers enrolled them in the independent study program, but we likely won't take a long trip like that until the kids are in college."

"It was good having them here," Harlan said. "I ain't realize how much I miss having young uns in the house."

"Well, you can have them as much as you want," Jesse said, smiling. "They love their mama and papa."

Harlan nodded, and then stood. He looked blankly at the wall, which told Jesse that Harlan had something on his mind. Rather than press for information, Jesse waited to see what Harlan would say. The wait was not long.

"Son, have y'all ever thought about moving to Knoxville?" Harlan said, still looking away.

To avoid seeming as if he wasn't answering the question, but not knowing *how* to answer it, Jesse merely said, "Umm."

"Sam and I were talking 'bout this," Harlan said, facing Jesse and taking a sip of his soda. "We really would like to see more of our grandkids. It would keep y'all from havin' to make that long trip from Virginia. For the mortgage y'all are payin' in Virginia, you could probably get a house for twice the size here in Knoxville. You could enroll your young uns in school here. You can travel as much as you want without having to take them out of school. And since Jennifer is a housewife, there's only your job that's a hindrance here."

"But that's a major hindrance," Jesse said. "I don't want to leave my church high and dry."

"Your father wants you to be pastor of the church when he retires," Harlan said. "At the rate he's going, that won't happen for 20 or 25 years. You could always go back to the church once the kids are grown."

"I'm a part of a ministry there, Pop."

"You can minister 'round these parts, Jesse. There are plenty of people in Knoxville who need help, who need a touch from God. Heck, just take a ride right up Magnolia to the Austin Homes. There's more people in need there than you can figure."

"Hasn't worked for you. What makes you think it'll work for anyone else in this town?"

Harlan's eyebrows went south. "What's that supposed to mean?"

"I've been ministering to you," Jesse said, undaunted, but quietly. "Yet, you're still gambling."

"I do the Lotto. It ain't the same thing."

"It *is* the same thing. It's like a heroin addict telling me he's freed from dope, and now he's just smoking weed."

Harlan set the soda on a table and drew so close to Jesse that Jesse could still smell the pizza Harlan had for lunch on his breath. "I used to drop half a paycheck every two weeks in gambling joints. Blackjack, poker, Texas hold 'em. Horses, football, baseball. You name it, I did it. I almost lost this house because of it. Now I spend four, no more than six dollars every now and then on lottery tickets. Now you tell me it's the same thing?"

"It's less of the same thing, but it's the same thing."

Harlan scoffed and turned away from Jesse. "Don't you give me any credit? I'm faithful to my wife. I love my grandchildren. I'm not out there shootin' people for a few bucks. I'm not a meth-head. I'm a good fella. Can't you cut me some slack on this?"

Jesse just looked at him without responding. He did not agree with Harlan, but he did not want Harlan to goad him into an argument, either. So he just kept quiet. He did not like confrontation. Just like his father.

Harlan walked over to his flat screen TV and opened the door to the cabinet on which it sat. He pulled out a thick stack of rubber-banded mail and handed it to Jesse. Jesse looked at it, confused.

"What's this?" Jesse asked.

"It's your mail."

Jesse slid the rubber band off the package and flipped through the stack of 85 envelopes. "How did you get our mail?"

"You had it forwarded here. See the yellow sticker on the envelopes?"

"No. I had the mail held at the post office in McLean."

"Well, it's been coming here for about a month. We figured it was something *you* did."

"No. It wasn't." Jesse walked to the foot of the stairs and called for his wife. When Jennifer came down the stairs, he showed her the envelopes and said, "Did you do anything to have our mail forwarded here?"

"No." Jennifer flipped through the envelopes. "I left all that up to you. I thought the mail was being held."

"It was. But for some reason, it's coming here."

"I'll call the post office for you, find out what's going on." Jennifer went to the computer, and within three minutes had found the telephone number for the post office in McLean. She dialed the number on her cell phone, then handed the phone to Jesse.

Jesse waited until the clerk answered, then said, "Yeah, this is Jesse Kane, spelled K-A-N-E. I live on 6609 Bynum Drive. I placed a request to hold mail about two months ago, but for some reason the mail is coming to my in-laws' home in Knoxville, Tennessee. I'd like to know what is going on."

The clerk verified Jesse's address, and then put Jesse on hold. After four minutes, she returned to the line and said, "Yes, we do have a hold request. But we also have a forwarding order filed on January 4 to forward your mail to the Knoxville address. So, all of your held mail went to that address."

Jesse placed the call on speakerphone so that Jennifer and Harlan could hear. "Who filed that order?" Jesse asked, shaking his head and looking at his wife.

"It was filed online by you, sir."

"Wait a minute." Jesse switched the phone to the other hand. "I don't know what is going on, but I was in Haiti on January 4. I didn't file any forwarding order."

"Well, someone filed it, sir. And we use credit card verification for orders placed online, so it was someone with your credit card and mailing address. Could someone have gotten hold of your card?"

"No," Jesse responded. "I had it with me the whole time. I used it just last night."

"You can come into the post office and cancel the order, if you want."

"I can't do that. I'm still out of town," Jesse looked at Jennifer for some ideas, but received only a blank stare. "I'll be back in town tomorrow morning, so I'll come to the post office then."

"Very well, sir. Is there anything else I can help you with?"

Jesse immediately had a thought. "You say the order was filed online?"

"Yes," the clerk answered.

"Then they would have to give an email address. What was the address they gave?"

"I can't reveal that over the phone."

"Okay. I'll give you my email address. Can you tell me if my address was used, or not?"

A sigh came through the phone. "What is the address?"

"JessandJen@jmail.com."

"Yes, that's the address."

"Would a confirmation have come to that address?"

"Yes."

"On January 4th?"

"Yes."

Jennifer moved immediately to the computer.

"Okay. Thanks. Appreciate your help." Jesse said goodbye to the clerk and then walked over to the computer, where his wife was perched in front of the screen, searching through her emails. After a few minutes of searching, she banged her fist on the computer desk and looked back over her shoulder at Jesse.

"We get about 10 or more emails a day, right?" Jennifer asked.

"Yeah," Jesse said. "Mostly junk."

"Look at this." Jennifer pointed to the emails on the screen. "We get 17 emails on January 3, and nine emails on January 5, but *none* on January 4. What's the chance of that happening?"

"Slim."

"And I told you the emails were being marked as read. So, someone is reading and *deleting* our emails."

"Someone is hacking into our accounts." Jesse concluded, turning to Harlan. "We gotta go."

"Now?" said Harlan.

"Yeah." Turning to Jennifer he said, "Let's get the kids packed up and ready to go."

"Honey, if we leave now, we won't get back until after 2 in the morning," Jennifer reasoned. "We won't be able to do anything then. Let's just have supper, spend the night, and then leave in the morning."

"*Early* in the morning," Jesse insisted. "We need to be on I-40 by 5."

* * *

Present day, 2 p.m.

Lottie K pulled her Nissan Sentra into her driveway, climbed out, and grabbed her two plastic bags of veggies and meat from Harris Teeter. She studied the dull, badly dinged Ford F-150 pickup truck parked in the driveway of 6609 Bynum. Lottie K was certain she had not seen the vehicle when she left for work that morning. She knew the Kanes were due home any day now. Maybe the vehicle belonged to them or someone they knew, although she had never seen it before.

Lottie K managed to get inside her home and put the groceries away before curiosity got the best of her and she walked back outside. She pulled the lapels of her coat together, trying to guard against the 40-degree chill. She looked at the house to see if she could see any signs that the Kanes had returned. But the house appeared the same as always, except for the pickup truck in the driveway. Since the Kanes had appointed her the official guardian of their home, Lottie K felt obligated to investigate further.

She strode across Bynum Drive and approached the house by way of the driveway, walking past the pickup truck along the way. The two-car garage was straight ahead of her, with a flawlessly white bay door guarding the entrance. Above the garage were the two bedrooms belonging to Aiden and Ashley. Lottie K looked up at the windows. For a moment, she thought she saw one of the curtains move, but she quickly dismissed it, guessing that it was the central heat shuffling the curtains. Directly to the left of the garage, alongside a wall at a right angle to the bay door, was a storm door leading to the guest room in the basement. Lottie K looked at it and saw nothing out of place.

To her left were five brick steps leading past the window of Jesse's home office. Lottie K took the stairs, and then continued along a brick walkway to five more steps leading to a covered porch. The front door was outfitted almost entirely in glass, with translucent flourishes, sidelights, and genuine mahogany framing it. It was set at a slight angle so that anyone inside could see the entire porch, while having an entire view of the southwestern lawn. Lottie K looked through the door, which gave her a view of the right portion of the living room, the double-door mahogany coat closet, and the hallway leading to the rear of the house.

Lottie K rang the bell, but she heard or saw no activity.

She would ring it three more times before giving up and heading off the porch, past the office, and back down to the guest bedroom. She knocked on its door several times with no response.

There were several more doors to check. One was the doorway leading from the rear deck to the family room. The other was a door on the west side of the home, also leading to the family room. Lottie K came up empty on both doors.

There was only one more door to check. The basement door directly under the deck led to the laundry and storage area. Lottie padded down the stairs to check this door, and then suddenly froze in place.

The door was partly ajar. She heard rustling noises for a few seconds, and then silence.

Fear shot through Lottie's body, and her heart began to race. Her first and only thought was that the Kanes' house was being robbed.

She followed every bit of advice she had ever received from law enforcement about what to do in such a situation. She backed up the steps and away from the door and hurried across the east lawn to the white siding and brick home next to 6609. She knocked frantically on the front door.

Tabita Beloo, an immigrant from Cape Town, South Africa who was married to a prominent Virginia cardiologist, answered the door. Tabita was popular in the neighborhood, chiefly because of the lavish parties she threw every Fourth of July and Christmas, to which she invited the entire block. She did this mostly to ingratiate herself to the neighbors, since her household was one of only five African American households within a 10-block radius. She had been in the country for 18 years, and lived on the block for six years. She shared the home with Simon, her husband of seven years, and Jaron, her 25-year-old son by her ex-husband, whom she divorced a year before she married Simon. Jaron lived in the guesthouse on the other side of the backyard pool.

"Hello, Miss Lottie." Tabita greeted her with a prominent Afrikaans accent. She was barefoot in blue jeans, a linen blouse over her full frame, and a kente cloth head-wrap. Her smile formed her dark cheeks into jolly rounds.

"I need to ask a favor. May I come in?" urged Lottie.

"Sure." Tabita stood aside and allowed Lottie onto the foyer of her home. From the foyer Lottie looked over the living room decorated in bright blues and oranges, and wide enough to park a Cessna inside.

"I need to use your phone. I think someone is breaking into the Kane residence," Lottie said.

"Oh, no." Tabita pointed Lottie to the phone, after which she locked her front door and then ran to the west bedroom. From the window of this bedroom, she had a complete view of the driveway side of 6609. She looked and, seeing nothing other than the pickup truck, ran back to Lottie, who had dialed Jesse Kane's cell phone number from memory.

* * *

Jesse Kane's cell phone chirped "Amazing Grace" from inside the right pocket of his khakis. Jesse shifted in the driver's seat so that Jennifer could reach in his pocket and grab the phone.

"Jennifer, this is Lottie. Are you home?"

"No," Jennifer said, placing the call on speakerphone. "But

we aren't far. We just got on 66, so we're about an hour away."

"Oh, god."

"What's wrong?" Jennifer asked.

"I think someone's broken into your home. There's a strange pickup truck parked in the driveway, and your basement door is open, and I heard noises."

Jesse increased his speed to 80 miles per hour.

"Did you call the police?" Jennifer asked.

"I didn't. I didn't know if it was you or not."

"Please call them Miss Lottie. Now!"

Lottie K wasted no time being polite. She hung up the phone immediately and dialed 911.

Jennifer looked back at the kids. Fortunately, they were asleep and had not heard the exchange. She then looked at Jesse, whose attention was firmly on the road.

"You think this is connected to our problems with the email?" Jennifer said.

"Either that, or we are having the worst welcome home anyone could ever have," Jesse said, hoping that all the state troopers that patrolled I-66 for speeders were busy at donut shops.

* * *

Within five minutes of Lottie's call, two Fairfax County police cruisers containing two officers each screeched to a stop in front of 6609. The doors of the cruisers popped open, and the four officers filed out and got into position. One of them slunk along the west side of the house, under cover of the chest-high shrubs, and took position in the rear yard where he could cover the exits from the family room. Another stood on the east front of the house, just beyond the garage, covering the guest room door and the front door. The other two officers approached the basement door, finding it ajar just as Lottie had told the dispatchers. They drew their weapons and carefully entered the basement, yelling "police officers" frequently as they entered the laundry room.

The officers heard loud voices respond from the recreation room just beyond the laundry. "We're in here!"

Two doors led to the recreation room. Each officer entered a door, both hands on his weapon, pointed ahead. They encountered a man and a woman, both middle-age, standing next to a couch facing a wall-mounted flat screen TV.

"What's going on?" The man looked at both the officers with confusion.

The officers briefly looked at each other. Officer Wilkinson continued to look around while the other, Sergeant Gwynn, ordered the couple to assume the position against a wall. Once he had searched them and verified they had no weapons, he holstered his weapon.

"We received a report of breaking and entering at this address," Sergeant Gwynn said. "Do you live here?"

Without hesitation, the couple answered in unison, "Yes, we do."

"Is there anyone else in the house?"

"No."

"What are your names?"

"I'm Bernard MacNichol, and my wife is Amber."

Sergeant Gwynn looked at Officer Wilkinson, who nodded that the basement was clear and he was about to go upstairs to check the first floor. Sergeant Gwynn nodded back, then got on his walkie-talkie and alerted the officers outside that the basement was clear and his partner was checking out the ground floor.

"Do you know why one of your neighbors would believe there was a break-in occurring at this address?" Sergeant Gwynn asked.

"I don't know," Bernard answered. "We had just fallen asleep in front of the TV. We weren't doing anything unusual."

"Your neighbor said she knocked on several doors and rang the doorbell. Why didn't you answer?"

"As I mentioned, officer, we were sleeping."

"You often sleep with your basement door wide open in the middle of winter?"

"It's a safe neighborhood. We didn't find it a concern."

That answer didn't sit well with Sergeant Gwynn. He decided to press. "Why didn't you just close your door?"

"Actually, we forgot it was open."

"How long have you lived here?"

"Three years."

"You own this home?"

"No. We rent it."

Sergeant Gwynn listened as his walkie-talkie chirped and the other officers told him the upstairs was clear.

"Okay, I'll need to see ID for the both of you."

Bernard nodded. "Certainly. I have it upstairs in my bedroom."

"Let's go." Sergeant Gwynn directed them to the staircase, while he followed. When they got upstairs, only Officer Wilkinson was present. The other officers, seeing no immediate threat or danger, went back to their cruiser.

The officers waited with Amber in the living room while Bernard went to the master bedroom at the rear of the house to retrieve his ID. When he returned with it, the officers examined it and found it to be a valid Virginia state driver's license with Bernard's correct name and the address listed as 6609 Bynum Drive. His wife retrieved two bills from the kitchen. Both bills were listed in the name of Bernard MacNichol, at the same address. That was all the officers needed to see to decide no crime was taking place. The officers apologized for the intrusion, handed the license back to Bernard, and left out the front door. Before they left the scene, they dialed Tabita's home number and asked to come to her house to speak to their complainant.

Lottie K had been watching the action from Tabita's bedroom window, but was unable to tell who was inside the house or what had happened. Lottie came out to the living room just as Tabita had let the officers into her foyer.

"Are you Mrs. Koch?" Sergeant Gwynn asked Lottie.

"That's me."

"Mrs. Koch, what gave you the idea that a burglary was occurring next door?"

"Because the owners of that house are out of town. I just spoke with them a few minutes ago."

"The people in the house claim *they* live there."

Lottie shook her head vehemently. "No. No. No one else lives in that house except the Kanes. They asked me to watch the house while they were gone."

"You sure about that? No one else living in the house, I mean?"

Adverse Possession

Lottie looked at the sergeant as if he had just called her a dirty word. "They are my neighbors. Their kids play with my grandkids. Of course I'm sure."

Tabita chimed in. "I agree. No one lives there except for the Kanes."

Officer Wilkinson feverishly wrote in a small notepad as they spoke.

"Well, the two people there have bills and driver's licenses to prove that the house is their rightful residence, so we cannot, by law, ask them to leave," Sergeant Gwynn stated.

"Who are they?" Lottie asked.

"I can't reveal that, ma'am," Sergeant Gwynn said. "All I can tell you is that they have proven to my satisfaction that they have a right to be on the premises."

"We also ran the tags on the truck in the driveway," Officer Wilkinson said. "The truck is registered to that address. And there were no signs of forced entry to the premises."

Lottie and Tabita looked at each other. For several seconds, neither had any idea what to say. Finally, Lottie walked past the officers to the telephone, picked it up, and dialed.

Jesse and Jennifer were 45 minutes away from McLean when Jesse's phone chirped again. Jennifer answered it quickly, hoping that Lottie K had some good news.

"Jenny, this is Lottie. They're saying that there are two people living in your house, and they have bills and ID and everything with your address."

"What!" The tone of Jennifer's voice startled Jesse and stirred the kids, but was not enough to wake them. "What do you mean someone is living in my house?"

Jesse found a safe place to pull the car over in case he had to get on the phone.

"I mean the police are telling me two people are living in your house," Lottie said. "I don't know who they are. But the police are telling me the people can prove they live there."

"No! That's crazy. No one is supposed to be in my house!"

Jesse stopped the car on the side of I-66 and motioned for Jennifer to give him the phone. Jennifer looked at him, her eyes wide. She was acknowledging him, but was not yet ready to give him the phone.

"Who are these people?" Jennifer asked.

"The police won't tell me."

"Let me talk to the police."

Lottie K passed the phone to Sergeant Gwynn. Jennifer introduced herself, and she and the sergeant talked for five minutes, going over everything that had happened. When the conversation was almost over, Jennifer was screaming, and she was almost in hysterics. It was then that Jennifer finally relinquished the phone to her husband.

"Officer, this is Jesse Kane. I'm Jennifer's husband. Is it possible for you to stick around until we get there? We're only about 45 minutes away. We can prove we own the house, and you can help us get these people out of my house. I promise you, these people do not live there."

There was a brief pause before Sergeant Gwynn responded. "Forty-five minutes, you say?"

"Yeah. We're just passing Haymarket now."

"Okay, we'll wait, Mr. Kane," Sergeant Gwynn said. "But there still may not be much we can do about your situation."

"Okay, just hang around 'til we get there."

When Jesse had finished speaking with the sergeant, he met the worried look of his wife with a feigned expression of confidence.

"Don't worry, honey. We'll get it straightened out."

"What is going on?" Jennifer asked. "We go away for two months, and suddenly all this happens?"

"Let's just pray about it," Jesse said, putting the SUV in drive and merging into the traffic headed east toward Washington, D.C. "Let's just pray to the Lord that this is some kind of mistake, misunderstanding, or whatever."

Jennifer grabbed Jesse's cell phone and called their house telephone. To her dismay, the phone was off the hook.

Jesse hugged the fast lane of I-66 and thought about his options.

What he was thinking was not pleasant.

* * *

Forty minutes later, the Kanes' Nissan Armada shot down Bynum Drive and screeched to a halt in front of the police cruiser parked outside their house. Tabita and Lottie, who were still inside Tabita's house, recognized the Kanes' vehicle and came outside.

Jesse looked back at Aiden and Ashley, who were awake now and wondering why a police car was in front of their house.

"Kids, I need to take care of something," Jesse said to them. "You stay in the car with your mother."

"But we have to go to the bathroom," Aiden protested.

Jesse looked at his wife. She was focusing her attention on

their house. The only thing that seemed to have changed was the presence of the grungy pickup truck in the driveway. She saw nothing else out of place.

Jesse then looked back and saw Tabita and Lottie approaching their car. He laid a gentle hand on Jennifer's shoulder to draw her attention. "Honey, could you ask Lottie if we could take the kids over to her house until we get this squared away?"

Jennifer looked at him, nodded her head slightly, then turned to Aiden and Ashley. "C'mon, kids. We're going over to Miss Lottie's for a few minutes. Don't take any of your things." The last sentence was meant to express her confidence in her husband's ability to resolve this issue, although she already felt violated.

Jesse grabbed his keys and got out of the car. He hugged both Tabita and Lottie, limiting his words to just "Hi" and "Thank you," and moved past them to greet the officers, who had gotten out of their vehicle and met him halfway between the two cars.

Jesse extended his hand to shake Sergeant Gwynn's hand. "I'm Jesse Kane. We own that house." He reached into his rear pocket, removed his wallet, took out his driver's license, and showed it to the officers.

Sergeant Gwynn looked at the license briefly, noted the name and address, then nodded for Jesse to put it away. Just 15 minutes before, Sergeant Gwynn had a detective at his station check land records to verify that Jesse Kane was the owner of the house. "So, you say these people have no authorization to be in your house?"

"No. Absolutely not. Who are they?"

Adverse Possession

"Bernard and Amber MacNichol. You know them?"

"No, never heard of them." He turned to Lottie, who was standing next to him. "You?"

"No," Lottie answered.

"What about your wife?" Sergeant Gwynn asked.

Jesse turned to call his wife, but paused when he saw her and Tabita scoot the kids across the street to Lottie's house. He turned back to the sergeant. "I can't tell you for sure. I doubt she knows them. But even if she did, they don't have any permission to be in my house."

"You gotta admit, Mr. Kane, that this is a very strange situation. Forgive me for being facetious, but it isn't often we encounter husband and wife burglary teams breaking into houses in ritzy neighborhoods in broad daylight."

Jesse shook his head and rubbed his forehead with his left hand. "I don't know how to respond to that."

"I mean, Mr. Kane, these people didn't even bother to hide themselves when we entered the house to check out the breaking-and-entering complaint. They acted as if they lived there."

"Trust me, they don't. I need them out of my house."

"Well, let me explain the law to you." Sergeant Gwynn paused, pondering his words, as he knew what he was about to say would not be received well. "The only way we can get them out of the house is if there's reasonable evidence that a criminal act has taken place, such as trespassing, or breaking and entering. There were no witnesses that actually saw this couple breaking into your home. There were no signs of forced entry. They didn't attempt to hide when we approached them in the basement. There didn't seem to be anything out of place.

And, they had government IDs with this address on them, a car registered to this address, and utility bills with their name and this address."

"You gotta be kidding me." Jesse looked at Lottie with disbelief, then back at the sergeant. "I guarantee you everything they showed you is fake."

"Well, after we spoke with you on the phone, and we found out through land records that you owned the home, we engaged them again, and they presented us with the keys to your home, and a copy of a lease agreement they have with you."

"What?" Jesse's tone carried down the block. He was glad that his wife was not there to see his mounting exasperation. Lottie tapped him gently on the arm, trying to calm him down. "This is crazy. This is absolutely insane. I did not give them keys, and I did not sign any lease agreement."

Sergeant Gwynn nodded calmly. "The fact is, we cannot effect an arrest when there's evidence that a tenancy is in place. If we did, it wouldn't even last beyond the preliminary hearing. They'd be out in 24 hours."

Jesse sighed hard and looked toward his house. "Sergeant, I know you're doing your job. But this is nuts. You're telling me I have to let these people stay in my home."

"What I am telling you is that I cannot arrest them. There's no evidence of a criminal act. If you want them out, you're going to have to go through the courts."

Jesse could not, would not, accept this. "Officer, we can go into my house. I can show you all my stuff, all our clothes, all our paperwork. My kids' clothes and all their stuff. I can prove that *we* live there, and not *them*."

Adverse Possession

Sergeant Gwynn kept his patience, though it was being tried. "You may live there, sir, but that doesn't mean that they don't. Again, they have documentation stating that they live there."

Jesse took some deep breaths and tried to calm down. Frustration had already set in, and he was just a couple of clicks away from outright anger. He turned to the officers, his hands in front of him, at chest level, his fingers spread, trying to convey a sense of earnestness. "Listen to me. I am a minister. My wife and I went on a two-month missionary trip to Haiti. We left the kids at my father-in-law's place in Knoxville. We asked our neighbor Lottie to watch the house while we were gone. When we came back, we noticed that someone had hacked into our emails, and even forwarded our mail to my dad's house in Knoxville. I don't know how these people got IDs and all that with my address, but it is obvious there's some type of identity theft going on. These people are not tenants of mine, and they do not belong in my house."

"Mr. Kane, I know this is hard to wrap your head around," said Sergeant Gwynn, "But ... ."

Jesse interrupted. "What if you just take them in for questioning or something? That gets them out of the house. Nothing saying I have to let them back in, is there?"

Sergeant Gwynn smiled, amused at Jesse's question. If he were in the same situation, he likely would have thought the same. "Nothing saying they have to go in for questioning, unless there is a charge. But even if they do, they will have a right to come back to the house unless a judge says otherwise. They could call the police on you and have the police order you to let them back in."

Jesse hung his head, shaking it slowly.

"Mr. Kane, we can try to talk to them and see if they will leave voluntarily," Sergeant Gwynn said. "But if not, there's nothing we can do."

"Let's do that," said Jesse, and then added, facetiously, "I can't *wait* to meet them."

Jesse, Sergeant Gwynn, and Officer Wilkinson walked to the front door, and Sergeant Gwynn banged on the wooden part of the door in typical cop style. Jesse felt weird standing on his porch, watching a cop knock on the door of his own house. From the porch, Jesse could see his living room through the window. Everything appeared the same as he had left it, except that he had closed the curtains before his trip overseas. He was annoyed that they had pulled back the curtains.

Jesse offered Sergeant Gwynn the key to the home. Sergeant Gwynn waved it away.

"I can't enter a house unless I have a warrant, or a suspicion that a crime is taking place," Sergeant Gwynn explained.

"But *I* can enter," Jesse said.

"Only under certain circumstances."

Jesse wanted to question the officer further about this, but Bernard MacNichol came to the door. He looked out at Jesse and the police officers, and then hesitated before opening the door. Jesse started to move inside, but Sergeant Gwynn halted him by holding up his hand.

"Mr. MacNichol, do you recognize this man?" Sergeant Gwynn asked.

"Yes, I do," Bernard answered quickly. "He is the owner."

"This is the man you signed a lease with?"

Adverse Possession

"Yes."

Another sigh came from Jesse. "I have never seen this man before in my life. I did not sign a lease with him. He has no authorization from me or my wife to be in my house."

Sergeant Gwynn told Jesse to stay on the porch with Officer Wilkinson while he walked into the house with Bernard. They moved into the office, just beside the foyer, and Sergeant Gwynn spoke in hushed tones.

"Listen, I don't know what's going on here, but if this guy is telling the truth, you may want to think a bit." Sergeant Gwynn looked around. "Look at this house. This is a very nice house. That means they have some money. They can hire attorneys. They'll sue you until they bleed you dry. They will still get their house back. Then, they'll have you locked up for identity theft and signature forgery. Is this how you want this story to end?"

Sergeant Gwynn studied Bernard's blank expression. Seeing no flex, he said, "You can pack up your stuff, give him back the keys, and walk out of here now, and avoid a lot of trouble later. This guy is a minister. Do you really want to go to war with a minister and his family?"

Bernard looked down, which Sergeant Gwynn interpreted as a sign that at least he was thinking about it. After a few seconds, Bernard looked up again and said, "This is my house. I live here. I'm not doing anything wrong."

Sergeant Gwynn looked at Bernard tersely. He knew Bernard was lying, but he could not do much about it. He could effect an arrest and hope that it would shake Bernard out of his fantasy. However, that meant he would have to lie on the report and say that there was sufficient evidence to support a trespassing charge. There was *no* evidence. If he said there was, and they discovered the lie, he would lose his job. With three kids, a wife, and a mortgage that took half his sergeant's pay, it was not a chance he could take.

"Okay, sir. I'll be back in a few minutes. Wait here." Sergeant Gwynn turned and left the office, and met Jesse and Officer Wilkinson on the porch.

"He's not budging, Mr. Kane," Sergeant Gwynn reported. "There's nothing we can do from here. My advice is to get yourself an attorney." He pulled a business card from his jacket pocket and handed it to Jesse. "Give me a call if you need anything further."

Jesse was quick and terse with his response. "I do need something further. I need to speak to your commanding officer. There's no way I'm leaving these people in my house."

With no expression, Sergeant Gwynn turned to his partner. "Get Lieutenant McGee down here." He watched as Officer Wilkinson unsnapped his walkie-talkie and walked toward their cruiser. He turned back to Jesse and gave him a reassuring look.

"No worries," Sergeant Gwynn told Jesse. "I would have done the same thing." He tapped Jesse gently on the back. "Our duty officer will be here shortly." He headed toward the cruiser and stood just outside it, watching the house as Officer Wilkinson radioed the duty officer on his walkie-talkie.

Seven minutes later, another police cruiser pulled up, and another uniformed cop climbed out. Jesse, who was still on the porch, watched as the duty officer conferred with Sergeant Gwynn and Officer Wilkinson, their voices hushed such that

Jesse could not make out what they were saying. After five minutes of conversation, Lieutenant McGee headed up the walkway toward the porch where Jesse was standing. Jesse and Lieutenant McGee introduced themselves, after which McGee looked inside the open door of the house and noticed Bernard standing near the foyer.

"You say that these people have no right to be in your house?" Lieutenant McGee asked Jesse.

"No," Jesse responded, sounding tired. "I don't know them."

"May I have your ID, please?"

Jesse frowned for a moment, wondering why the officer needed his ID again. Nonetheless he reached for his wallet, pulled out his ID, and handed it to Lieutenant McGee.

"Wait here." Without another word, Lieutenant McGee walked into the house and started talking with Bernard. Once again, Jesse could not make out the conversation, but watched them closely. After a minute, they both walked toward the kitchen.

Jesse's cell phone rang. He pulled it from his pocket and saw Lottie's number on the caller ID. He answered, not surprised to hear his wife's voice on the other end.

"Honey, what's going on?" Jennifer asked, a shaky nervousness evident in her voice.

"They're still saying there's nothing they can do, but I called in a commanding officer," Jesse explained. "He just went in to talk to them, so hopefully it'll get worked out."

"I hope so."

"How's the kids?"

"They're in the basement with Lottie and Tabita."

"Good. Keep them there. I don't want them seeing this and getting worried."

"What about me?"

"I don't want you getting worried either."

Jesse heard voices coming from the house and turned to watch Lieutenant McGee exit the home and shut the door behind him. Shutting the door was not a good sign.

"I'll call you back, honey." Jesse hung up the phone, shoved it in his pocket, and hoped that Lieutenant McGee was approaching him with good news.

"I just examined the lease agreement this guy has," Lieutenant McGee explained. "I checked the signature against the one on your ID. It matches."

"That's impossible," Jesse said. "I never signed a lease."

"So, you're saying they forged your signature?"

"Yes. Can I see the lease?"

"I asked him that. He refused."

"He refused because the lease is a fake. He knows that, and so do I."

"If that is the case, then seeing the lease won't change the facts on the ground. But, here are the facts from my perspective." Lieutenant McGee guided Jesse off the porch and down the walkway, away from the house. "You may not want to accept this, but there is nothing I can do."

Jesse opened his mouth to protest, but Lieutenant McGee quickly silenced him by continuing to talk. "If we were dealing with a stolen car, this would be easy. But we're dealing with homes, landlords, tenants, lease agreements, and a law that is very pro-tenant. Because of that, there are limits on what police officers can do. And one thing we can't do is eject people from a home when there's evidence that a tenancy is in place. Otherwise, anytime a landlord or owner decides he doesn't like a tenant, or the tenant is not paying rent, they could call the cops and have the person evicted without due process."

"Officer, you have to believe me." Jesse's voice was low yet shrill, as if it had lost all of its power. "This guy does not live here. He is not a tenant. You've got to believe that."

"It's not about what I believe. It's about what I can prove." This was a statement that Lieutenant McGee had made umpteen times in his 15-year career as a police officer.

"I can prove it!" Jesse's voice was louder now, almost carrying. "Talk to the Beloos next door. Talk to Mrs. Koch 'cross the street. Talk to anybody on this block. They will tell you that I live here."

"I'm sure you do." Lieutenant McGee nodded and averted his eyes away from Jesse. "My point is that there is no proof that the MacNichols *don't* live here."

"Talk to my neighbors! They'll tell you they've never seen these people before."

Lieutenant McGee turned his shoulders away. He had lost his patience. "Sir, this is not a police matter. That's what I'm telling you. This is a matter for the courts. My advice is to find someplace else for you and your family to sleep tonight. Then, call an attorney tomorrow morning. But there's nothing further I can do. Good day, sir."

Jesse watched helplessly as Lieutenant McGee walked back to his vehicle and drove off, followed by Sergeant Gwynn and Officer Wilkinson. Jesse looked back at his house just in time to see Bernard slam the front door.

Louis N. Jones

Here he was, locked out of his own home, an American dream turned into a nightmare. For a moment he stood there, stunned, unsure how to react or respond. The only thing he could think to do was to knock on the door again, hoping that Bernard would come to the door and at least talk to him. What did Bernard want? Did he want money? What was going on in his mind that he would pretend to be a tenant in a home he had no right to occupy?

Jesse's frantic knocks went unanswered for almost six minutes. He looked at his house key, tempted to use it to enter the home. However, he thought about what Sergeant Gwynn had said. He could only enter the home under certain circumstances. But what *were* those circumstances?

Jesse was convinced that Bernard had a screw loose. He had to be crazy, touched in the head. It was that realization that convinced him not to try to enter the home, at least not alone, at least not now.

He walked across the front yard and continued across the street to Lottie K's house. The quietness of the late afternoon street contrasted with the turmoil going on inside him. He felt violated and raped. Some stranger had co-opted his prized possession, and there was nothing immediate that he could do. His fate would be in the hands of another stranger, a judge in a courtroom.

For a twinkling, fleeting moment, Jesse thought about Haiti, the earthquake damage, the abject poverty, the kids running around with nothing to do, the gangs. He wondered if things weren't a lot better there than they were here.

Jennifer had been watching the goings-on through Lottie's

living room window. When she saw that the officers were not arresting the strangers in her home, and noticed the dejected look on Jesse's face as he walked toward Lottie's house, she knew that she would not be spending the night in her own bedroom. She glumly walked to the front door and opened it for Jesse as he approached. "Not good news, is it?"

Jesse shook his head, feeling defeated, and more than a little embarrassed. He walked inside, shut the door, and looked to see where the kids were. Jennifer explained that they were in the basement with Lottie and Tabita. Feeling confident there were no eavesdroppers, he explained the situation to his wife. She received the information calmly, as she was already prepared for bad news.

"What are we gonna do?" Jennifer asked.

Jesse looked away blankly, thinking aloud. "We have to find somewhere to sleep tonight. Tomorrow, I'll go to see my Pop, see if he can connect me with Joe Lippman."

"We ain't gotta worry about a place to live," Jennifer said. "I spoke with Lottie. She said we can stay here as long as we need. She's got two empty bedrooms downstairs, so that'll be perfect for us. This way, we ain't far away from the house."

"That'll be good."

"She also gave us the keys back, too. That was my concern, that maybe Lottie lost the keys somehow, and the people in our house found them."

"Well, apparently they have keys anyway. Who's to know where they got them."

"You think they are going to steal from us, if they ain't already?"

"I don't know. But I don't want to take my eyes off that

house tonight, just in case they get cute and decide to move out at 2 in the morning with half our stuff."

Tabita came upstairs. "What happened?"

Jesse told her.

Tabita shook her head and scoffed. "This country is so crazy. Somebody breaks in your home, and you have to go to court to get them out."

"Sign of the times," Jennifer said.

"Well, I will do what I can for you." Tabita inched toward the door. "My husband and my son will be home in 30 minutes. I need to finish dinner. If you like, you and the kids can come. We have plenty. That is, if you like *babute*, African food."

"I'm sure we'll enjoy whatever you cook, Mrs. Beloo," Jennifer said. "But in case the kids are a little finicky, maybe I'll just get 'em some hamburgers from Fuddruckers."

"Of course." Tabita smiled and opened the front door. "We eat at 7, so come before then." She left, shutting the door gently.

Jennifer watched Tabita through the window as she walked across the street. "She's a sweet woman."

"Yeah, that was nice of her to offer us dinner," Jesse said. "But I'm going to have to pass."

"Why?"

"I want to get some sleep, wake up about 10 or 11, then keep an eye on the house."

"All night?"

"Yep. I don't want them to haul away all of our stuff overnight. Tomorrow, after I speak with Joe, I'm getting a U-Haul, and a few of the men from the church, and we are going to move all our stuff out of that house."

"Can you do that?"

"I'm *going* to do it. I may not be able to get them out of my house, but there's no law that says they have to use our stuff while they're there."

God? Why?

* * *

At 2 in the morning, Bynum Drive became as quiet as an empty rustic cabin, deep in the West Virginia woods. There was a major highway just eight blocks way, but it did nothing to diminish the neighborhood's placid serenity. Jesse sat in Lottie's living room, the window ajar just enough so that he could hear any noises outside, but not enough to remove the heartening warmth of the living room. He sat beside the window, fully dressed in jeans and a T-shirt, reading one of Lottie's *Good Housekeeping* magazines in the soft glow of a nearby floor lamp. Occasionally, he would glance out to see if there was any activity at his house. Curiously, all the lights in his house were still on.

He wondered if this was all some type of strange, vivid dream, from which he would awaken any second and find himself in bed, beside his wife, in his own home. What kind of world was he living in that someone could break into his house, and then get to stay for who knows how long?

Adverse Possession

He thought maybe this was a sign that he should not have traveled to Haiti. It was risky, and his father had advised him against it. Department of State travel advisories had warned against travel to Haiti, because of the violence, the robberies, the cholera, the weather. He felt uneasy about taking his kids out of school for two months. Nonetheless, he pressed forward, because of his passion to help children in third world countries. Now was God punishing him? If not, what in the world is God doing? He had helped so many children make a better life for themselves, and now God was denying his own children their rightful home.

This was really bothering him. The combination of frustration and helplessness created a strange concoction of unrelenting anger and forbidden thoughts. He knew it was normal to be upset in such situations, but he felt something akin to rage. He was ashamed that his mind considered a solution that would have been unsavory for a minister, much less another Christian believer. Nevertheless, it seemed the easiest solution, which was why he had not totally dismissed it. Yes, he could spend time, money, and effort to hire an attorney, go to court, and drag this issue out for months; or he could deal with it in a way that could be immediately effective, but could have long-range repercussions.

Jesse had never been a violent man. In fact, he abhorred violence. In his mind, there was always another solution than violence, even if it did not seem so at the immediate moment. He struggled to raise his kids that way, despite raising them in a society and among people who embrace violence as problem-solving and as entertainment. He knew there was a great culture of violence in America, and he tried his best to avoid it, through his faith in Christ and through constructive thinking. Yet now, backed into a corner, with a total stranger enjoying his home and rifling through his personal effects, his reasonable mind teetered toward a quick—if only short term—solution.

Now, here he was, sitting awake at 2 in the morning, watching his house while the intruders were likely asleep in the bed he had planned to enjoy this night. *Life was notoriously unfair.*

Jesse wanted to go to bed, embrace his wife, and forgo this vigil. After all, if they planned to take anything, they likely would have taken it by now. Should anything go missing, the cops had their names, driver's license numbers, and vehicle registration. It might not be an ideal situation for thieves. Even if they were to steal, Jesse would only lose his belongings. He could always replace those.

He found himself hoping that this was an extended burglary. *Just take what you want, and give me my house back*, he thought.

Jesse's desperation was visceral, palpable. He wanted a perfect solution, but there were none. He wanted an option that did not involve sacrifice, and there weren't any. Just thinking about it gave him a headache and caused him to drop the magazine to the floor in front of his bare feet.

Enough was enough. He decided to go to bed. He likely would have a fitful sleep, but it would be sleep nonetheless. Whatever happened, he would not let this stranger control him any more than he already had. He would get up in the morning, talk to Joe Lippman, and then go on to remove from his house whatever belongings remained. Until then, he needed the comfort of his wife, who was waiting up, unable to sleep, sitting in bed, in a dark room, hoping that her husband would come to bed, hoping to have the opportunity to pray with him and settle their minds and spirits with the peace of the Spirit.

Dusk arrived a few hours later, bringing with it overcast skies and a mist in the air that was almost like a cold steam.

Jesse lay in bed until after rush hour, then showered, and dressed. He decided not to wake up his wife, as the events of the previous day made her wearier than usual. He went to his car and started the 30-minute trip to Harvest of Righteousness.

Rodereck was sitting in his office reading the Bible and preparing for the night's Bible study, which he preferred to teach personally. He had given instructions to his secretary to hold all calls and visits while he was studying. However, such orders rarely included his son, who was the only person — other than the secretary — who had a free hand to walk directly into Rodereck's office without the secretary first announcing his visit.

Rodereck was diligently studying a scripture in First Peter when Jesse entered the office. Normally, his son's entry into his office was a non-event. However, seeing him this time was special. This was Rodereck's first time seeing Jesse since he returned from Haiti. Rodereck placed the Bible on his desk and stood to his feet.

"Son! You made it back!" Rodereck walked over to Jesse and they embraced. Jesse wore a pair of blue jeans and a green polo shirt. It was the cleanest outfit he had in his luggage, and it was still heavily wrinkled from the claustrophobic three-day trip in his luggage. "How was your trip?"

"Swell." Jesse sat in a wing chair in the counseling corner of Rodereck's office. "It was a bit of a culture shock, and I got bitten by at least 15 species of bugs while we were down there. But nonetheless, the Lord's blessings were on that trip."

"Hmm." Rodereck feigned interest.

"I mean, we spent most of our time down there in the mud and the heat, building these two buildings. I could have all kinds of bad things to say about that experience, but what made it worthwhile was the kids." Jesse smiled as he culled his memories. "When they saw their new school building, which was nothing more than four walls, a roof, and a blackboard, they were excited. It was like Christmas for them. They jumped. They danced. They sang. They were so grateful for their new school. In comparison, kids in America are so spoiled. If they don't get the latest iPad, their Christmas is ruined. In Haiti, these kids acted like this school was the best thing ever to happen to them."

Once Jesse had finished, Rodereck said, "That's wonderful. Are you coming to church tonight? I would love for you to give a report to the congregation on your trip."

How hypocritical was that statement, Jesse thought. His father had vehemently opposed the trip to Haiti. Now suddenly he wanted to wave the victory banner. Jesse did not want to go down that road. Anyone that wanted to know about the trip could ask him personally. Besides, he was a little preoccupied.

"I need to get in touch with Joe," Jesse said. "Is he still representing the church?"

"Why do you need him?" There was a time when Rodereck

would not have asked his son that question, at least not at first. He would have gone straight to the Rolodex, plucked out the number, and asked questions later. Now, Rodereck needed to gauge Jesse's need for an attorney, mostly because Jesse had signed the church to a 10-year lease on the Trudeaus' home without Rodereck's permission. Rodereck's trust in Jesse had dwindled to practically nothing, and he would take no chances that Jesse was up to his usual tricks.

Jesse did not want to go into details, so he simply said, "Squatters broke into my house while I was overseas. Now I have to hire an attorney to get them out."

Rodereck removed his glasses. "Squatters?"

"Yeah. They were there when we came home yesterday. The police can't do anything because they say it appears the squatters have a legitimate tenancy. So, I have to go through the courts."

"How did they get in?"

Jesse shook his head. "I don't know. The police said they had a key, but how they got it, I don't know."

"So you and the squatters are together in the same house?"

"No. We are at Miss Lottie's, across the street. The police advised us not to try to share the house with them, which made sense. I don't want my wife and children in a home with complete strangers who have already shown they don't have our best interests in mind."

Rodereck opened the door to his office and called on his secretary, Elena Ruiz, to find Joe Lippman's number. Once he had it, he gave it to Jesse with a disclaimer. "Joe is mostly a corporate attorney. He has some experience in landlord and tenant, but not sure if he's ever been involved in any L&T

litigation."

"Let's hope it won't matter." Jesse headed for the door. "Once these squatters know we're serious, I hope they just pack up and leave rather than let things get ugly."

"Well. Joe Lippman ain't cheap," Rodereck said. "That's a lot of money to spend because you didn't want to listen."

Jesse was almost out the door. When he heard Rodereck's remark, he turned. "What are you taking about?"

"I told you not to go to Haiti. If you'd listened to me, it—"

Jesse walked back inside the office and slammed the door so hard it startled the blinds on his office windows. "I can't believe you are going to say I told you so at a time like this."

"Yeah," Rodereck said, unrelenting. "Because if you had listened to me, there wouldn't have *been* a time like this."

Rodereck had a way of taking Jesse to the edge. But Jesse remembered that Rodereck was still his father and deserved his respect. Jesse took two deep breaths, calmed his spirit, and spoke quietly. "You're trying to make what happened yesterday a consequence of my trip to Haiti, and that's unfair. Not only is it unfair, it's unsubstantiated. Squatting can happen to anyone. It can happen to you at your apartment while you're sitting in this office."

Rodereck moved around to his cherry wood double pedestal desk and sat down in his leather executive chair. "Son, sometimes when we fail to obey God, there are consequences," he said.

"I didn't fail to obey God. I failed to obey *you*. There *is* a difference."

Rodereck looked down at his Bible. "Son, I have to get ready for Bible study tonight. I have no wish to argue. I'm glad you made it back safety, and I hope you get your squatter situation worked out."

Jesse cringed at his father's dismissive statement. It was as if Rodereck could care less that his family's home was being violated. Were it one of his other loyal church members in this predicament, Rodereck would have demonstrated care and compassion and moved heaven and earth to help. It seemed like the kind of insensitive thing someone would say to another person whom they knew they would never see again. He knew his father was not that uncaring, but that was how it came across.

He left his father's office, said goodbye to Elena Ruiz, and walked out into the parking lot. Once he approached his car, he pulled out his cell phone and made three calls. One call was to his wife to make sure the house was okay, and to instruct her to call a few of his friends from the church to help; the second was to Joe Lippman, whose voice mail picked up; and the third was to the rental truck place to make sure they had a large moving truck. He left his car in the church parking lot and walked two blocks to the rental center.

About an hour later, Jesse parked the moving truck in front of 6609 Bynum. He looked around and saw four cars parked at the curb adjacent to Lottie's house, which meant that his friends from church had arrived. He did not see anyone in the cars, so he trusted that they were in Lottie K's house with his wife, waiting on him.

The MacNichols' truck was still parked in the driveway, so he could not back the massive moving truck up to the garage door. He settled with leaving it parked at the curb, the plane of its rear door lined with the lengthwise center of the driveway. He climbed out of the truck, opened the rear door, and looked around. Almost everyone who lived on the block was at work, so there were no curious neighbors he had to explain himself to. But he needed to hurry. It was already 11 a.m., and it would take several hours to clear out the house, and another several hours to get everything unloaded in a nearby storage facility. He hoped to finish by dinnertime, as he had promised he would take his wife and kids to dinner at the Olive Garden restaurant in Tysons Corner.

Jesse made a quick call on his cell phone to his wife, and told her to have the men meet him near the truck. Seconds later, they came pouring out of Lottie's house—three strong, muscular men, none more than 30 years of age, all participants in the church's jobs program, all of whom worked part-time renovating the church's dining room. Another man also emerged, late forties, not as muscular as the other men, but healthy and able, which was all Jesse needed. Jennifer followed, wearing blue jeans, a thick sweater, and the same work boots that got her through many a muddy work site in Haiti. They gathered around Jesse for a quick huddle.

"Okay, guys, I'm going to go in and label everything that's ours," instructed Jesse. "You guys just go in and grab whatever's labeled. Jen's going to go in and pack up and label whatever loose items belong to us that she thinks we should take. Jen, there are lots of empty boxes in the back of the truck." Jesse looked toward the house for a few seconds, and then turned his attention back to the group. "Do not say anything to the people in there. Absolutely nothing. No conversations. No small talk. Do not take any instructions from them. Don't let them give you anything. If you need clarification on something, ask me or Jen. Is that clear?"

They all nodded agreement.

"I really appreciate you guys helping me out like this on such short notice," Jesse said. "But the quicker we do this the better. Let's go."

Jesse walked up the driveway, his team following like soldiers headed into battle. Once they reached the front door, Jesse noticed the curtains were drawn, although the glass in the front door allowed them a clear view of the foyer. There appeared to be no one in view. Jesse started to put his keys into the lock, but Jennifer stopped him.

"You gon' wanna knock first," Jennifer said.

"I'm not going to knock on the door of my own house," Jesse protested.

"You wanna knock first," Jennifer repeated, now a command rather than a suggestion. "If these folk are crazy enough to do this, the last thing you want to do is startle them."

That was Jennifer, always the voice of reason. Jesse acquiesced to her request and knocked loudly on the door. After four rounds of alternating knocking and ringing the bell, no one answered.

"Maybe they left," one of the men said.

Jennifer shook her head. "They're there. I know it."

"Well, I've knocked enough. If they're in there, they know we're here. I'm going in." Before Jennifer had a chance to protest, Jesse pushed his key into the door lock and twisted. The key did not move. He twisted again in the other direction. Nothing. He jiggled the key, but the cylinder would not budge. He pulled out the key and looked incredulously at his wife. "They changed the locks."

Jennifer exhaled hard. "They probably knew we were going to try to get in. Honey, let's … ."

Before Jennifer could finish her statement, Jesse walked past her and marched down the walkway to the driveway and the guest room door. He tried his key in the storm door with no luck. Jesse's keys were also ineffective on the basement door and the sliding glass doors leading from the deck to the family room.

Jesse's recourse was quick and decisive. Without a word to the group, he walked out to his vehicle, opened the driver's side door, and reached inside to press the remote garage door opener. The garage door slowly slid upward. Jesse walked up the driveway toward the garage and motioned for the group to follow him. They looked at one another and then reluctantly followed Jesse into the garage.

Once they arrived, Jesse tried to unlock the wooden door leading from the garage to the laundry area, but was unsuccessful. Exasperated, Jesse sighed.

"How did these people have time to change all the locks since yesterday?" Jesse wondered aloud.

"They didn't do this yesterday," Jennifer offered. "Five'll get you 10 they are the ones that's been reading our email, and they are the ones who forwarded our mail to Knoxville. They've been in there at least a month. They probably got into your computer 'cause you like to leave it on all the time, so I reckon that's how they got access to our email."

"A month? Lottie never noticed? No one on this block noticed?"

"Honey, if they're coming and going at night, ain't nobody gonna notice them."

Jesse grabbed a flat head screwdriver from his still-intact tool kit on a shelf in the garage.

"What are you gonna do?" Jennifer asked.

"Gonna jimmy the lock."

"That ain't illegal?"

"Jen, this is my house. They aren't going to arrest me for breaking into my own house."

"Honey, I got a funny feelin' about this. Maybe we should wait 'til we talk to Joe."

Jesse ignored her, inserting the screwdriver between the door and its jamb, at the level of the latch plate. He jerked the screwdriver back and forth, up and down, hearing some faint crackling of wood, then some heavier cracking. He then removed the screwdriver and gently pushed open the door. The laundry room was dark, and the opening of the door allowed a beam of daylight to shoot across to the far end of the room. The double doors leading to the recreation room were directly to his left. Jesse walked inside, motioning for the others to follow him.

"We're going to start down in the basement, move everything out through the garage," he said, slowly opening the double doors to the recreation room and peering in. The room was much brighter than the laundry room due to the overhead windows, on the far wall, drawing in the muted late morning daylight. The eggshell white carpet was as clean and soft as always and enabled Jesse to walk across the rec room floor without making a sound.

His first order of business was to make sure that his

beloved 50-inch Toshiba LCD flat screen TV — the one that he had bought nine months ago for $900 at Walmart — was still hanging on the wall to the right of the double doors. Once he confirmed it was still there, he sighed and started toward the TV, intending to unhook it himself.

Suddenly his wife let out a piercing scream.

Jesse jerked and quickly turned in her direction. He followed her frightened stare to the open door directly across the room from the double doors, the one leading to the basement bedroom.

Standing in the doorway was a woman, holding them at rapt attention with a .38 caliber handgun pointed directly at Jesse's head.

Adverse Possession

Get out of my house!

* * *

Bernard MacNichol walked out the front doors of Inova Fairfax Hospital, prescription in hand. Some days he would have the hospital staff call him a taxi; other days, like today, he would walk from the hospital along Gallows Road to the strip mall directly across Route 50. His favorite place there was the Fratelli Pizzeria. It reminded him of his teenage years when he would go to the Fratelli's in Philadelphia with his friends. He would win brownie points because he had enough money to buy pizza for all his friends and, occasionally, mugs full of beer.

He had another reason for liking this Fratelli's. It had become a pastime of his to sit at the teakwood bar during lunchtime, nurse a couple of drinks, and check out the pretty corporate ladies coming in from various offices around the area. It reminded him that only nine years ago he became a part of that corporate environment. A large construction association had hired him as a computer technician after he had spent several years working dead-end jobs at various construction sites around Philadelphia.

He had never made it up to the suit-and-tie class. He was only a 41-year-old low-level techie sitting in a nondescript windowless corner office surrounded by monolithic boxes with flashing lights and humming fans, keeping the bits and bytes flowing at the pleasure of the higher pay grades. Nonetheless, he felt as if he was part of the club, though no one ever asked him out for drinks at happy hour like most of the other office wonks.

The woman who would eventually become his wife worked on the same floor, but in a different department, four doors down, near the loading dock. Her job was to handle all incoming and outgoing mail and packages. She knew the mail carrier, the FedEx lady, and the UPS man by name. She would take their deliveries, sort them, and distribute them to their recipients via a thrice daily mail run. She would also take any outgoing communication, address it, label it, and send it out. She would often joke that she made a fair living simply because all of the 160 employees of the association were too highfalutin to lick their own envelopes.

Except for the maintenance department, which had their offices at the far end of the hall and had established their own little clique, Bernard and Amber were the only employees who worked on that floor. They naturally became good friends soon after he started working there. The males in the office described Amber, in frat boy vernacular, as "cute," "hot," a "babe." She was a tall brown-haired woman with blue eyes and a basketball wife body that was often hidden in the baggy blue jeans, thick blouses, and smock she wore as part of her job. Several men from the company would visit her daily just to talk, and a fair amount of them would hope for something more. Amber would sense Bernard's brooding jealousy every time he walked in her office and saw her chatting with one of the "upstairs guys," as he called them. However, Bernard was always polite, never intrusive, never angry, never showing his greener tendencies to her visitors, though Amber could see right through him. She found him sweet and attractive, and decided to ask him out for drinks and dinner one day after work. They spent the rest of the evening at a pizzeria — similar to the one in which he now sat — sipping on mojitos, munching away on deep-dish pizza, and chatting about everything from work to past relationships.

They would marry a year later. No pomp, quick, quiet, a justice of the peace, a few family and friends. No one at work knew they were married, and Bernard and Amber wanted to keep it that way. There was no policy on fraternization, but Bernard and Amber knew that couples within the company faced greater scrutiny because of conflict of interest and favoritism issues. Their jobs were largely quiet and drama-free. They had no desire to add any controversy to the mix.

Now that job was done. The layoffs happened suddenly. The company claimed financial issues because of the recession, and gave 40 workers their pink slips. It was largely an opportunity for the company to get rid of their underperforming employees. Though Bernard was a knowledgeable and capable employee, he knew it was because of his cancer that he made the cut. Amber eventually quit in protest of Bernard's firing.

Bernard spent the next three years in and out of work. He would stay at a job long enough until the malaise and frequent doctors' visits due to his illness made him a liability at the job. Because he was a high school dropout, he could only find blue-collar employment, and his illness would make it difficult to maintain those jobs for long.

Amber found another job as a mail clerk, and could put Bernard on her company health plan. Since they did not have kids, the insurance was not prohibitively expensive. Nevertheless, Amber soon lost that job, finding herself the victim of a layoff just like her husband. They struggled to make the COBRA payments for their health insurance, and the policy eventually lapsed.

They would eventually travel to the D.C. area for the funeral for Bernard's parents. Bernard and Amber decided that, rather than return to Philly, they would make a go of it in northern Virginia, hoping to take advantage of the burgeoning tech market. However, employers could see right through him, and nobody wanted to take a chance on hiring a sick employee.

Bernard pulled the prescription out of his front pants pocket, slipped on his glasses, and read it again. Because of his doctor's horrid penmanship, he could not make out the words. He placed it on the bar, took a couple more sips of his beer, paid the bartender, and waited.

A man wearing blue jeans and a down ski jacket entered the restaurant. It was not difficult for the man to find the person he came to see. He had been told to look for his meet in the bar area, and Bernard was the only one there.

The man approached Bernard, looked around cautiously, and then said to him, "You who I'm looking for?"

"Yeah," Bernard answered. "You're the one who did the

online ad, right?"

"You ain't never done this before, have you?" the man said, looking around again. "You ain't a cop, are you?"

"No."

"Let's step outside."

Bernard left his payment for drinks on the bar, grabbed the prescription, and headed outside with the man. They headed to the center of the parking lot.

The man looked around again and said, "What you need?"

"I don't know." Bernard handed the man his prescription. "I can't understand the handwriting."

The man looked down at the prescription for two seconds, and then looked up and said, "It's oxycodone." He handed the prescription back to Bernard.

"Can you get that?"

"I can get anything."

"How much will it be?"

"Hundred and 20 pills, about 20 dollars."

"Not bad."

"That's because I'm not giving you my street price. If I was, you'd be paying 240 dollars."

"Twenty's good. It's less than the drug store."

"Almost ain't worth my time. But since you are one of the few of my customers who ain't trying to get high or bulked up, I'll hook you up."

The statement was partly true, but mostly a lie. He could get the first batch free through some of his contacts. He was hoping to win Bernard as a future customer, at which time he would return to his customary pricing.

"So, when do you think you'll have it?" Bernard asked.

"Give me two days. Meet me back here. About 8. But not inside. I don't meet inside."

"Okay."

The man looked at Bernard, but did not move.

"What?" Bernard said.

"You gonna give me the money, or what?"

"Oh, I thought I paid you when the pills came."

"Naw. Money up front."

"Well, how do I know you'll come back with the pills?"

"C'mon, dude. If I was gonna take you, I'd take you for a lot more than 20. Two days, you'll get your stuff. Trust me on that."

Bernard reached in his pocket and grabbed some bills. He pulled the only 20 off a small fold of fives and ones and handed it to the man. The man quickly took the money, shoved it in his pocket, and then walked away toward Gallows Road.

Bernard hated this. But with no insurance, he had no choice. He had just plunked down $500 for his latest round of chemotherapy at Inova, and he was almost flat broke. If it wasn't for the $450 he found in a lockbox in the Kane's bedroom closet, he wouldn't have been able to get his treatment this month.

He checked his money and figured he had enough to catch a taxi back to 6609 Bynum. There was a hotel nearby, and he knew he could find plenty of cabs there. He shoved the money back in his pocket and started toward Gallows Road for the long walk to the hotel.

* * *

"Get out of my house!" Amber MacNichol yelled, a nervous tremble in her voice. She stepped out of the doorway, the gun still trained at Jesse's head, her taut expression convincing Jesse that she could pull the trigger at any moment.

Jesse was most concerned about his wife. He nodded to her, without taking his eyes off Amber, and said, "Honey, get out."

Jennifer was most concerned about her husband. She did not budge.

Jesse spoke to the men surrounding Jennifer. He figured Amber would feel less threatened if fewer people were in the room. "Fellas, take my wife outside, please."

"I ain't goin' nowhere until you come with me," Jennifer said.

"I'm coming. I'll be right out."

One of the men gently laid a hand on Jennifer's shoulder and nudged her toward the exit. She reluctantly turned her body to leave, but never took her eyes off Amber until she was almost out the door leading to the garage. The men followed her, but were concerned about why Jesse was not immediately following them.

"You go too!" Amber yelled at Jesse.

"Okay, I'm going." Jesse moved slowly toward the rec room door, keeping his eyes fixed on the gun. When he was standing in the doorway, he said, "Listen, we own this house. Me, my wife, and kids don't have anything. I was just getting a few things that we need."

"You don't get a moving truck just to get a *few* things," Amber snapped.

Jesse thought it best not to argue. "You're right. But my

family has nothing. Can I at least get a few things out of the kids' rooms?"

"You tell me what to get. I'll leave the stuff outside. But you have to get out of my house, or I swear I'll shoot."

Jesse noticed how delusional she was. She kept referring to the house as *her* house. *Did she really believe that?* "Okay, I'm leaving. I just need the kids' clothes. If you could just put them in bags and set them outside the garage, I'll come get them."

"Okay. Now get out!"

Jesse hurried out the door of the garage and headed down the driveway to where Jennifer and the men were standing near the moving truck. He looked back just in time to see Amber flick a switch that closed the garage door.

"Honey, are you okay?" Jennifer asked.

"Yeah, I'm fine," said Jesse.

"I called the police."

"Thanks, hon, but I doubt it will do any good."

"She pulled a gun on you."

"We also broke into the house. A house that the police already believe belongs to them." Jesse nodded toward the house as he said the word *them*.

Jennifer went from concerned to doleful in less than five seconds. She watched as Jesse went over to the rear of the moving truck and pulled down the gate. "Jesse, what are we gonna do?"

"Little else to do," Jesse said. "We have to get in touch with Joe. Other than that, we have to pray like never before."

One of the men spoke up. "I say we do that now. Let's pray now. Right here in front of the house. Let's not wait."

Jesse nodded, appreciating his sensitivity. They gathered in a circle, held hands, and prayed, right at the edge of the driveway of 6609. It was a long, pleading prayer for mercy, for strength, and for understanding.

Amber watched them through parted curtains from the window of the master bedroom.

Adverse Possession

Desperation

* * *

Amber called Bernard on his cell phone when Jesse, Jennifer, and their friends had left. She was shaking and frightened, not so much from the break-in itself, but because of the need to brandish the gun Bernard had left her and the possibility that she would have had to fire it.

Bernard asked the taxi to drop him on Chester Street, which was the nearest street behind 6609. Once he paid the taxi driver, he walked up a driveway between two houses. He traversed a back yard, maneuvered around a grove of trees, and stepped onto the rear yard of 6609. This way, he could enter the house without anyone, especially the Kanes, seeing him from Bynum. He knew they were temporarily living directly across the street and likely paying rapt attention to them.

He entered through the basement door and called his wife's name so she would know it was he entering the house. He found her in the rec room, sitting on the couch, looking at

TV. The gun was sitting on the couch next to her. He picked up the gun, checked it, and pursed his lips.

"Probably should have had a round in the chamber before you used this," Bernard said.

Amber shot him an annoyed look. "How was I supposed to know that? You told me to just point and shoot, just like a camera."

"Thought the cylinder was full." Bernard slipped the gun in his pocket. "Worked anyway, though. I knew they would try *something*."

Amber frowned and looked away from him. "Did you get your medicine?"

"No. Another couple of days." Bernard started toward the stairs, but stopped when he heard Amber's voice again.

"Where are we going with this?"

Sensing his wife's ambivalence, Bernard turned and headed back toward her. He sat next to her and wrapped his right arm around her shoulder.

"Look, I know this is hard right now," Bernard said. "The Reclaim Network said this was to be expected. This is a very nice house, and the Kanes are not going to give it up easily."

"But we gotta know we can't keep this place," Amber complained. "Sooner or later we are going to have to leave. And now I'm pointing guns at the people who want it back. It seems kind of convoluted to me. So, what's the point?"

"You know the point, Amber," Bernard said, standing up. "We discussed this. You're just having some doubt right now, and that's to be expected. But it's going to take years for them to kick us out, and by then, we'll have squatters' rights."

"No." Amber shook her head vigorously, her blonde hair

brushing her shoulders. "This is more than just a strategy to stay off the streets. This is personal. This was your mom and dad's house, wasn't it?"

Bernard looked at her intensely. "How did you know that?"

"I looked up the land records on this house," Amber said, changing the channel on the TV. "They're online, you know. The records say that this house was bought two years ago by Harvey and Mildred MacNichol. It also says that the house was foreclosed on 15 months ago, and that it was bought by the Kanes 12 months ago." Amber turned to him just in time to see his face go from anger to downcast. "You never told me your parents once owned this house. You never told me they lost it in foreclosure. You *did* tell me that they moved from this home because it was too expensive, and moved to an apartment, and that was where the fire happened. So, stop lying. Why didn't you tell me what really happened with your parents?"

The revelation hit Bernard like a ton of bricks. He had not expected Amber to find out about his parents, at least not so soon, not now. He wondered what motivated Amber to check the online land records for the house, but that was not relevant now. The point is, *she knew*.

Bernard paced the floor for a few seconds before he spoke. "I didn't tell you because I didn't want to ruin your memory of them."

"What would ruin my memory of them?" Amber said. "They were lovely people. I adored them."

"I wanted to keep it that way." Bernard took a deep breath. "Fact is, it's enough that I'm sick, and can't find a job. Here we are trying to scrape together whatever morsels of funds we can find to make a living. But for you to hear about my parents losing their home and becoming homeless, it would have been too much. I was afraid you'd think, 'the apple doesn't fall far from the tree.'"

"How did they lose the home?"

"Got caught up with a bad loan they couldn't afford," Bernard explained. "You didn't know this, but my dad's online company folded two years ago, roughly the same time they bought this house. He gave it a good fight, and stayed afloat for a long time, but could never recover from the dot-com bubble burst. So, here he was, with no real income, and a brand new 5K mortgage on this house. After that, Dad started drinking heavily. I mean, he was known for tipping them back now and again, but now it was completely out of control. It was as if he didn't care anymore. I think he was cheating on Mom, too, but Mom never said anything about that. Pride, and all."

Bernard sat back down on the couch. Amber lightly and sympathetically stroked his hand. She could tell this was difficult for him to recount.

"Well, worse led to worse, and they lost the house, and most of their stuff," Bernard said. "They had to move to a cheesy one bedroom apartment off Route 1. One night, Dad was half-drunk, trying to cook something on the stove. He fell asleep, left the stove on. Smoke detectors in the apartment didn't work … ."

"They said at the funeral it was arson," Amber remembered.

"That's what they wanted everyone to believe. It was a better, more dignified story than saying, 'Dad was drunk and caught the apartment building on fire.'" Bernard shook his head. "They were once making six figures a year and giving to four charities, only to die penniless and drunk in a Section 8 apartment."

Both pain and regret were etched on Bernard's face, and he started to rant. "This was my parents' dream house. They worked hard to be able to afford the down payment. And they only enjoy it for nine months? Did anybody around here help? Did anybody care? This is one of the richest counties in the United States. Any one of these neighbors could have wrote a check to my parents for 30 grand like it was a cup of water." His volume lowered, and his voice started to crack. "I got guilt, too. I couldn't do anything to help them. I was their son, and I couldn't do anything."

Amber started rubbing his shoulders and back as Bernard doubled over and started to cry, saying over and over, "couldn't do nothing, couldn't do nothing." When he was done, Amber gripped his face with her hands, wiping his tears with her fingers. Bernard looked into her eyes and saw compassion and understanding, and that strengthened him.

"So, yes, this is personal," Bernard continued. "This was my parents' house. Now it's ours. The Reclaim Network will help us. My parents put 90,000 dollars down on this house. And nine months later, they have nothing. That's not right. I don't care what the property records say. This is my parents' house. By extension, it's our house. So, the Kanes will have to find someplace else to live, because we aren't going anywhere."

* * *

Adverse Possession

Joe Lippman sat in the conference room of his eighth-floor corner office, one of several in a gigantic, glass-enclosed office building in the heart of Tysons Corner. Jesse and Jennifer sat directly across from him on the other side of the conference room table. Joe listened with great interest while Jesse relayed to him the story of the takeover of their house, and their encounter with the gun-wielding Amber MacNichol the previous day. Joe asked many questions, but let the Kanes do much of the talking. When they were finally done, and Joe fully understood the situation, he stood up and paced in front of the window, ignoring its picturesque view. This gesture did not instill in Jesse a great deal of confidence.

"Factually, the police were wrong," Joe said, stopping his pacing. He stood there, all 6' 1" of him, towering over the Kanes. His eyes, which drooped slightly on the outer corners, tried to convey compassion. "But legally, they were right. They can't take any action if it might be a legitimate tenancy. They don't want to risk getting sued."

"So, what are we talking about here?" Jesse said. "What are our next steps?"

"Well, I could see about a court order to retrieve your personal belongings," Joe surmised. "Certainly no rental agreement is going to include your personal effects. At the same time, we start the process to go to court for unlawful detainer."

"How long will that take?" Jennifer asked. She was seated close to her husband, her hand grasping his.

"Could take up to six months, and that's if they don't appeal. If they do, and they likely will, it could be 9 or 10 months before you regain access to your property."

Jennifer let out a hard exasperated breath. Jesse shook his head in disbelief. He had hoped the process would only take a month or two.

"So, they get to stay in my house scot-free for almost a year?" Jesse said.

"I wouldn't say scot-free," Joe stated. "Once they decide this case in your favor the judge will likely refer the matter to the State's attorney for prosecution on the fraudulent lease. They'll likely go to jail. Of course, you could also sue them for losses and punitive damages."

"If they're taking over my house, I don't reckon they're gonna have the money to pay a judgment," Jennifer said.

"You're probably right." Joe allowed his towering frame to settle in a chair across the conference room table from the Kanes. "But I gotta tell you. If you are going to do this, you'd better do it quick. If you wait too late, you'll be in the middle of winter before the matter is referred to the sheriff's office for eviction. Sheriff won't evict if it's raining or snowing outside. You don't want to give them extra days inside your house just because of the weather."

"How much is all this going to cost us?" Jesse asked.

"Well, since you're relatives of Pastor Kane, I'll discount my usual fees," Joe said. "I'll need a 2,000-dollar retainer, and then 200 dollars per hour, plus expenses." He paused to see how Jesse and Jennifer would react.

Jennifer met Jesse's eyes just long enough to give him the "it's up to you" look. Jesse hung his head slightly and considered his options. It was either a year of putting Joe's kids through college, or put matters in his own hands, which so far was not working.

Adverse Possession

Jesse recalled the moment where the police answered the call to his house just after Amber had ejected them from the house at gunpoint. The cop who answered, a young cadet just out of the academy, had obviously been briefed on the situation at 6609 prior to arrival. Jennifer had thought that a different cop answering the call might see things their way and put the MacNichols out of their house. She showed the officer all of the forwarded mail they had received at her parents' house in Tennessee. Surely, it would be proof that they lived there.

The cop would simply repeat the same line that Lieutenant McGee had told them the day before. There is no proof that the MacNichols are trespassers on the property. The cop's only response to Amber's holding them at gunpoint was to knock on the door and talk to Amber. Of course, Amber did not answer, the cop declared there was nothing he could do, and he urged them again to call an attorney.

Jesse looked at Joe and nodded his head gently, which Joe interpreted as reluctant agreement with his fees.

"Have you seen the lease?" Joe asked.

Both Jesse and Jennifer shook their heads.

"That's probably good," Joe commented.

"Why?" Jennifer asked.

"Plausible deniability. At some point the MacNichols are going to have to produce the lease. The judge may ask if you recognize the lease and if you signed it. You can say 'I've never seen this lease in my life,' and not be lying about it. I'll have to get a handwriting expert to examine the lease and testify that the signature is not real. That could cost a few more hundred dollars."

Jesse looked at his wife, who gave him a half smile and a slight shrug of the shoulders, and withheld any comment. Jesse pulled his checkbook out of Jennifer's purse and started to write a check, payable to Joe Lippman Associates. He could literally feel a sharp twinge in his arm as he wrote the words 'two thousand' on the check. By the time he signed it, there was not one positive feeling in his soul about Bernard and Amber MacNichol. Not one.

* * *

Jesse and Jennifer left the meeting with Joe committed to telling their children what really happened. They had been avoiding telling them the full truth, hoping that the situation would be resolved quickly and they would not have to tell their children such traumatic news. Until now, they had explained that some people were staying in their home temporarily and they did not want to move back in until they left. The kids would have plenty of follow-up questions, but Jesse and Jennifer would always quickly skip the subject. Now, since Joe told them that their situation would not be easily or quickly resolved, they needed to answer the many questions their children were asking.

Lottie K was at work that day, so the Kanes had asked Tabita to babysit the kids at her home. Tabita had them seated at the kitchenette just inside her spacious marble counter kitchen, and was preparing tuna fish sandwiches for the kids when the Kanes knocked on the door.

"Come on in," Tabita said, stepping aside to allow Jesse and Jennifer inside. The kitchenette was fully visible from the foyer. Jesse and Jennifer greeted Tabita and then walked directly to Aiden and Ashley. Jennifer kissed and hugged both of them longer than usual; if the kids were older and smarter, they would have realized it was Jennifer's way of preparing them for bad news. Jesse sat at the table with them, while Jennifer remained standing.

"Kids, there's something mommy and I need to tell you," Jesse said. "When we were away in Haiti, some people broke into our house and are now living there. We called the police, but the people who broke in lied and said we had given them permission to live there. But we didn't, so the police don't know who to believe. So, a judge has to figure it out."

"Like *Judge Judy*," Aiden blurted out.

"Something like that," Jesse continued. "Anyway, judges are very busy, and they have a lot of decisions to make, so it will take a long time before the judge says that we can move back in."

"What about our stuff?" Ashley asked, seemingly on the verge of tears.

"That's just stuff, honey," Jennifer chimed in. "We can get more stuff."

"Mommy's right, kids," Jesse said.

"Are we homeless?" Aiden asked.

"No, Aiden, we are not homeless. Miss Lottie will allow us to stay here as long as we need. We are going to be all right. We are a family, and we will get through this together. You know how I know?"

"How?" both kids asked at once.

"Because God says so," Jesse said. "In the Bible, the writer of the 37th Psalms says he has never seen the righteous forsaken, nor his seed begging bread. That means that God will never give up on us, and he will take care of us."

Jesse stopped to observe them and gauge their reaction. Both sat stone-faced, looking downward with no discernable expressions. Ashley swung her legs back and forth, her bare feet sweeping the floor tile. Aiden looked up.

"How long is it going to take to get our house back?" Aiden asked.

Jesse looked at Aiden, and then quickly cut a glance over at Tabita, who was stirring a bowl of tuna fish at the counter, but still passively listening in on the conversation.

"It could take a year."

Tabita quietly muttered "Jesus" under her breath.

Jesse watched the kids as they tried to process what he was saying. He knew that understanding was difficult for them. A year was a long time to most adults, but to a child, it was like an eternity. He thought about when it would be appropriate to have follow-up talks with his children.

"The good news is, y'all get to hang out with Miss Lottie and Miss Tabita much more," Jennifer said, trying to put a positive spin on things. "In another week, you'll start back to school."

Knowing that good food could inject good spirits into any glum occasion, Tabita brought in seven tuna fish sandwiches on a platter, more than enough to feed everyone.

"One thing's for sure," Tabita said, her warm smile already lifting the mood. "You will never go hungry. Not while Tabita is here." She stood between Ashley and Aiden and took their hands. "Come, let's pray for the food."

Jesse and Jennifer joined in the prayer circle, and they lifted up prayers for the food, for the fellowship, for the children, and for God to move upon the situation at 6609.

Jesse did not close his eyes like the rest of them. He had gone from being irritated at the MacNichols, to full-blown anger. It was one thing to inconvenience him, but it was another to confuse and hurt his children. Maybe he deserved it.

But they didn't.

Empty Prayer Closet

* * *

"Funny how things go."

When Jennifer spoke, Jesse was in bed for the night, his eyes were closed, and he was almost asleep. Without stirring, he asked groggily, "What do you mean?"

Jennifer sat up in bed. The glow from an overhead street lamp filtered through the brush outside the window and cast freckles of light against the walls. The room itself was barely big enough to hold a waist high mahogany dresser, a nightstand, and the double bed they lay in. "In Knoxville, when I had my little apartment after I moved out of my parents' house, I was always close to eviction. I would ask my boyfriends to help pay the rent, but they would always let me down."

"Why buy the cow when you can get the milk for free?" Jesse turned on his left side, his back to Jennifer.

"Anyway, I've been sued for eviction so many times, I honestly thought every judge at that courthouse knew my name. But I always found a way out of it. I never got evicted, even though I was always broke."

"You would steal the money, right?" Jesse remembered the stories she had told about herself before they started dating.

"Or borrow it from friends, and never pay it back. Pretty much the same thing. Point is, now I'm married to a man who makes 80,000 a year as a preacher, and we *still* get evicted from our own home. I guess money don't necessarily buy you security, right?"

Jesse was silent. Jennifer leaned in close and placed her lips close to his right ear.

"You know what you told the kids today?" Jennifer whispered. "That we're gonna be all right? I want you to really believe that. I've been in worse messes than this, and I can tell you, this ain't nothin'. We got each other, we got a place to stay, and we got money. Maybe we don't have all our stuff. But that's okay. We can use this time to get closer to one another, to get closer to God. This can be like a fast, kinda. Sometimes having a bunch of stuff distracts us from what's important. We can make this work for us. It can be like a continuation of our Haiti experience."

Jesse said nothing. He understood her point but struggled to agree. He wanted to punish the people who stole his livelihood and the livelihood of his family. They made him feel completely ineffective. His kids had always thought of him as a hero. What were they thinking now? He could not get out of his mind the disappointed looks on their faces at Tabita's table.

He wanted Bernard and his wife to hurt. He wanted payback. Turning lemons into lemonade would just make it more difficult, less justifiable, to hate those who put him in this situation. He might even become thankful for them having done it, and that was something he simply could not fathom. This thing was wrong, and the MacNichols needed to know how wrong it really was.

"What do you think, honey?" Jennifer's hand snaked under the covers, under his T-shirt, found his chest, the place closest to his heart.

Jesse exhaled at the pleasure of her touch. *Jennifer was always the voice of reason.* "I understand," he said, acknowledging her wisdom.

Yet, he could not be influenced by it.

Not this time.

* * *

Jennifer awakened the next morning to strong sunlight pouring through the small window in the bedroom. That was a sign that it was at least 8 a.m. and time for her to get up, though it was Saturday and she could choose to sleep in. She turned over to her left to rouse Jesse, but found his side of the bed empty.

She sat up quickly and noticed that he was not in the bedroom. This bothered her, as Jesse rarely got out of bed in the morning without their saying a prayer together, even if it was only a few minutes. It was one of those not-so-secret secrets to which she attributed the success of her marriage. *Always pray together each morning,* a minister in Tennessee had once said to her. *Even if you're angry at each other.* It was a stalwart habit of their marriage. They would pray even before making love. Jennifer would often play on the words of the famous book *Eat, Pray, Love*. In her marriage, it was more like *Pray, Love, Eat*.

Maybe there was an emergency with the kids, she thought. She got out of bed, pulled a long terry cloth robe out of her luggage, and walked into the hallway. The kids' room was directly across the hall, so she quietly opened the door and looked inside. No Jesse, but the kids were sleeping soundly in their separate twin beds. She shut the door gently, deciding not to awaken them yet.

With the quiet gait of bare feet on carpet, she moved to the open area at the end of the hall, next to the stairs. The click-clank of dishes and pots and the robust smell of freshly-brewed dark roast meant that someone was upstairs in the kitchen. Jennifer decided to go upstairs, hoping the mystery cook was her husband.

She found Lottie in the kitchen, placing various types of pastries and cold meats on the table. When she noticed Jennifer watching, she said, "I thought we'd have a German style breakfast this morning."

"That's great." Jennifer smiled at Lottie and passed by the kitchen, searching the dining room, then the living room, then looking out of the living room window onto the porch. Seeing no signs of Jesse, or of their car, Jennifer turned to Lottie. "Have you seen my husband?"

Lottie answered without taking her eyes off the boneless ham she was slicing. "Well, he was in and out quite a bit last night."

"Really?" Jennifer said, moving closer to Lottie, pressing her for an explanation.

"Yeah. Left around 1 this morning, came back around 5, left out again at 6."

"You were up to see this?"

Lottie pointed to the alarm panel near the front door. "I turned off my burglar alarm when you started staying here, because I want you to be able to come and go as you please without fussing with it." Lottie plopped a few pieces of ham onto a platter. "But the alarm panel in my room still beeps whenever that front door is opened. I'm a light sleeper."

Jennifer felt embarrassed. "I'm sorry, Miss Lottie. We didn't mean to keep you up at night."

"It's okay, dear. After the third beep, I just got up and took the battery out of the darned thing. *Ärgerlich*." Lottie turned to her. "Does he do this kind of thing often?"

"Never. At bedtime he's like a rock. He'd probably sleep right through the Second Coming."

"Well, at 6, after I took the battery out of the chime, I looked out the window, and it looked like he was just sitting in the car. I watched TV until about 7:30, and then I heard the car start, and he left."

Jennifer shook her head. "That's so unlike him."

Lottie stopped slicing enough to console her. "Honey, he's probably just worried. It's not every day that a man comes home from a long trip and finds a stranger living in his house."

"You're probably right," Jennifer said, accepting her answer, though it did little to cease her own worry.

Bernard decided not to take the taxi or public transportation this time. Instead, he drove his pickup truck to the strip mall and parked near Fratelli's Pizzeria. He peered at his watch:

Adverse Possession

7:58 a.m. Two minutes early. Looking around, he saw only nine other cars sitting in the mall parking lot. Most of the vehicular traffic was coming and going from the McDonald's drive-thru just a few yards away. It was a Saturday, so the workday traffic was sparse.

Bernard turned off the ignition. There was only an eighth of a tank of gas in the truck, so he tried to save as much of it as possible, even if he had to do without the heat. That was one of three reasons he rarely drove the truck. Another reason was that it was once his parents' truck, so it was more sentimental to him than practical. It was his parents' only possession after the foreclosure, and the truck keys were the only thing recoverable from the charred apartment. He also never drove the truck because he had no insurance, and he didn't want to risk any accidents driving among the D.C. area's manic and aggressive drivers.

The time ticked on, and the truck grew cold quickly: *8:00 ... 8:10 ... 8:15 ... .* He was starting to see his breath, and he was beginning to think that his dealer would not be returning with his medication. Fortunately, he had kept his prescription, and he could still fill it legitimately. However, the $80 price tag would quickly chew up the remaining funds he had earned performing day labor at various sites around town.

... 8:30. Bernard was beginning to chalk this up as a lesson learned. He should have known better than to trust a person who sold prescription drugs without a prescription. Especially one who advertised online. Yet somehow, the man seemed legit about wanting to help him. Otherwise, why would a drug dealer risk jail time for $20?

A minute later, he noticed his dealer running across the

heavy trafficked Route 50 and heading for the parking lot. Bernard started to get out of the truck, but the dealer held up his hand, signaling for Bernard to remain inside.

The dealer got in the passenger side of the truck. He pulled a small white bag out of his inside coat pocket and handed it to Bernard.

Bernard opened the bag. "You're late."

"This ain't a job interview, dude." The dealer's eyes scanned his surroundings. "Patience is a virtue."

Bernard pulled out a sandwich bag filled with round yellow pills. "Can you get more?"

"I can get as much as you need. Cost in the future gonna be more than 20 dollars, though."

Bernard scoffed, amazed that the idea of a loss leader was applicable even in the world of illegal drugs. He put the pills back in the bag and shoved the bag under his seat. "Thanks for this."

"No problem. So, you need more?"

"Maybe later. Not right now."

"Cool. You know how to get in touch with me." The dealer got out of the truck and hurried across the parking lot in a different direction from where he came.

Bernard felt a strange and dubious sense of accomplishment. *My first drug deal.* Wasn't as difficult as he thought, and he would use his dire financial situation and his failing health as excuses against any encroaching guilty feelings. He started the truck and drove toward the Gallows Road exit. He would drive past the graves of his parents before he headed home.

* * *

Adverse Possession

They had been married for 10 years, yet this was the first time Jennifer sat down to breakfast without having any idea where her husband was. In 30 minutes of sitting at Lottie's table with her kids, she managed to eat only a slice of ham and a Kaiser roll. Lottie K tried to keep the breakfast conversation lively, and engaged the kids by asking them about their studies while they were in Knoxville. Lottie K knew that Jennifer was in a funk, and knew why, so she did not bother pressing Jennifer into joining their talk.

Jennifer allowed the kids to go downstairs with Lottie K after breakfast and watch TV. She wanted to be alone anyway. She stayed upstairs and tried to put herself in the right frame of mind. She alternated several unanswered, straight-to-voice-mail calls to Jesse's cell with calls to the church office, to Rodereck's cell, to Joe Lippman's office, to relatives, to friends, and anywhere else she thought he might be. Her mind could not bear the thought that Jesse had a suspicious, immoral, or clandestine reason for leaving the house without telling her. She tried to stay positive, though it was difficult for her to justify Jesse not informing her of his actions, or turning off his cell phone. That was what stuck with her the most. He had been through some stressful situations before, but he had never reacted like this.

She recalled the conversation in the car on the way to her parents' house. *I would never cheat on you.* She remembered the call on Jesse's cell, and the immediate hang-up once she said hello. She remembered how the night before, after rubbing his chest, which usually got him started, he had no interest in lovemaking. If he had a clandestine lover, she imagined that he could not wait to spend time with her after being apart from her for two months. Maybe this house situation was a convenient ruse for him to step out on her.

The thoughts made no sense, but they came so fast and furious, they were difficult to ignore. They were as voices, soft and sweet, dipping with sincerity, passion, and conviction, reminding her of her inadequacies and imperfections. She struggled to make sense of this, but somehow, Jesse's infidelity was the only thing that made sense.

Rather than dwell on Jesse's lack of presence in their prayer closet this morning, Jennifer decided to pray on her own. "Father, I don't know what my husband is doing right now. But you know. I pray that you guide his heart and his mind, so that he makes righteous choices. I pray wherever he is, that you will keep watch over him and keep him safe. In the name of Jesus."

She then sat on the couch, looked out the window at her house across the street, and tried to allow faith to triumph over uncertainty and worry.

* * *

Jennifer was sitting on the couch reading one of Lottie's housekeeping magazines when she heard the front doorknob jiggle. She jumped up, dropped the magazine, ran to the foyer, and flung open the door. Jesse was standing at the door, looking tired and worn, wearing wrinkled blue jeans and the Florida A&M hoodie that he had bought at the airport gift shop in Fort Lauderdale.

Jennifer did not waste any time with greetings. "Where have you been?"

Adverse Possession

Jesse stepped inside and gently closed the door. "Honey, let's sit down for a moment."

Jesse stepped ahead of her and sat in a Bordeaux-colored Queen Anne armchair near the couch. Jennifer remained standing.

"Where have you been? It's almost noon."

Jesse sighed. "I couldn't sleep last night, so I took a walk, started thinking about some things. And I ... "

"That was a long walk," Jennifer interrupted. "And you couldn't tell me you were going for a walk? You couldn't answer your cell phone? And don't tell me you didn't want to wake me."

Jesse held his hands up in a gesture of part-surrender, part-defense. "Jen, will you let me finish?"

Jennifer went to the couch, sat, crossed her arms, glowered at him, and waited.

Jesse took another deep breath. "I was thinking. There has to be some way to end this situation without waiting several months. I couldn't sleep, so I walked around the neighborhood for a bit. Finally, I had a thought. What if we could get some dirt on this guy? Cheating on his wife, whatever. Something that he wouldn't want anybody to know. We could use it as leverage to get our house back. And I found something."

Jesse waited for her to respond, but Jennifer said nothing and just glared at him. He continued. "Around 7:30 this morning, I saw him leave out. I decided to follow him to see where he was going."

Jennifer heard him clearly, but asked anyway. "You followed him?"

"Yeah."

"You do realize you have a wife and two young uns, right?"

"Yes."

Jennifer was not sure she believed him, but humored him anyway. She leaned forward. "So, what if he had caught you following him? His wife already pointed a gun in your face. What makes you think that he wouldn't do the same thing if he caught you following him around?"

Jesse could not argue. She was right. It made sense. It was reasonable. *Jennifer was always the voice of reason.* But he didn't need reason. He needed results. That was why he didn't tell his wife about his plans, or answer his cell phone. He knew she would talk him out of it, but this was a decision he had to make for himself. He took steps to make sure Bernard did not notice him, such as staying at least two cars behind, and wearing his hoodie so Bernard would not recognize him easily. That was all that was needed.

Jesse sidestepped her questions. "Listen, guess what I found out?"

Again, silence. A stare, as cold as hatred.

"This guy's doing drugs."

"How do you know?"

"Well, I don't really. But it certainly looked like a drug deal."

Jennifer shook her head. "This just gets worse and worse."

"Listen, I took precautions. I didn't get close. In fact, I was in the parking lot across the street when I saw it."

"Saw what?"

"This guy runs across Route 50, gets in MacNichol's car, stays in there for about a minute, gets back out."

"How do you know one of them wasn't lending the other

money? Or anything else?" Jennifer stood. "Jesse, that could have been anything. You can't prove it."

"No, it was a drug deal. I know it."

With more emphasis, Jennifer repeated, loudly, "You can't *prove* it."

Jesse raised his voice to match hers. "I may not need to prove it. It may be enough for him to *think* I saw a drug deal. I can use it as leverage; tell him I'll go to the police if he does not get out of my house."

Jennifer's hands were flailing, pleading, her tone just shy of an outright shout. "Jesse, this is not good. If you did see a drug deal, then you are messing with drug addicts and drug dealers, including one that has a gun."

"Do you have any better ideas?"

"Yes, I do. Trust God. Leave this up to Him and the lawyers."

They heard the basement door open, turned and saw Lottie at the foot of the stairs.

Lottie exchanged concerned glances between the two. "Everything okay up here?"

"Yeah, we're fine," Jesse did not take his eyes off Jennifer.

"Because if not, I can take the kids outside. They really don't need to be hearing this."

"I'm sorry, Miss Lottie," Jennifer said, her head down. "I didn't know we were that loud."

"No problem. Do you want me to take the kids out? It's not that cold out."

"No, we're okay," Jesse said.

Lottie went downstairs, closing the basement door firmly.

Jennifer sat back on the couch. She looked at him for a long moment, searching his eyes, observing his demeanor. He didn't carry himself like a guilty person, like he was doing something he wanted hidden from his wife. She knew about those kinds of men; she had met plenty of them in her lifetime. Jesse was not evasive, was not trying to avoid her, and his story was easily verifiable and too intricate to be a lie. "I think you need to talk with your father."

Jesse laughed. "My father?"

"Yes. He may not be perfect, but he is your pastor, as well as your father."

"You know what my Pop told me when I told him about what was going on?" Jesse said. "Basically, it was: 'serves you right for going to Haiti.' Then he gave me Joe's number and basically said good luck. I don't think my Pop has a lot to contribute here."

"Well, Elder Williams, then. Ain't you close to him?"

"We've talked quite a bit."

"Well, him then."

Jesse nodded. To keep the peace, he would talk to Elder Williams. Not because he felt as if he needed to. If it weren't for his wife's insistence, he would not be consulting with Rodereck, Elder Williams, or anyone else in his circle. They would only tell him what was on the heart of God.

Jesse wasn't sure he wanted to hear that right now.

Adverse Possession

The end of compassion

* * *

Jennifer decided to cook dinner that night to have something to occupy her mind, and further to bind her family together. With her mother's down home recipes firmly in her memory, she prepared pot roast with carrots, peas, and onions, and homemade wheat rolls. The savory scent of the meal permeated the entire house long before it was ready, stoking the hunger of Jesse, Lottie, and the kids, who could not wait to gather around the dinner table.

Confident that she had effectively shown her family that she had not lost a beat in the kitchen since she had been in Haiti, Jennifer went to the basement with the kids while Jesse drove to the church to seek out Elder Williams.

Jesse pulled up at Harvest of Righteousness at 6:45 p.m. He stepped out of his vehicle and took a quick survey of the number of cars in the parking lot. He estimated 40, which meant that the two classes scheduled that night would be well-attended, which was rare for a Saturday night. A man and a woman stood talking near the faux steeple at the front of the building. Rodereck had built the steeple to make the building look more like a church and less like the stand-alone grocery store it had once been. Despite Rodereck's efforts to erase the building's past, there were still subtle reminders of its former use, such as the loading zone striping still faintly visible along the front entrance to the building.

Jesse waved to the man and woman at the front of the church, but decided to enter the church through the left side door, which was the normal entrance for pastors and ministerial staff. Three doors down the blue and gray carpeted hallway was a door with a brass-colored sign reading "Classroom 1A." Jesse peered in through the door's glass panels and saw the classroom was empty. That was strange. Normally Elder Williams would be in his classroom by that time, preparing to lead his recovery support group.

He walked farther down the hallway and through a glass door to the lobby, which was on his right. On his left were two sets of solid double doors that led to the sanctuary. On the wall above the doors was a four-foot illustration of the church logo, a large cornucopia, inverted, with people of various races at the open end, a cross centered in the background, and the word "Harvest" in a crescent shape at the top of the logo, and the words "of Righteousness" at the bottom.

A teenage black female with a bouncy, curly hairdo sat behind the lobby desk, plugging away on Facebook until she looked up and saw that Jesse was there.

"Oh, Pastor Jesse, hello." She turned around to face him, situating the high back of her chair so that it hid the computer screen. "I'd heard you were back. Welcome."

"Thanks, Claire." Jesse decided to ignore her Facebooking even though using social media was forbidden while on the clock. "Have you seen Elder Williams?"

There was a long pause from Claire before she spoke. "I guess you don't know."

"Know what?"

"Elder Williams is no longer with this church."

"Since when?"

"He quit yesterday."

"Why?"

"I don't know. You'll have to ask Pastor Rodereck."

"I'll do that. Thanks."

Jesse walked back down the hallway, made a right at the next corridor, and walked all the way to the door at the end, which led to the pastor's office suite. Jesse walked in, passed Elena Ruiz's desk, and gently knocked on Rodereck's door. He heard his father's voice through the door saying, "Come."

Jesse walked in and found his father sitting on the couch flipping through files. "Don't you ever go home?"

"Too much work to do." Rodereck looked up at him. "Notwithstanding the problems you are having, when can we expect you to hop back in the saddle here at church?"

"I understand that I'm not the only person who has fallen off his horse," Jesse said.

"What do you mean?"

"What happened to Elder Williams?"

"He's no longer with us."

"I know that. What happened?"

Rodereck ignored him and went back to flipping through his files.

Adverse Possession

"I could always call him directly and find out," Jesse said. "But I would rather hear it from you."

Rodereck dropped the files on the couch and removed his glasses. He found it annoying that none of his son's visits of late were cordial. "He and I had a disagreement."

Jesse saw that he would have to extract the information from his father piece by piece. "What kind of disagreement?"

"The disagreeable kind."

"Pop, don't get flip with me."

"Not my fault that you can't take a hint that something is none of your business."

"Pop, I'm director of evangelism and missions. Elder Williams' recovery class is under my department. So, how is it not my business?"

"This doesn't pertain to E&M. This pertains to a personal disagreement between Elder Williams and me. He felt so strongly about his position that he left the church."

"What was his position?"

Rodereck saw that Jesse would not give up. Given his persistence, Jesse would likely find out anyway." At our meeting earlier this week, we discovered that the lease for your in-laws' house in Knoxville expires in two months. Elder Williams' position is that we should renew the lease for another five years."

"And your position?"

"Let the lease lapse."

"And what will happen to the Trudeaus?"

"They'll likely have to leave the house. The owners won't rent directly to them."

Jesse let out a big sigh, and his face twisted into a scowl.

"Pop?"

Rodereck came quickly to his own defense. "Son, we have been giving the Trudeaus subsidized rent for 10 years now. We can't say we haven't helped them. But, nothing lasts forever. I'm sure you'll agree that for this church to lose 800 dollars a month for a house we don't own and is not even in our jurisdiction makes for bad business."

"I agree, Pop. It *is* bad business."

That statement surprised Rodereck. He studied Jesse to make sure he wasn't being facetious. "You agree?"

"Yeah, I agree. It's bad business. But this was never a business arrangement. It was a mercy arrangement. It was benevolence. Now, you're basically putting them out in the street."

"Son, the Trudeaus have had 10 years to pull their act together. *Ten years*. They can't use the church as a crutch forever. At some point, they have to start walking for themselves. Sometimes people don't find out how strong they really are until the thing that supports them is taken away."

Jesse struggled for valid arguments to his father's points, but none came. He was right. Ten years *was* a long time to pay someone's rent, particularly if they could fend for themselves. If the discussion were about anyone other than his in-laws, he would not have conflicted with his father's decision.

Rodereck saw that his son was mulling over his remarks. He stood and laid a hand on Jesse's shoulder. "Son, this church's call is to fulfill the Great Commission. With this church, and any other organization, its finances should be used for that purpose. When a philanthropist gives a grant, he gives to causes that he believes in. Causes that achieve goals that he wants, in the way that he wants them. When we give money, it has to either help the preaching of the gospel, or lead to people being saved through the gospel. The question I have is: how has this assistance to your in-laws helped fulfill the call of the church?"

Jesse's response was quiet and uncertain. "I think part of the call of the church should be compassion toward those in need."

"But where does that compassion lead?" Rodereck said urgently. "Does it lead to saved souls? Does it lead to involvement in the church? Does it lead to better lives? We've been paying the Trudeaus' rent for 10 years. Not *once* have they donated to any of our programs. Not *once* have they participated in any of our outreaches. Not *once* have they visited our church. And by your own confession, they don't seem interested in a relationship with Christ. And I hear that Mr. Trudeau has a gambling problem. That's a major concern to me. We've been doing this for 10 years. How long should our hearts bleed?"

Jesse walked over to the window and looked out at nothing in particular. "So, you think they are taking advantage of us?"

Rodereck banged his fist in his hand. "Exactly."

Jesse remained quiet. Seeing that he was upset, Rodereck drew closer to him. "I know this is hard for you to hear. I know you love your in-laws. And this will likely put you in a difficult situation with your wife. But it has to be done."

"So when will they have to leave?" Jesse asked.

"Elder O'Reilly's working on contacting an attorney in Knoxville," Rodereck said. "Once that happens, we'll give them a 60-day notice. After that, they'll probably have another

30 days before eviction. So, they'll have 90 days to figure out where to go."

Jesse continued to look out the window, though he could see in the reflection his father looking at him. Normally he would have argued with his father, but this turn of events completely took the fight out of him. First, he was kicked out of his house. Now he hears that his in-laws may be kicked out of theirs. It was too much to bear. He was not certain that his shoulders were strong enough to handle two major problems. There were not many options. Never in his life had he felt so impotent.

Jesse decided to deal with the Trudeaus' problem later. Now, he needed to focus on the reason he came to the church in the first place.

Jesse turned to face his father. "I have another issue ... ."

* * *

Jennifer was playing Boggle in the family room with the kids when Lottie K came down to the basement. Jennifer watched Lottie tilt her head toward a far corner of the basement, in an area out of earshot of the kids.

"Kids, I'll be right back," Jennifer said to them, and then walked over to the corner of the basement where Lottie was standing.

"I was upstairs thinking—and I know this is none of my business—but why don't you and your husband go on a date tomorrow night?" Lottie suggested. "It seems like you two are pretty stressed out, and that may be the perfect way to keep your mind off things."

Jennifer smiled appreciatively. "Yeah, that sounds like a good idea."

"Yeah. I'll watch the kids. You two go to dinner, go to a movie, and if you feel so inclined, check into a hotel." Lottie feigned embarrassment. "I know you don't feel quite comfortable here, with the kids and me hanging around."

"I hope my husband agrees."

"Of course he will. Why won't he?"

"I'll have to buy something to wear. All of my good clothes are in our house."

"Then do that. Buy something that will light his *fire*." She said the word *fire* straight from her gut, with a seductive growl.

Jennifer laughed. "Miss Lottie, you shouldn't oughta be talking like that to us good ol' Christian folk."

Lottie scoffed. "Honey, please. I'm too old to be that naive."

Jennifer laughed again. "Thanks, Miss Lottie."

"No problem. Let's just hope that man of yours recognizes this as an opportunity and says yes."

"Well, God willin' and the creek don't rise, he will."

Breaking Point

* * *

Jennifer was delighted that Jesse had agreed to the date, and she woke up the next morning as excited as if it were their first date. She looked forward to spending her morning taking the kids to Sunday school, while Lottie caught up with her chores. Jesse went to the pastor's office for the ministry staff's regular Sunday morning prayer, but not before agreeing to watch the kids after church while Jennifer went shopping.

Once service was over at 1:30 p.m., Jennifer borrowed Lottie's car and drove alone to Tysons Corner Center, a huge indoor shopping mall just a few miles from Bynum Drive. She parked in the parking lot next to the entrance of the Nordstrom Rack store. Jennifer always felt strange walking into the upscale Nordstrom Rack store. Growing up, she had always been a Kmart type of woman, with occasional forays into JCPenney or Belk. Even now, she preferred the hustle and bustle of Walmart to the trendy extravagance of Tysons. But it all changed one Christmas, when her mother-in-law bought her a red jacket dress from Nordstrom's, and she got rave reviews whenever she wore it Sunday at the church. After that, she decided to add Nordstrom to her repertoire of stores for special events.

She would certainly make this a special event.

She walked in, and poked and prodded through the women's racks, looking for something that was sexy but not overtly so, conservative and sophisticated but not matronly. After 15 minutes of searching, she found a sheath dress, adorned with lace and sheer lace sleeves. It was size six, her size, and it was purple, which was her husband's favorite color.

She found a dressing room and tried on the dress. It fit her snugly, accentuating her curves without being too tight. The hem of the dress hung about two inches above her knees.

It was perfect.

She took the dress and a pair of high-heeled purple pumps to the checkout line. She proudly presented her husband's Visa check card and watched as the sales associate rang up her $256.12 bill. *Back in the day I could get six outfits for this price,* she thought.

The register beeped, and the sales associate peered at it inquisitively. No receipt printed out for her to sign. Jennifer knew this meant trouble.

The sales associate handed her back the card. "I'm sorry, ma'am. There's a problem with your card."

Jennifer had heard these words often before in her life. But they seemed strange now, given that she and Jesse's account balance was at $11,056 when she checked it online the day before.

"Are you sure?" Jennifer said. "Please try again."

The sales associate recognized the sincerity in her words. She knew Jennifer was not one of those customers who, too embarrassed to admit they did not have the money to pay, tried to play it as if it were some type of mistake. "Yes, ma'am." She scanned the card again. Again, it came up declined.

Jennifer knew she did not have the cash in her purse to pay. She and her husband had eschewed credit cards many years before, preferring to pay for everything with their check card. Jennifer tried to think of her options.

The sales associate helped her. "You can put this on hold until the store closes today. After that, we have to return it to the rack."

Jennifer gave the associate a flustered nod. "Thank you." She filled out some paperwork, got a receipt, and hurried out the store. Her watch read 2:36 p.m. The bank was right around the corner, near the escalator leading to the first floor. She walked to it, at a pace that was just shy of running.

The bank was closed, but the ATM was open. She stuck the card inside, ran a mini-balance, and checked it. To her dismay, she saw a check listed that had cleared the day before. She had no idea what the check was. Her inclination was to blame her husband. After all, the check had cleared on the same day that Jesse was out playing his spy games.

She rushed to the parking lot, got in the car, and drove back to Lottie's to check their accounts online.

Her only purpose in life, right now, was to find out why Jesse had written a $10,000 check on their account, and to whom, and why Jesse had not told her.

Adverse Possession

* * *

When Jennifer returned, Jesse was finished with his after-church meetings and was in their room catching a nap. Before Jennifer woke him, she checked on the kids, who were in their room napping as well. She then went straight to Lottie's computer in the basement family room, accessed her account online, and studied the recent activity.

Both the $10,000 check and the $2,000 check that Jesse had written to Joe Lippman and Associates had cleared, causing a $1,000 overdraft. Jennifer pulled up a copy of the check on screen, and then went to wake Jesse.

Jesse, bleary-eyed, came into the family room with her. Jennifer pointed to the image of the check on the computer and said, "What is this?"

Jesse looked closely at the check. When he saw the amount, he exclaimed, "What?"

Jennifer pressed. "What is the Reclaim Network, and why would they get 10,000 dollars of our money?"

"Jenny, I have no idea what this is, or what's going on."

"You didn't order this check?"

"No!" Jesse responded, almost yelling.

"Then who did? Looks like a cashier's check."

Jesse took over the computer mouse, clicked around for a bit, and came up with answers. "This check was sent through the electronic bill pay. It was ordered a few days ago, but was paid Friday."

"Why didn't I see it before now?"

"It's like any other check. You won't see it on the account until it clears."

"So, who ordered it? I changed all the passwords on our accounts as soon as I found out that our email was compromised."

"It was probably ordered before you did that."

"Then, the check would have been ordered while we were still overseas."

"Yeah."

Those voices returned again, whispering to Jennifer's soul, sly and convincing, weaving a lie of her husband as an adulterer. First, he disappears at odd hours without telling her. Now, 10 grand disappears from their account. Jennifer studied him long and hard, searching his eyes for any hint that he was lying.

"Jen, the MacNichols did this."

Jennifer frowned. *Does he actually expect me to believe that? Maybe that was why he married me, thinking I'm some kind of dumb hick who would swoon on his every word.*

"How would they do that, Jesse?" Jennifer asked.

"The same way they got into our email. You said I left the computer on. Maybe that's how they got into our account."

"But we have to enter a user name and password to get into our bank account," Jennifer reminded him. "That information is not stored in the computer, and it is not written down. There's no way they could have gotten into our bank account without knowing that information."

"Then they did it some other way," Jesse guessed. "They have access to our house. That means they have access to our personal papers. They know our names, our social security numbers, and our birthdates. They know our kids' names, social security numbers, birthdates. They have access to our bank statements, our account numbers. They have access to our entire financial history. I'm pretty sure, with all of that information, they figured out how to get money out of our account."

"So, what is the Reclaim Network?"

"I don't know, Jen. I didn't write the damn check!"

Jennifer drew her head back slightly, giving him a *I can't believe you said that to me* look. "Don't cuss at me."

Jesse exhaled and hung his head down. In his religious upbringing, and in Jennifer's, that word was a curse word, pure and simple, and was not to be uttered in polite company, except when preaching about hell. But the more he thought about it, the word seemed appropriate, since that check was putting a wedge between him and his wife. Nonetheless, he regretted not choosing his words more carefully.

"I'm sorry, Jen." Jesse looked up at her. "I didn't mean to cuss at you. I just feel like you're accusing me. I can assure you, I did not have anything to do with that check."

Jennifer looked at him, not sure whether to believe him, or those voices. They were stronger and more urgent now, reminding her of her days in Knoxville, of all the married couples she knew. Trusting their husbands was the undoing and peril of every married woman who had ever been cheated on, lied to, stolen from, beaten up, divorced, or scandalized. They all wanted to *believe*, as she wanted to now. But she couldn't ignore reality. Strange things were going on, and Jesse's being a pastor, a man of integrity, did not satiate that conflict.

Jennifer decided to reserve judgment for later. Right now, all she cared about was finding out about the Reclaim

Network and why they were getting $10,000 of their money.

Jesse tried to remain calm on the outside, but inside him was the wrath of a hundred bloodthirsty soldiers. "Jen, you know, Lord help me for saying this, but right now, all I want to do is go across the street and beat the snot out of this guy."

Jennifer, looking down at the floor, said, "Jesse, you're a minister. You can't go around beating up people. Just call Joe and find out what we need to do." Having a thought, she looked up at Jesse in desperation. "I hope our savings is still intact."

"There's no online access to that, but I'll check the bank tomorrow."

Jesse went back to the bedroom, grabbed his cell phone, and came back to the family room. He dialed Joe Lippman's cell number, and then said to Jennifer, "This has to be over with quick. I can't take much more of this."

* * *

Two hours later, Jesse and Jennifer were sitting in front of Joe Lippman's desk while Joe poured over the paperwork that Jennifer had printed out from their online account. Joe had planned to spend the afternoon relaxing at home, but the desperation in Jesse's voice convinced him to abandon his plans to watch the NBA All Star game, throw on some khakis and a grey T-shirt, and head to the office to meet them. "What is the Reclaim Network?" he asked.

"No clue," replied Jesse. "Jen tried to look them up online, but she didn't find any information. All we have is the address, a PO box in D.C."

Adverse Possession

Joe leaned back in his chair and pulled off his glasses. "You have any proof that the MacNichols did this? It seems like the kind of people that would do something like this would be south of the border by now."

"Who else could have done it?" Jesse shrugged. "They're the only ones that have access to our personal information, because they're in our house."

"Yes, but can you prove it?" Joe stood up, walked over to the front of his desk, and sat on the edge of it. "Once you report this to the bank, the bank can trace the transaction to the exact PC where it was made. But that's the best they can do. They can't prove, substantively, who was at the keyboard typing at the time the check was ordered. If the MacNichols say they didn't do it, there's no witnesses, no records, that can refute that. Unless you can tie the MacNichols to the Reclaim Network and prove they benefitted somehow from the check."

"So, you're telling us that the MacNichols are going to get away with this?" Jesse was seething.

"No." Joe's voice was a calm contrast to Jesse's. "The bank will investigate. If this were a 60 dollar or 70 dollar loss, the bank likely wouldn't bother. Isn't worth their time. But a 10K loss? I think they'll take that seriously. They probably have to refund your money, and they'll want it back. What you need to do, first thing on Monday, is call your bank's fraud department and file a claim. They'll advise you whether or not to call the police. They'll also give you a case number. Get that number to me. I'll follow up and use the case to strengthen our unlawful detainer filing."

Joe and Jennifer watched Jesse as he massaged his hands

and looked down at the floor. "I was going to take my wife on a date tonight." Jesse spoke slowly and methodically. "We had reservations at Legal's in Tysons, then we were going to go to a movie. Now, I can't do that, because I have no money. We gave up our credit cards years ago. I mean, I have money in a money market account, but I can't access that until tomorrow. And there's no guarantee that the MacNichols didn't get to that, too. Two people that I don't even know kept me from going on a date with my wife. People I don't know are trying to make my life a living hell."

Jesse decided that now was the time to reveal the results of his conversation the previous day with Rodereck. He had not told Jennifer that Elder Williams was no longer with the church, and he had not told her that he sought advice from his father. He was afraid of how Jennifer would respond to his father's advice, but now, after this latest violation of his security, he no longer cared.

Jesse gave them both a serious look. "You know what my father said to me about this? He spoke to me out of Nehemiah Chapter 4, about the rebuilding of the wall in Jerusalem. The wall in Jerusalem represented the security of the Jews. But the enemies of Jerusalem didn't want that to happen, and they fashioned plans against it. But Nehemiah, while building that wall, posted guards, with spears, swords, and bows. Then he said to them, 'Don't be afraid of your enemies. Remember the Lord, who is great and awesome, and fight for your families, your sons and your daughters, your wives and your *homes.*'" He placed emphasis on the last word.

Jesse turned to his wife. "This is a satanic attack against us, against our family. It is a direct threat to our security. My

Adverse Possession

Pop said that I would not be a man of God if I allowed this to happen. Since the MacNichols are now taking our money, I have to take action. I have to rebuild our wall." He turned to Joe. "You can file your case. But I'm not going to wait for several months until a judge gets around to deciding our fate. I'm going to find the smoking gun, and I'm going to find it now. This has got to end."

Jesse rose from his chair, turned to Jennifer and tilted his head toward the door. Jennifer got up, and they started toward the door.

"May I give you my legal advice?" Joe said, stopping them just before they opened the door. He did not wait for their answer. "Filing this case is the only legal way you're going to get your home back. Anything else could complicate your case, and may even cause the judge to decide in their favor. You need to take care of this through legal channels."

Jesse looked at Joe without acknowledging his comment. He then turned and opened the door to leave.

"Jesse?"

Jesse and Jennifer stopped and again gave Joe their attention.

"Nehemiah also trusted God. I hope you won't forget the importance of that."

Without further comment, Jesse and Jennifer turned and left.

* * *

"So, your Pa thinks you should fight to get the house back?" Jennifer said to Jesse on the way home in the car. "I thought you weren't gonna talk to your Pa. I thought you preferred to talk to Elder Williams."

"Elder is no longer with the church." Even as he said it, Jesse realized it was a dangerous comment. No doubt Jennifer would probe further, which would compel him to tell her why Elder Williams had left. Given the brewing tension between him and his wife, he did not want to travel down that road. Yet he felt he had to tell her that much, as she would likely find out through the rumor mill at some point. He hoped that no one at the church knew the specific reasons why Elder Williams had left. If Jennifer found out, then she would force Jesse to do something about it. His shoulders were simply not big enough to handle two mounting problems.

"Why?" was Jennifer's inevitable question.

"Some sort of theological disagreement," Jesse explained, choosing to be as vague as possible. To throw her off the trail, he followed up with, "At some point I have to call Elder Williams at home and find out exactly what happened."

"Hmm." Jennifer sat back in her seat as Jesse steered the Armada onto Bynum Drive. "Elder Williams was a good man. That's a huge loss for the church."

"Maybe I can get him to agree to return."

"I hope so. And I hope you have a chance to talk with him as well about what's goin' on. I'm not sure I'm okay with your Pa's advice."

"Jen, this is not surgery. I don't need a second opinion."

"So, what are you planning to do?"

Jesse backed the car into Lottie's driveway and looked directly across the street at their home. Everything looked normal, except that almost every light was still burning in the home. The beat-up pickup truck was still in the driveway.

"I got two leads," Jesse said. "One is the drug thing. I need some more on that, in order to give it some bite. But my biggest opportunity is this Reclaim Network."

"How's that?"

"They must be awful special to the MacNichols that they would send this company 10,000 dollars. I'll bet there is some connection there we need to know about."

"But how are you going to find out more? There's nothing about them online, not even in D.C.'s online records. The only thing we know about them is their PO box number."

Jesse switched off the ignition and removed the key. "Did you look up the PO box online? Or just the company name?"

"The company name."

"Let's get down stairs to the computer. I got an idea."

* * *

Jesse and Jennifer scrambled inside, slowing just long enough to ask Miss Lottie, who was in the kitchen preparing dinner, where the kids were. They disappeared to the basement immediately after Lottie told them the kids were at Tabita's.

Jennifer sat at the helm while Jesse hovered above her, looking at the screen. Within a few minutes, Jennifer had Googled the Reclaim Network's PO box address and found several references to a company called Estate Ventures, LLC. Jennifer accessed D.C. city online records and found that the company had a registered agent named Perrin Houton.

Jesse studied the address of the registered agent. "Most

registered agents are attorneys. That doesn't seem like an attorney's address."

Jennifer went back to work on Google again and pulled up a photograph of the home.

"Not an office," Jennifer commented. "Private home."

"Nice one, too," Jesse noted.

"Doesn't mean an attorney doesn't live there."

"It's possible. Kinda doubt it, though."

"This guy Perrin doesn't own the home, though. It's owned by some guy who lives in Bethesda. Looks like he's owned it for close to 20 years."

"Perrin's probably renting."

"What are you going to do?"

"I'm going to go there."

Jennifer swiveled in her chair to face him, hoping that she would find a smirk on his face and evidence that he was in a joking mood. Her hopes were dashed when she saw that he was as straight-faced as an undertaker. "You can't be serious."

"I'm quite serious."

"You heard what Joe said. You can't get too involved with these people."

Only then did Jesse laugh. "Jen, it's not like I'm going to go up to the front door, knock, and demand that they tell me who they are and why they got 10,000 dollars of my money. I'm going to be a little clandestine about it."

"Like you did with Bernard's drug deal?"

"Something like that."

"Jesse." Jennifer sighed with the desperation of a wife who had completely lost the ear of her husband. "This sounds like something really dangerous. I really wish you'd let God and the courts handle this."

"Jen, I'm a man of God. I have to take action." He smiled again, trying to instill some confidence in his wife, and failing miserably. "Trust me. They'll never know I was there."

The Reclaim Network

* * *

Jesse kissed his wife goodnight at 11:30 p.m. and hung around the basement watching TV, passing time until he had to leave. At exactly 1 a.m., he grabbed some of Lottie's old rolled up newspapers, and headed out to the Armada. He opened the driver's side door and popped open the rear hatch. On his way back to the rear of the car, he looked across the street at 6609. All the lights were still on, and there was no activity apparent in the house, although he knew the MacNichols were there. Weird.

He flipped down the rear seats of the Armada, and then opened the newspapers, spreading them on the rear floor area. He then shut the hatch and climbed into the driver's seat to get ready for his trip to D.C.

Interstate 66 was surprisingly populous for that time of morning. Jesse did not know whether that was normal; he was usually in the house by 10 p.m., except on special occasions. Traveling around the D.C. area at cricket's hours was something he did not do often.

The air was mild, and the sky clear, so Jesse cracked open his driver's side window to let some fresh air into the vehicle. He had a tinge of guilt for saying no to his wife's request to join him. He knew how much she wanted to be involved, but his protective nature would not let her go along. He had to deal with this. He planned to make this trip as often as he needed to get what he was looking for.

It was 30 minutes later when Jesse arrived at Morgan Place, in the northwest quadrant of Washington, D.C. Morgan Place formed one side of a triangular block, with Porter Street and Harvard Street being the other sides. Neatly-kept row houses lined both sides of the one-block, tree-lined street. The front stairs extended from their porches directly to the sidewalk, and on each side of the stairs were stone-fenced patches of earth, no more than five-feet square, sprouting various types of shrubbery. Jesse double-parked in front of 456 Morgan and carefully looked around to make sure no one was watching him. It was the main reason he wanted to do this so late; no nosy neighbors, no curious onlookers, everyone either in bed, surfing for porn, watching TV, reading, having sex, or some combination of the above.

Jesse looked carefully at 456 Morgan. It was what many Washingtonians called a Wardman-style row house, with a brick veneer, covered porch, columns holding up the porch roof, three double-hung windows on the second floor, and a dormer set into an almost vertical slate roof. All the lights were off, except a flicker of television lights through the shrub-shielded basement window. He looked around the front area of the house, but did not see what he was looking for.

He drove slowly up the block, counting the number of houses until he reached the corner. He turned the corner, and then pulled into a narrow alley. He counted houses again until he was sure he was in the rear of 456 Morgan. Fortunately, the green supercan at the end of the driveway leading to the house was emblazoned with the number "456," a confirmation that he was at the right house. He checked the windows. No lights, no blinds with slats ajar, no one apparently looking. The neighboring homes also appeared to be silent, no faces appearing in windows, no doors creaking slightly ajar at the behest of eavesdroppers. At this time of morning, even the night owls had ceased to monitor the goings-on outside. Jesse was ready.

He switched off the lights, but left the vehicle running. He popped open the hatch, then scurried around the front of the car to the supercan. He flipped open the top, gently and quietly, and removed two bags, one a black plastic garbage bag, and the other a smaller, white plastic bag. He placed the bags in the rear of the Armada, setting them carefully on the newspaper so they would not spill over. He then gently shut the hatch, closed the top to the supercan, climbed in the vehicle, and pulled off quickly.

Once he was clear of Morgan Place, he dialed his wife's cell phone. He opened his window to release a pungent odor that started to emit from one bag, something that smelled like stale onions and mold.

"Hi," she answered, alert. Her voice was clipped and taut. She was obviously still annoyed.

"You up?"

"Yep. I couldn't sleep."

Adverse Possession

"Well, stop worrying. I'm on my way home."

"You got it?"

"We'll see."

At 2:30 a.m. Jesse arrived back at Lottie's house, pulled the garbage bags out of the vehicle, and took them and the newspapers around back to the porch adjacent to the basement door, looking over his shoulder at 6609 to make sure he wasn't being observed. Jennifer, wearing a nightshirt and a robe, turned on the porch light and stepped outside.

"Turn out that light," Jesse directed. He wanted to do this in cover of darkness, so his neighbors were less likely to notice.

Jennifer went back inside, switched off the light, then came back out. "How are we s'posed to see what we are lookin' at without a light?"

"We can do this in the morning, if you'd rather," Jesse offered.

"No, let's do it now. Maybe I'll sleep better if I know there was some good reason you went traipsing off to D.C. to steal trash at the dead of night."

They dumped the black garbage bag onto a spread of newspapers lining the porch. Jesse, using a twig he found in the yard, plucked through mostly kitchen garbage, finding only two papers.

"This stuff stinks," Jennifer exclaimed, earning her a look from Jesse that said, *It's garbage. What do you expect?*

They quickly wrapped the newspapers around the garbage and threw it away in a trashcan sitting on the porch.

The white garbage bag seemed to contain mostly office paperwork. They moved the bag inside the house, and dumped the contents on the basement cocktail table, rooting through the papers thoroughly.

Jennifer pulled out a couple of papers of interest. "Look at these."

Jesse drew closer to her and peered at the papers in her hand. The letterhead showed line art of a boxy gabled home along with the words "Reclaim Network" and the PO box address. The body of the letter was an invitation to a support group meeting Tuesday, at 7:30 p.m., in the basement of an Episcopal church not far from Morgan Place. The papers appeared to be draft copies, scribbled with various notes and highlights.

Jesse and Jennifer dug further and found thank you letters for donations, among old catalogs, bill stubs, empty envelopes, Starbucks coffee cups, and printouts of web sites. When they had finished routing through the papers and bills, the story had started to come together.

The Reclaim Network was a trade name for the main activity of Estate Ventures. Though the company was listed in city records as a real estate consulting service, it was actually a fee-based support network providing resources and advice to people interested in taking over vacant and foreclosed properties and claiming them as their own. Perrin Houton was a facilitator of the project.

The project had an anonymous online blog, called "Reclaim Now!" which contained several rants and diatribes about the rich and corporate greed, and advocated turning over the wealth of the rich to the poor. The blog skewered rich politicians, over-paid corporate executives, famous entertainers, greedy megachurches, Wall Street, and almost any bank with more than a million dollars in assets. Some of the blog entries linked to pages full of unrecognizable gibberish, which Jesse and Jennifer assumed was a technical error. In fact, it was information contained in code, which only members of the group could decipher, so that the network could distribute information widely, without anyone else knowing what it was.

They could find no information proving Bernard MacNichol's connection to the group. But they knew that the MacNichols were likely receiving advice and technical assistance from the Reclaim Network, and that the $10,000 was probably payment for those services.

It was 4 a.m. before all of their research was done. Sitting back on the couch with Jennifer, Jesse said, "I knew this guy wasn't smart enough to do all this on his own."

"Yeah, but is it worth 10,000 dollars?" Jennifer asked. "Do they really charge that much? It seems to me that for 10,000 dollars, you could rent a legit apartment for about as long as you have a prayer of taking over someone's house."

"They may be promising something they can't deliver. They may be telling their members that they can get permanent access to a home. That would certainly be worth 10,000 dollars, if the occupiers get to keep the home they occupy."

"Yeah, but that doesn't make sense. They had to have broken into our home before they knew we had the money, or knew they could even get access to our money. And what group charges 10,000 dollars to poor people who can't afford their own housing? If they can't afford housing, how can they afford 10,000 dollars?"

Jesse started cleaning up the papers on the table. "A lot

of this doesn't make sense. Which is why we need to look further into this."

Jennifer frowned. "Don't tell me you're thinking of going to that Tuesday meeting."

"Not me, but I know someone who may be interested."

"Who?"

Jesse was silent, but looked directly at his wife. Jennifer had known him long enough to be able to read his thoughts in his face.

"Jesse, not your father."

"Yep."

"Seriously?"

"It'll be perfect for him."

"You're gonna send your filthy-rich father into a room full of these people? That's like gift-wrapping the road runner and handing him to the coyote."

"My father's mission has been to help people achieve financial prosperity. Groups like this exist because it's not always easy to be prosperous. What better place for him to learn that?"

"You're kidding me, right?" Rodereck removed his preaching robe after officiating over a memorial service in the sanctuary. "You want me to go to a meeting of people who specialize in taking over other folks' homes?"

"Pop, it's just a meeting," Jesse said. "You go to meetings all the time."

"Yeah, but I usually don't go to meetings with a bunch of socialists."

Adverse Possession

"I'm not asking you to join. I'm asking you to attend and gather information. And besides, socialist is probably a strong word."

Rodereck unfastened his tie. "Why can't you go?"

Jesse grabbed his father's robe, a black crepe garment with gold panels on each side of the center affixed with Latin crosses. He also owned a purple robe and a white robe, which he often wore on less solemn occasions. "Bernard MacNichol has already seen me. So has his wife. If either of them is there at the meeting and recognizes me, things'll start getting hush-hush. Bernard's wife has seen Jennifer, and both of them have probably seen Jennifer walk in and out of Lottie's house."

"Jesse, I've been on TV. There's a chance they would recognize *me*."

Jesse hung up the robe in the closet. "These don't seem like the type of people who would hang on the words of TV preachers," he noted. "Billy Graham could probably walk in that room, and they wouldn't know who he was."

"What makes you think I'd be welcome at this meeting?"

"That, I don't know. I'm grasping for straws here. I need as much information as I can get. It's either that, or spend more nights digging through these people's trash."

Rodereck's chuckle reflected his astonishment. "I can't believe you did that." He slipped on his suit jacket and reached on his desk for his car keys. "I have to head out to the repast, so I have to run. I'll think about it."

"Thanks, Pop." Jesse walked his father to the door and saw him to his car. Once Rodereck pulled off, Jesse hung his head. *I'll think about it.* That was Rodereck's way of saying *There's not a chance in a million I'll be caught dead at this meeting.*

Jesse hoped his father would come around and agree to his request. But if he were a betting man, he wouldn't have waged even a penny on that happening.

With no certain answer from his father, Jesse was determined to find out more information about the Reclaim Network on his own. He drove back to 456 Newton again at 1:30 a.m. on Tuesday morning, pulling the trash in the same manner as before, finding nothing more than old porn magazines and printouts of web pages.

But this time, he saw human activity. After rooting through the garbage can in back, he pulled around front and noticed two people in the shadows on the porch. He drove past at normal speed, looking only briefly at the two people, who were sitting in wooden folding chairs, facing each other, almost knee to knee, as if in deep conversation. He stopped at the next intersection, made a U-turn, and slipped into a parking space along the curb a few doors up from the house, on the opposite side of the street. Here, he could have a clear view of the porch from his driver's side windshield without drawing any attention. He readied the digital camera, which he had borrowed from the church, and placed it near his right hand on the passenger seat. He had already set the camera to low-light mode, which would enable him to take night pictures without using a flash.

He sat there, watching, waiting for something to happen. He was not sure what he was waiting for. Two people sitting together on a porch was not unusual, after all. Nevertheless, desperate for something to happen with his housing situation, he would wait to see what, if any, opportunities this would give him.

Jesse thought to call his wife to let her know he would be arriving home later than usual, but decided against it. She would be too much of a distraction right now. He needed to focus. He needed his head in the game. Any moment missed could needlessly prolong his suffering and the suffering of his family.

Ten minutes later, the people moved from the shadows and started to walk down the stairs. Jesse could see that it was a man, about 40 years of age, and a woman, no, a girl, or at least she looked like a girl. *Yes, she was a girl.* To Jesse, she looked no older than 15 or 16, maybe older, but not old enough to be an adult. Jesse was trained to think positively about people unless they showed him otherwise, so Jesse's first guess was that the girl was the man's daughter. They walked down the stairs toward the sidewalk, the girl wearing a puffy North Face jacket and the tightest of blue jeans, the man wearing what appeared to be pajama bottoms, slippers, and a heavy wool pea coat. Jesse saw nothing to pique his curiosity, and he reached for the keys to start the ignition, intending to go home. When he looked up again, he moved his hand away from the keys, seeing something very interesting.

Is he kissing her?

Jesse leaned forward and craned his neck to get as close a view as possible in his car. Yes, the girl did reach up, wrap her arms around the man's neck, and kiss him passionately on the lips. The man responded by reaching around her and kneading her derriere, pulling her closer to him as he hungrily devoured her lips.

Jesse could not watch. He turned away, glancing at them only briefly every few seconds to see if they had finished. He was disgusted, but he was also angry. Even if she were the age of consent, he was still too old for her, and thus extremely shallow.

As he looked away, he noticed the camera sitting on the passenger's seat, and almost instantly, a thought came to him. What if this man making out in the middle of the sidewalk with an underage girl was Perrin Houtin, the organizer of the Reclaim Network?

He spotted an opportunity.

He quickly grabbed the camera, reset its shutter speed, aimed, and clicked. Again, he clicked, and a third and fourth time. He reviewed the photos in the camera monitor. They were a bit blurry and dark, but still clear enough to identify the subjects.

Jesse watched until the man and girl finished their affectionate public tryst. His eyes followed the girl as she hurried across the street and walked up the stairs to another house. He looked at the man, who stood there watching her until she was safely inside the house. He was about medium height, light-skinned, with a head full of long manicured dreadlocks tied together in the back of his head like a ponytail. Jesse quickly snapped a photo of him. The man, unaware that Jesse was there, moved quickly up the stairs of 456 and disappeared inside the house.

Jesse smiled. He now had a strategy, although he hated having to sully himself with other people's private details to get it. He pulled his cell phone out of his pocket, set its alarm to 7:30 a.m., and placed it in the cupholder next to him. He adjusted his seat so that he could recline comfortably. After a check of the fuel to ensure there was enough to keep the vehicle warm, he leaned back and tried to get some shut-eye.

A 5:30 a.m. call from Jennifer awakened him earlier than expected. He knew this was the worry call, the call of concern, the call during which Jennifer would interrogate him about why he had not called to tell her he would be delayed coming home. The phone would never stop ringing if Jennifer could not reach him, so Jesse answered.

"Hey, hon."

"Where are you?"

"Still in D.C. I got a lead we may be able to use."

"I was expecting you home by 2. Why didn't you call?"

"I didn't want to wake you."

"Jesse, that's lame."

"Seriously, I didn't. I didn't want you up half the night worrying about me."

"I *am* worried."

"I'm okay." Jesse tried to focus her. "Don't you want to hear about the lead I have?"

"I want my husband."

"You have me."

"No, I don't. You care more about the house than me. We haven't talked, or spent any time with each other."

Jesse sighed. Just the night before, Jennifer was excited about finding out more information about the Reclaim Network. Now, she was turning on him. *Women are so fickle.* "That's not true. I care about you. But I have to fix this. We weren't able to even go on a date because of this."

"Jesse, why are you giving these people that much power?"
Jesse did not follow. He silently awaited an explanation.

"We could have still gone on our date. It might not have been what we wanted, but it would have been time spent together nonetheless. We could have scraped up enough money to go to McDonald's, and a movie. I wouldn't have cared what we did, as long as we were together. But you let these people cheat you out of that. You're letting them ruin our relationship."

Jesse found Jennifer's statement rather dramatic, but he did not argue. It was almost 5:45, just 30 minutes until dawn. He needed at least another hour of sleep, so that he could follow the lead he had been given. "Jen, do we have to talk about this now?"

Jesse heard a hard sigh come through the phone, followed by her terse voice. "I'm sure we'll talk *whenever* you decide to come home."

Click.

Jesse looked at his phone. That was only the second time Jennifer had hung up on him during their 10 years of marriage. The first time was a jealous streak during the first year of their marriage. Jennifer suspected that a woman from the church had her eyes on Jesse, and Jesse seemed to do nothing to deflect the attention. She found out, during a routine phone call to Jesse at the church, that the woman had taken Jesse out to lunch. This resulted in an argument, and then the hanging up. Jennifer later apologized, realizing that Jesse's job was to deal with all types of people, including those that may have crushes on him. She had inadvertently imposed Rodereck's sins upon her husband.

Adverse Possession

Jesse put the phone in his pocket, deciding not to call her back. He replayed her last statement in his mind. *I'm sure we'll talk whenever you decide to come home.*

"That's the problem," Jesse said loudly to himself. "We don't *have* a home to come home to."

Jennifer had been tossing and turning most of the night, and she found she could not get back to sleep after she hung up on Jesse. She had hoped that Jesse would call her back to settle the matter, but he seemed intent on fulfilling whatever it was he was doing.

She sat up in bed, trying to deal with her conflicting feelings. She had hoped that returning home from Haiti would give them an opportunity to focus on one another after spending months absorbed helping the less fortunate. They had spent many days working in mud and dirt and the hot sun, helping to build schools. They spent the nights in cramped living quarters, with only a cot and a few blankets, the threat of robbery or kidnaping always looming around them. She yearned for the peace and tranquility of home. She looked forward to it; she *pined* for it. It excited her to think of Jesse taking on one of their special dates, which would always be something unique and different. She remembered one day when he came home from the church, asked her to get dressed, and surprised her with tickets to a concert of her favorite group, Third Day. Another time he awakened her at 5 a.m. and announced that he was taking her on a shopping spree in New York.

But, easily the most special date was the least extravagant

one. On the evening of their fifth anniversary, he took her to a remote area of Virginia Beach just off Sandpiper Road, to a lonely swath of beach owned by a friend from another church. There, they had a picnic of fruits and vegetables, along with a bottle of Iron Horse Chardonnay, after which they watched the sunset together and, confident that no one else was around, made love at the edges of the surf.

She understood his intent, she understood his passion, and she tried to suppress her feelings of neglect, because she knew Jesse was fighting for their family home. On the other hand, she felt that losing their home had taken away his passion for her, his spontaneity, his doting manner. She felt that God was showing her what really *was* the number one love in Jesse's life, and it was not her. That bothered Jennifer. If this thing lasted several months, as Joe stated, she was not sure she could stand being disconnected from her husband that long.

She got up at 6:45 and walked across the hall to the kids' room. She looked in on them and saw they were sleeping soundly. They seemed to be adjusting to this better than the adults, though they occasionally yearned for the belongings they missed. Lottie K had done a great job in keeping them occupied so they would not have time to dwell on the things they did not have.

Jennifer walked back into her bedroom, stood in the middle of the room, and talked to God. "Lord, I don't know what you're doing. But I know you have a master plan behind all this, and I pray that you would reveal your will to us. Help us to come together and focus on you and your desire for us during this time. Help us to draw closer to you. In Jesus name."

Adverse Possession

Feeling better after she had prayed, she opened the well-worn Bible she had taken with her to Haiti, and flipped to a passage of Scripture she had read often. From Matthew 6:21, it read, "For where your treasure is, there will your heart be also."

Pursuit

Jesse was jerked awake by the sound of a car horn blasting. He quickly sat upright and looked at the clock. It was 7:45 a.m. The alarm on his phone had gone off at 7:30, but because it was in his pocket, he never heard it.

He looked around and noticed a blue sedan a few yards ahead, double-parked, its engine running, hazard lights blinking. A middle-age black woman, wearing pink scrubs, climbed out of the car and motioned *hurry-up* toward a house on that side of the street.

Jesse adjusted his driver's seat and looked intently at the woman. A few seconds later, the young girl that he had seen earlier that morning emerged from her house, hurried down the steps, and got into the waiting car. The girl was carrying a backpack, and appeared to be wearing the same jeans and coat as the night before. The woman got back in the car, and the hazard lights stopped blinking. Jesse smiled and prepared to pull his vehicle out of its parking space.

This was a good sign.

The blue sedan pulled off and made a left turn at Porter

Street, the next intersection. Jesse followed, hanging back two or three car lengths so that he could avoid suspicion. The Nissan made a right turn at busy Connecticut Avenue and drove past the University of the District of Columbia, with its wheat-colored masonry buildings. Fortunately there was enough traffic out such that Jesse's presence behind did not attract much suspicion, so he pulled within a car length of the sedan.

The sedan's left turn at Albemarle made Jesse nervous. This street consisted of many stop signs and traffic lights. He had to widen the distance, so if the occupants of the sedan looked back, he did not appear to be following them. When the sedan made a right turn on Nebraska, and then a left on Chesapeake, Jesse was half a block behind.

On Chesapeake, he saw the sedan pull left into a driveway up ahead. Jesse drove past the driveway and pulled into a no parking zone just beyond it. He put the car in park, looked back and saw the girl climb out of the blue sedan and head toward the western entrance of Woodrow Wilson High School. Jesse pulled out his camera, adjusted the settings, and took a telephoto shot of the girl just as she was about to enter the double doors of the school.

Perfect, Jesse thought. He put the camera away and, with a yawn, put his car into drive and pulled off. Before he went home, he needed to make a stop at Joe Lippman's office.

* * *

Joe Lippman examined the photographs on Jesse's camera and listened as Jesse explained all of his activities over the past day.

"You're a regular Columbo, ain't ya?" Joe leaned back in his chair. "How does all this help your case?"

Jesse paced about the office. "If this guy is Perrin Houtin — and I'm willing to bet he is — then the last thing he wants is to go to jail for having sexual relations with an underage girl."

"And that's why he slobs her down and gropes her like a loaf of bread on a public sidewalk." Joe's remark was pointedly ironic.

"Ah, but it was early in the morning. He didn't expect that anybody was going to be watching him. Not anyone that cared, anyway." Jesse sat in a chair across from Joe's desk and leaned forward. "So, if that were Perrin Houton, what kind of confessions do you think he would make in exchange for not having his business with this girl put out on the street? And I'm not just talking about the police. How do you think her mother would react, knowing that her daughter is mixing it up with a 40-ish man?"

Joe stood. "I see where you're going with this. But Jesse, I gotta tell you. This thing is pretty weak, legally and otherwise."

"Weak?"

"Yeah. Okay, you saw the girl go into a high school with a backpack. So, that means that she attends the school. But the legal age of consent in D.C. is 16. So, she could be 16, 17, 18. She could even be an underachieving 21-year-old for all we know. You don't have the facts to establish that something illegal was happening on that sidewalk. And any attorney would likely argue that the kiss was not sexual in nature and intent. It was just the two of them saying goodbye, after which she went to her own home. So, proving sexual contact is iffy."

"Did you not just hear me say he touched her rear end?" Jesse stated. "He didn't just touch it. He—"

Joe interrupted. "I heard you. I'm just telling you how this thing is going to go down in a court."

"I'm hoping it doesn't get to a court. I use this as leverage against this guy, get him to tell me what I need to know to get these people out of my house."

"Then I have to warn you." Joe's face became stark. "Confronting someone, especially someone you don't know, with their sins could be dangerous. What's to stop this man from shooting you right then and there, ridding himself of the problem?"

"That's why we have to be careful how we do this."

"I recommend we not do it at all. My process server served notice on the MacNichols today. They have 30 days to leave, or else we'll seek an unlawful detainer. Let's play this out through the courts."

"Joe, I can't wait months to get my house back," Jesse grabbed his camera. "The MacNichols do not get to win like this. You can work it through the courts. But there's always more than one solution to every problem."

"And just as many consequences," Joe added.

Jesse shot a final look of contempt at Joe before he turned to leave.

* * *

Jesse called his father from the car. "Dad, you don't have to worry about going to the Reclaim Network meeting tonight."

Rodereck, answering the phone from his car, was relieved,

only because he didn't have to tell his son he had no intention of going to that meeting. "What changed your mind?"

"I got some new information. I think I'm going to go to this meeting myself."

"What if they recognize you?"

"That doesn't matter now."

It was 11 a.m. when Jesse finally made it back to Lottie K's house. On his way to her front door, he stared a long time at his house. Everything seemed okay; nothing had changed from the night before, except that Bernard's pickup truck was no longer in the driveway. He noticed that Lottie's car was also absent, meaning that she had gone somewhere.

He used his key and walked into Lottie's house. Shutting the door behind him, he noticed that the first floor was quiet. No lights, no noise, no lingering odor of breakfast. Either no one was at home, or his wife and kids were all down in the basement. He walked slowly to the basement door and opened it. There did not seem to be much noise down there, either. Jesse found this unusual, as his kids were usually a rowdy bunch when they were at the peak of their morning energy.

He walked down the basement stairs and found it still. No TVs. No video games. No radio. *No one's at home*, he thought. He set the camera down on the cocktail table, removed his jacket, and tossed it over the rear of the couch. He pulled off his shoes, lay on the couch, and turned the TV on with the remote. With any luck, he could relax for about an hour or so before his wife got home.

He heard the bedroom door creak, which startled him and

made him jump up. Jesse looked around the corner and saw Jennifer, still in her nightclothes, coming toward him.

With a face void of expression and a voice as ominous as a doctor's death announcement, Jennifer looked in his eyes and said the four most dreaded words that any red-blooded American husband could hear from his wife.

"We need to talk."

Confrontation

Bernard parked his pickup truck on a side street and sneaked around the back of 6609, as usual. He entered through the basement door, walked across the laundry room into the rec room, and saw his wife sitting on the couch in nothing but her bra and panties, chain-smoking Winstons and working on her second glass of Scotch.

"What's the matter?" Bernard asked, removing a navy blue bomber jacket with the pocket fasteners missing and a wispy white stain on the rear shoulder that came from brushing against a freshly painted wall. "Drinking at 11 in the morning?"

Amber reached over to the cocktail table, picked up a piece of paper, and then slammed it back on the table. Bernard walked over, picked it up, and read it.

"It's the 30-day notice to vacate," said Bernard nonchalantly. "Perrin told us to expect this. He said simply ignore it. Then they'll have to take us to court, and that's when the plan will kick in."

"The plan, huh?" Amber placed her still-lit cigarette on

top of the inverted Scotch bottle cap. She had tried to quit smoking, but had picked up the habit again recently. "I just spoke to Perrin about an hour ago."

"What'd he say?"

"He told us not to contact him for a while."

"Why?"

"He thinks he's being investigated."

"What makes him think that?"

"He said he talked to his neighbor this morning, and his neighbor told him he saw someone come through the alley and take the trash out of his garbage bin. He figures that no one would be that interested in his trash unless they were checking on him. He thinks it has to do with that 10,000 dollar check."

Bernard's face curled into worry. "So, what about the plan? What about our attorney?"

"Perrin says he's gonna work all that out. Just don't contact him until he contacts us. He's cancelling the meeting tonight as well, but he's gonna stick around and watch, just to see if anyone uninvited shows up."

"Why do I get the feeling this creep is trying to stiff us?" Bernard flopped in a chair next to the couch. "We send him 10Gs, and all of a sudden, he wants to go underground."

Amber finished off the last of her Scotch, and then poured more in the same glass. She pushed the glass over to Bernard. "Might as well have a drink with me. Somehow, this doesn't sound like it's going to work out too well for us."

"What do you want to talk about?" Jesse headed back to

the couch and reclined on it. Jennifer stood in front of the couch, blocking Jesse's view of the TV.

"I want to talk about us." Jennifer was stonefaced, her arms folded.

"Where are the kids?" Jesse asked.

"They're at Tabita's. Now, can we talk about this?"

Jesse yawned. "Jen, can this wait until later? I've been up half the night trying to get our home back, and I'd like to get some rest."

"You mean, you've been tryin' to get your *house* back?"

"Same thing."

"No, it ain't. *We're* your home. Your wife and your children are your home. That thing across the street is just an organized pile of bricks and wood. You're neglecting your home, tryin' to get a house."

"So, do you just want me to let the house go?"

"No. We can pray. We can let the attorneys deal with it, and let God do the rest. Otherwise, we get on with our lives, without lettin' the MacNichols, or anybody else, take any piece of it. Then, we have the true victory."

Jesse lay on the couch, staring up at the ceiling, saying nothing.

"I want us to go out tonight."

Jesse sat up. "Tonight?"

Jennifer knelt down in front of him. "Yes, tonight. Since the MacNichols didn't get access to our savings, we have money. We can go out, spend some time with each other."

Jesse winced. "Jen, I have that meeting tonight."

"What meetin'?"

"The one with the Reclaim Network."

"I thought you asked your father to do that?"

"I told him I would do it. I think I have a lead that will get us out of this mess." Jesse observed the dejected look on her face. "What about tomorrow?"

"Tomorrow?"

"Tomorrow. I should be finished with this mess by then. I promise."

"I've gotta see if Tabita or Lottie can watch the kids."

"Do that. But this thing should be done and over with by tonight. Trust me on that."

* * *

A man with dreadlocks pulled his gray Chevy Malibu into the parking lot of Grace Episcopal Church, a three-story Romanesque building, at 7:15 p.m. The parking lot was adjacent to the right side of the church, allowing the man to see the side entrance of the church from his vehicle. He shut off the ignition. His best friend, Charlie Heard, sat in the passenger seat and observed the other cars in the parking lot.

"Lot of cars here," Charlie Heard noted. Charlie was a thick black man with a goatee and a full head of shiny curly short hair. "You sure you cancelled the meeting?"

"They got some other church meeting going on here tonight, but that's about it," Perrin Houton said. "If anybody shows up, but comes back out, we know they came here for our meeting. And that's someone we need to know about."

"All right, man, but I can't hang out too long tonight."

"Why not?"

"Got Paris Brooks coming over."

"Who's Paris Brooks?"

"The girl who came to our Reclaim meeting last month. The one with the body like Nicki Minaj."

"Nicki who?"

"Nicki Minaj. That girl rapper from Trinidad."

"Oh, yeah."

"I been trying to hit that for a month. Looks like tonight is the lucky night."

"Good for you."

"How's that thing with Yvette going?"

Perrin noticed a Nissan Armada pulling into the parking lot from Connecticut Avenue. He kept a close eye on it as it circled the lot searching for a parking space.

"Per?"

Perrin's concentration was broken. "Yeah?"

"How's Yvette treating you?"

"Going good. She was over last night. Her mom had to work a couple of hours into the midnight shift at the hospital."

"How old is she again?"

Perrin studied the man getting out of the Armada — a white man with well-coiffed black hair, leather jacket, button up shirt, and casual black slacks with black oxfords. "She said she was 18."

"Man, that girl don't look a day above 15. D'you check her ID?"

"Her body looked grown. That's all the ID I need."

"Better hope her moms don't find out."

Perrin watched the man walk to the church entrance. "This cat's got Virginia tags."

"Yeah. What that mean?"

"Probably nothing. But if this is our man, he's probably not a cop."

"How you know he ain't one of them private detectives? He look like he could be one. All he needs is a trench coat."

Charlie went on jabbering about how he managed to get Paris to go on a date with him, but Perrin was not listening. His attention was on the church's side entrance. If his guess were right, the security guard would immediately tell the man that the meeting was cancelled, and he would return instantly to his car. As expected, three minutes later, Jesse left the church and returned to the Armada.

"Like I thought." Perrin interrupted Charlie's diatribe. "That's the dude that's watching me."

"What you gonna do?"

"See where he goes."

Perrin waited until Jesse got inside his car and pulled out of his parking space before he started his own car. He waited until Jesse had passed by him and had turned south on Connecticut before he pulled out of the parking lot and followed him.

"Man, we don't know if this is the guy who's been checking up on you." Charlie was worried that he would miss his date with Paris. "For all we know, he might have gone into that church asking for directions."

"Naw. This cat has got Virginia tags."

Charlie scoffed. "So what? This is Washington, D.C. At any given moment you might see two or three cars in this city with Virginia tags."

"You know Booz?"

"Yeah, your neighbor."

"You know Booz lives in a basement room. He told me he saw an SUV with Virginia tags come down the alley about 2 in the morning and take the trash out of my trash can. He said whenever someone comes down that alley, the lights shine right in his bedroom window. That's what made him go to the window and look."

"Booz was up that late?"

"Booz don't get in until like 1:30 in the morning. He drives the Metrobus, the AF line, evening shift."

"I still think you're paranoid."

Perrin would get the last laugh when the Armada made a left turn on Porter, crossed Beach Drive, and then made another left on Morgan Place.

"Hey, man, he's going right past your house," Charlie noted.

Perrin darted into an alley off Porter and then pulled headfirst into the driveway behind his house. He then shut off the ignition and waited. Two minutes later, the Armada rolled slowly down the alley from the opposite end.

"Let's find out what's up," Perrin said to Charlie. Together they got out of the vehicle and waited until the Armada was just in front of the driveway to 456 Morgan. Charlie then stepped out in the alley to block the Armada's way while Perrin approached from the driver's side. Perrin motioned Jesse to roll down his window. Jesse complied, verifying his doors were locked, but only opening his window about three inches, enough for voices, air, and not much else to pass through.

"What's up?" Perrin's voice was as menacing as he could muster.

Jesse avoided the man's eyes. "Just trying to drive through."

"Why are you checking up on me? I saw you try to come to my meeting, and now you're at my house."

Jesse took this statement as mildly sufficient evidence that the person he was talking to was Perrin Houtin, but he was determined to ask anyway. "Who are you?"

"Who are *you*?" Perrin retorted.

"I'm just someone trying to get back what's mine."

"Look, man, you'd better get from around my neighborhood, and leave me alone, or you gonna get jacked up."

Jesse looked in Perrin's eyes to see if he was serious, but he saw no real desire or intent. He looked in Charlie's malevolent eyes, and observed his clenched fists, and saw otherwise.

"Look, I'm not after you," Jesse explained. "I could care less about you and your business. But, you do have information that could help me get my house back, and I need that information."

"You need to get out of my face."

Jesse slowly reached to his passenger's seat and picked up a manila file folder. He pushed it toward Perrin through the slot in the window, but Perrin refused to take it.

"What's this?"

"Something you need to see."

"I ain't touching that, man." Perrin did not know whether Jesse was handing him a summons, and he was aware of the rules of service of process. If he did not touch the package, he could deny in court that he was served.

Jesse opened the file folder and removed one photograph, showing it to Perrin through the window. "That's you, last night, with a girl, looks to be about 14 or 15. I could be wrong, but I'm willing to guess I am not." Jesse replaced the photograph in the file folder and again shoved the folder through the slot in the window.

This time, Perrin took it.

He opened the folder, flipping through the pictures. The menacing look on Perrin's face slowly transformed into worry. Charlie drew close to Perrin so that he could see the pictures.

"The originals of those photos are in my attorney's office." Jesse's voice became stronger and steadier. He had Perrin's attention now. "Tomorrow, at exactly 9:01 a.m., I have instructed my attorney to deliver those pictures to the girl's mother, and to the police. Once the police are called, they'll do a rape kit on the girl, and they'll find out if there has been contact other than a freaky kiss on the sidewalk. At minimum, you'll get 10 years in prison."

Perrin looked up from the photos and glared at Jesse, not sure whether to acquiesce or beat him silly.

"But if you tell me what I want to know, those pictures never see the light of day," Jesse said.

Perrin looked at the photos again, as if he was searching for some loophole, some way to get out of his current conundrum. Finding none, he said, "So, what do you want to know?"

"Not now." Jesse pulled a business card from his shirt pocket and handed it to Perrin. "That's my attorney's address. Be there by 9 o'clock tomorrow morning. If you're not there by 9:01, don't bother showing."

Perrin simply glared at Jesse, saying nothing.

"And by the way, bring a cashier's check for 10 grand."

Perrin's mouth dropped open as if the tendons had

snapped. "For what?"

"You know what."

It did not take long for Perrin to realize that the $10,000 that Jesse was asking for was the same money he had received from Bernard MacNichol. Perrin cursed under his breath, knowing he had made a major mistake accepting money that could be traced. He should have asked for it in cash.

Perrin relied on a routine denial. "I don't have 10 grand."

"Five, then. You can give me the other five later, but the threat will remain active until you do." Jesse rolled up his window and drove away, leaving Perrin standing there holding the open file of photos.

Charlie peered over Perrin's shoulder at a photo. "Dag, man, you were feeling her up like that in the middle of the sidewalk? Should've checked that ID."

"Man, shut up!" Perrin slammed the file shut.

"You really gonna give him 10,000 dollars?"

"Not if I can help it. I need to talk to Les."

* * *

Jesse managed to drive four blocks away before he had to pull over and throw the gear into park. He leaned back and took several deep breaths, grabbing his chest in a fruitless gesture to calm the heavy beating of his heart. With eyes closed, he thought about how close he was to getting seriously hurt, and he thanked God for making it out of there unscathed.

When his heartbeat had calmed down, Jesse pulled out his cell phone and dialed Joe Lippman's cell.

After five rings Joe answered, "Hello?"

"Joe. Jesse Kane."

"Pastor Jesse, how are you?"

"Great, *now*. You got a minute?"

"Only a minute. My wife has company over, and she just made the most marvelous beef brisket pot roast."

"I need you at 9 tomorrow morning."

"Why?"

"What are those meetings you lawyers have, where witnesses are recorded in the office?"

"A deposition?"

"Yes. I have a witness that may help our case, and may even help us resolve it out of court. But I need to take his information in your office, and I need it to be recorded."

"Jesse, maybe we'd better talk about this when I have more time. How about tomorrow morning?"

"Fine. I'll meet you at your office at 8 tomorrow morning. But we have to be ready to meet this guy at 9."

"What guy?"

"Perrin Houton."

"No kidding? You found him?"

"Yes. And I have my leverage. I'll tell you about it tomorrow."

Adverse Possession

Less than a man

After having achieved a victory, of sorts, all Jesse wanted to do was go home and relax with his wife and kids. He pulled the Armada in the driveway behind Lottie's car, and then walked wearily inside the house.

Lottie was in the kitchen cleaning up after dinner. She saw Jesse trudge toward the basement door and said, "Got a plate for you in the oven if you want it. Jen really did a great job with the barbecue chicken."

"Thanks, Lottie," Jesse said. "I'll come up and get it later." He placed his hand on the knob to open the basement door.

"Jesse?"

"Yeah, Miss Lottie?"

"Your wife does not look like she's in a good mood."

"Well, I haven't been around much."

"Just so you know."

Jesse nodded his thanks to Lottie for the heads-up. He opened the basement door and slowly padded down the stairs. Jennifer, wearing gray shorts and a white T-shirt, was sitting on the couch listening to music through an iPod. When she saw Jesse, she removed the headphones from her ears and gave him a stern look.

Jesse removed his jacket. "Where are the kids?"

"Tabita and her son took 'em to the movies," Jennifer said, in an unsettling monotone.

"Hmm." Jesse placed his jacket on the couch and decided to move into some test-the-waters small talk. "Whatcha listening to?"

"*Through the Fire.*"

"Boy, if the Crabb Family had a quarter for every time you played *that* song ... ." Jesse sat down next to Jennifer. Rather, he *tried* to.

Jennifer abruptly stood up. Only the anointed words of the music to which she had been listening calmed her spirit to the point that she avoided slapping him square in the face. "You got a message."

Jesse looked up at her. "What message?"

Jennifer nodded toward the cocktail table. Jesse looked at the table and saw a small piece of paper with writing on it. He picked up the paper and read the note, in Jennifer's handwriting.

Elder Williams called.

Now Jesse knew why Jennifer was in such a foul mood. She had spoken to Elder Williams, and Elder Williams had likely told her about her parents' pending eviction. He put the note back on the table, and avoided looking up at Jennifer.

"Why ain't you tell me?" Jennifer's voice cracked with a hurt that made him tremble inside.

Jesse gazed up at her and tried to be as earnest as possible. "'With everything going on, I didn't want to burden you with extra bad news."

"Jesse, my parents are getting kicked out of their home," Jennifer said loudly. "That's somethin' you should have told me right away."

Jesse lowered his head in a moment of condemnation before he had a thought. "Wait a minute, How did you even know I knew about it?" Jesse asked. "I never spoke to Elder Williams."

"As soon as I got finished talkin' with Elder Williams, I called your father. He told me he had told you. *Days* ago."

That was a gotcha moment if there ever was one. Jesse took a deep breath, and waxed apologetic. "Jen, I … "

Jennifer interrupted. "I feel like I don't know you no more. You go out all times of the night. Most of the time, you don't tell me. You don't call me. I only know half of what's goin' on. You don't tell me about my parents. We ain't even *did it* since we got back to McLean. When's the last time we went a whole week without doin' *that*?"

Jesse scoffed. "Jen, we *are* in a stranger's home."

"That didn't stop you in Haiti," Jennifer replied. "Most of the time there, we were sleeping in tents, and you still found ways to hook up with me when no one was looking."

Because there wasn't much else to do most of the time, he thought. But Jesse held back from expressing that thought, knowing that to do so would be akin to tossing himself into a swamp full of crocodiles. Jesse just shook his head and did not respond.

"You are so obsessed with this house, and nothing else matters to you. Not your young uns, not your in-laws, not your church, not your wife … ."

Adverse Possession

That remark stung Jesse fiercely and shook him out of his malaise. Most of what she had said up until that point was true and undisputed. Now she was trying to judge his motives, and judge them wrongly. He jumped up from the couch and stared at her intensely. "Whoa, wait a minute! That was uncalled for. I am not going to let you tell me that I don't care for my family! Everything I am doing is for you and those kids. I risked my life today for you and those kids."

Jennifer dialed back her tone. "Well, I'd rather you *live* your life for us than risk it. Could you try *that* for a change?"

Jesse huffed, and turned away. She seemed to have no interest in hearing his unbridled tale of heroism, no appreciation for his valiance, and that pinched a nerve. From tightened lips, he decided to tell her anyway. "Y'know, I confronted Perrin Houtin today with the pictures. He had a friend with him. And both those guys looked like they could have tossed me all around Washington, D.C. without breaking a sweat. In fact, I'm sure they wanted to. But I did that because I don't want to see you and our kids living in someone else's basement."

"Jesse, I told you I don't give a hoot about that … ."

"But I do!" Jesse shouted. "I do! I'm supposed to take care of my family. Don't you understand? A man that can't provide for his family feels *less* than a man. I can't stand around and watch my wife living in a cramped basement. I can't watch my kids run over to someone else's house because they are bored out of their minds. I can't do that and I won't."

"So, taking care of this through the courts is an affront to your *manhood*?" Jennifer matched his tone. "The court system is some kinda feminist solution?"

"I'm not saying that. I'm just saying I can't sit around and wait."

"All good things come to them that wait."

"Yeah, well so do missed opportunities." Jesse then lowered his voice, but it was still loud enough to carry to Lottie's inquisitive ears upstairs. "And no, I didn't tell you about your parents. That was too much to bear when I had my own problems to deal with. I am responsible for providing for you. I can't be responsible for providing for them, too. And you shouldn't be either."

"You're soundin' more like your Pa every day."

Jesse shook his head. Jennifer really knew how to strike those blows that would leave him doubled over. He hated when anyone compared him with his father, and Jennifer knew that. That could have caused another argument, the second link in the chain of dissention. Instead, he glared at Jennifer, grabbed his jacket from the couch, and stormed off down the hallway toward their bedroom. Jennifer heard the door open and slam. Except the door she heard was not the bedroom door.

It was the basement door leading outside.

* * *

The Subaru Wagon pulled up to the curb about five blocks away from 456 Newton. It was white, circa 1988, with small patches of rust along the side moldings and front fenders, and had long since lost its luster. It had Maryland tags and tinted windows dark enough to shield everything except the shadow of the car's occupant. As the ignition was switched off, the car engine sputtered and coughed to a stop. It looked like one of those types of cars you saw struggling college students drive on the way to and from class.

However, Lester Hampton was definitely not a college student. He never went to college. After graduating from Wilson High School, he worked a handful of retail jobs, working his way up to manager, and saving up enough money to buy his first house, a tiny bungalow in the Wakefield area of Washington, D.C.

Two years later, his precious little house was sold at a downtown foreclosure auction house, and federal marshals came to put him and his possessions on the street.

Lester would blame his misfortune on a bad loan, one where the interest rates would suddenly explode, leaving him with a mortgage he couldn't afford. He had been attracted to the loan because they gave it to those with bad credit histories and featured a low down payment. But within 18 months, the payments were so high, he couldn't afford them.

The bank denied him a loan modification. The publicly stated reason was that his income was too low, and that giving him a modification would only delay the inevitable.

In private board rooms, however, they discussed how the housing costs were rising in the Wakefield neighborhood, and how this was an opportunity to rid themselves of this portfolio and make a tidy profit.

So, the 26-year-old retail manager found himself living in friends' houses, denying help from his parents, who were struggling hospitality workers. A few months later, he found an apartment on Connecticut Avenue, his homelessness permanently abated.

However, bitterness coursed through him, as thick as overgrown weeds. He would make the banks pay for their injustice. He would be the bane of their existence.

Two weeks after he obtained the keys to his new apartment, he and three friends drove to Annapolis to file paperwork to start a nonprofit organization called Keeping Our Homes D.C. The mission of the organization was to provide assistance and counseling to help struggling homeowners stay in their homes. Lester managed to build volunteer coalitions around the city to help him with the organization's work.

Shortly after, he felt the financial pressure again. He was laid off his retail management job. His solution was to make Keeping Our Homes fee-based, charging hundreds, and sometimes thousands, to struggling homeowners for his services.

Some homeowners actually paid, mostly out of desperation, willing to try anything to keep their homes. But Lester lost a lot of support after that. Many of his grassroots volunteers thought Lester was kowtowing to the same capitalistic tendencies that they felt caused the foreclosure crisis. They abandoned him in droves. Some of them contacted the media.

A TV news channel hopped on the story, investigating Keeping Our Homes and splashing the story on national airwaves exposing Lester's organization as a corrupt outfit taking advantage of struggling homeowners. By the time the story aired, the TV news reporters had found several instances of homeowners who had paid for services, but never received them. Lester became a typical victim of over-promising and under-delivering.

The negative coverage was embarrassing and debilitating.

Adverse Possession

Lester quickly shut down his operation and went underground for two years, working primarily from his apartment on telephone sales calls and various odd jobs, planting shrubs here, sweeping floors there. He had just enough money to keep the cupboard stocked with Ramen noodles and Kool-Aid. On one of his odd jobs, he met a man who was in similar financial straits, and had also been the victim of a predatory loan. They became good friends and eventually rented a house together once they both were evicted from their apartments for non-payment of rent.

It was Perrin Houtin who convinced his best friend Lester to reestablish the Keeping Our Homes program. Having not tired of his vendetta against the banks, he readily agreed, with a few changes. Perrin Houtin would be the face of the program, and the name would change to Estate Ventures. Since organizing as a nonprofit would draw unwanted attention, Lester and Perrin decided to incorporate as an LLC in D.C. To hide as much about the business structure of the organization as possible, they came up with the name "The Reclaim Network" to describe their efforts to help families reclaim foreclosed homes. But unlike Keeping Our Homes, Perrin and Lester kept the group hush-hush, working with just a few network members who paid up to $15K for the privilege of Lester and Perrin's expertise in overturning and nullifying foreclosures.

At least that's what they told everyone. Lester and Perrin had never actually overturned or nullified any foreclosure. They had never filed a case in court. But they did a very good job of convincing people that they went through a lengthy legal process to reclaim a foreclosed home. After all, if the people were stupid enough to give them thousands of dollars to reclaim a home, chances are they were too stupid to realize how fake their court papers were.

It was a perfect little scam. By illegally moving people back into foreclosed homes, they wrecked havoc on the banks, who had to hire lawyers and file court papers to get them out. By providing their assistance, they got paid, certainly not enough to be rich, but enough to survive.

Lester was dirty, and that made him paranoid and careful. He would conduct his business such that no one could tie him to it if they came knocking. In case someone was watching Perrin's house, they would never meet there to talk. Instead, they had an agreed-upon rendezvous point five blocks away from Perrin's house.

Lester pulled a pack of cigarettes out of his shirt pocket, lit one, took a drag, and then exhaled it out through a slightly opened driver's side window. As he did, he looked in the rear view mirror and saw Perrin approaching his car. He rolled down his window as Perrin looked in.

Lester was tall, solidly built and ruddy, his black hair cut short on the sides but layered on top. His paranoia was evident the moment he opened his mouth.

"I told you never to contact me on the phone. Use the blog." Lester's voice was smooth and deep, his words rolling off his tongue like the flow of honey.

"This was an emergency," Perrin told him. "I didn't want to wait around until you saw the blog."

"Anybody tail you here?"

"Naw. Drove through the park like you told me. Followed all those winding roads. Nobody was on me."

"So, you say this guy's been checking up on you?"

"Yeah. Don't know who he is, but he wants me to meet him at his attorney's office tomorrow morning."

"And why would you do that?"

"He got something on me."

"What?"

"This girl I'm seein'."

"What about her?"

"Jailbait."

"He saw you?"

"He got pictures."

"How'd he get those?"

Perrin shook his head, more out of stupidity than regret. "We spent some time together while her mom was at work. She was leaving around one in the morning, and we were saying goodbye outside. I didn't think anybody was watching. I kissed her and kinda felt her up a little bit."

Lester cursed.

Perrin continued. "So, he wants me to come to his lawyer's office tomorrow, and bring 5,000 dollars. If I don't, his lawyer is gonna release those pictures to the police and to her mother."

"How does he know who her mother is?"

"I don't know. He probably saw the house my girl went back to."

"And you have no idea who this guy is?"

"I think he may be the owner of that house the MacNichols are in."

"How do you know that?"

"Virginia tags. We only got one takeover in Virginia."

"What's your impression of this guy?"

"Cat's got no heart. He couldn't even roll down the window when he was talking to me."

Lester flicked the still-lit butt of his cigarette out the window and looked straight ahead. "You got heart?"

"No doubt."

"Good. 'Cause you're gonna need it for what I'm gonna ask you to do."

Adverse Possession

A Mother's love

* * *

Jesse drove around McLean and some parts of Arlington for several hours, trying to calm down, to clear his head, to work some things out in his mind. He had no destination, but he knew he couldn't go home.

He had arguments with his wife before, and usually he would acquiesce at some point, simply because he had no stomach for arguing. But this was different. She should have appreciated everything he was doing to reclaim their house, but he felt she was turning into one of his biggest detractors. What wife would not be supportive of her husband's efforts to save their family home?

For no other reason than the leading of the Spirit, Jesse wound up 30 miles away in Potomac, Maryland on Bit and Spur Lane. He needed someone to talk to, and he couldn't go to his father. After all, it was likely Rodereck's advice that caused the rift between him and his wife, and right now, he wasn't certain what God was doing or what he should do. He had never felt so disconnected, so alone.

The house was ahead on his right. All of the houses on this block reflected perfectly Potomac's reputation as an upscale town whose residents were solidly in the six-figure income range. The lawns were deep and wide and exquisitely manicured, the driveways so wide and long they were almost like side streets. The homes, some colonial, some Spanish-style, some French country, all huge and with values well over $2 million. If Jesse could afford it, he would move his family here without a second thought.

Jesse pulled the Armada in the stone driveway of the house midway down Bit and Spur Lane and parked across from the front entrance. The neighborhood was so quiet, the jingle of his keys as he opened the door and climbed out seemed to reverberate through the block. Jesse checked his watch. It was 11 p.m. He noticed that the only light on in the house was in an upstairs bedroom. She would definitely be surprised to see him, but she would not turn him away.

Jesse approached the ornate double wooden door, feeling as if he was about to enter into Buckingham Palace. He had to ring the doorbell three times before the porch lights came on and one of the doors slowly parted open. The woman stood there, in black silk pajamas and a long robe, looking at him with a combination of surprise and delight.

"Jesse, honey, is everything okay? Why are you here so late?"

Jesse walked past her and inside the foyer. "A lot of things on my mind, Ma. A lot of things."

Camille Fairchild started using her maiden name immediately after her divorce with Rodereck Kane was final. It was her way of severing most ties with the man she once called her husband. Jesse, her only son, remained the only visible connection to that turbulent period in her life.

Jesse walked through the foyer and into the living room, where he sat on a crème-colored leather couch. Camille shut the door gently and walked into the living room, her bare feet swishing on the Brazilian cherry floors.

"Jesse, what's going on?" Camille sat across from him on a matching love seat. The last she had spoken to him was when he had called her from the Trudeaus' home to tell her he was back in the country. "Where is Jen? Is she okay? The kids?"

"They're fine."

Camille eschewed any further questions, waiting until he was ready to talk. The wait was not long.

"I had an argument with her."

Camille nodded. "Must have been a pretty bad argument to send you over here so late."

"Did Dad tell you what was going on?"

"Now, you know I haven't spoken to that man since his alimony payments stopped."

"Well, I got back home from Haiti, and discovered that someone else was living in my home."

Camille drew back. She wasn't sure she heard that right. "Did you say someone else was living in your home?"

"Yeah. And the police can't do anything about it."

"Are you serious?"

"Yeah." Jesse gave her the entire story, from the moment they arrived at the Trudeaus' home and discovered their mail had been forwarded, to his visit to Perrin Houtin's home.

Camille had lots of questions, but for the sake of time and her sacrificed bedtime, she asked only a few. "You don't know these people?"

"No. Never seen them before."

"How did they know your house was vacant?"

"Don't know. I guess they were watching it."

"No newspapers piling up, or anything."

"No. Lottie took care of all that."

"Hmm. Sounds like something more than meets the eye."

Jesse leaned forward. "Like what, Ma?"

"Don't know. Something. Just watch your back."

Jesse nodded. He had always admired his mother's spiritual discernment. If she sensed something wasn't right, she usually was spot-on.

It was that same discernment that led to her break-up with Rodereck. Throughout their marriage, Rodereck insisted on keeping Camille as a housewife, while Camille felt called to be a partner with Rodereck in his business and church ventures. She was well-versed in business administration through her four years at Columbia University and subsequent management of Bishop Woodmore's church. But Rodereck was old-school. He felt that a woman's place was in the home. So, Camille kept her place, even though she felt a yearning from God to do much more than bake fritters and help Jesse with his homework.

For 17 years of marriage, Camille played the soccer mom, occasionally reminding Rodereck that she could be so much more. Having only one child was not as challenging as having two or three like other moms she knew, so she was confident she could handle the rigors of being both a housewife and a business partner.

For Rodereck, the issue was not her ability to handle both duties. He married Camille because he was attracted to her model-thin body, dark brown hair, and Caucasian skin with a dash of African American features. He wanted an excuse to have sex without feeling guilty, and Bishop Woodmore had told him that it was difficult, if not impossible, to pastor a thriving church without a wife at home. But Rodereck fell out of love with her once it became clear that Camille wanted to be more than a housewife, although he did a good job of pretending to love her for close to two years. Once Jesse was born, Rodereck retreated to the church, leaving Camille with the main responsibility of raising Jesse. Whenever he was at home, he would spent his time writing sermons, on counseling calls, or doing other things for the church at the expense of their marriage. Although they slept together, they didn't sleep together. Camille knew that Rodereck's many tasks were things that pastors do, but this was way past extreme.

Camille put up with it for 17 years, hoping that things would change. She didn't believe in divorce, so she kept praying and fasting, hoping that God would give her a breakthrough. But she knew she was tired of being a roommate to a man who was supposed to be her husband.

After Jesse went off to college, Rodereck found a lawyer and filed for divorce. It should have been devastating for Camille, but to her, God was giving her freedom.

She requested, and was awarded, $2,500 a month in alimony. She squirreled most of it away, eventually becoming a majority investor in a photo-based online social media site. The site took off, and so did her earnings. At a salary of $500,000 per year, Camille was able to afford her $3 million modern Spanish villa, which she had owned for three years. When Jesse brought Rodereck by to see the house, nestled on a 2.5-acre lot with wrought-iron fencing and fence columns made of Central American granite, he congratulated Camille, feigned smiles, left quickly, and hasn't spoke to her since.

"I'm trying to do what I can to resolve this situation," Jesse told her. "But it seems like my wife doesn't appreciate it."

"Hmm," was Camille's only response.

"Do you think I'm like my father?"

"I think in some ways you are. I think you try not to be, but you don't succeed. You're your father's son."

"I'm also my mother's son."

"Yes, but what I meant is that you're a man, like your father, which means the two of you share similar traits. Both of you come from a long tradition of hunter-gatherers. You're alpha males. Your worth is tied to your ability to be king of the castle, to bring home the prey. But sometimes, that makes you callous to the needs of those you're providing for."

Jesse's eyes narrowed. "What do you mean?"

"When I was married to your father, he thought that as long as he was putting a roof over my head and as long as we had money, he was doing his job. And that's part of it." Camille stood up and started to pace. She was one of those types of people who spoke more clearly and eloquently when they were moving around. "But in case you didn't notice, this is the 21st century. Roles have reversed, and a lot of women don't need men to be the breadwinner any more." She did a game-show model flourish toward her cavernous living room, illustrating her point.

"You've done pretty well for yourself," Jesse stated.

"Yes, but a woman needs more than just that. She needs attention, caring, love. She wants her man to be there for her, not *out there* for her. That's all a part of providing for her. She's not appreciating what you're doing because that's not what she needs right now. She needs you. She's just as afraid and concerned about that house as you are. She just won't show that to you, because if she does, and you're not in the right place, it'll drive you further away from her."

Jesse shifted in his seat. "You ever miss Dad?"

Camille sat back down. "Your father never gave me a lot to miss. I'm happier without him than I was with him. You are the only good product of my relationship with him. But I don't want you to become like him, so ambitious you can't focus on what's important. Jennifer needs you at home. She needs you to agree with her in prayer, because ultimately, only the grace of God is going to solve this situation with your house."

Jesse sat silently, looking away, immersed in his thoughts. Camille, feeling she had said all she needed to, stood up. "You and your family can stay here if you want. I have plenty of space."

Jesse stood to his feet. "Whatever possessed you to buy a six-bedroom house, when it is only you?"

"It's an investment." Camille moved toward the door, cueing Jesse that it was time to leave. "Besides, if I get bored with one side of the house, I can always move to the other side."

It was the first time Jesse had cracked a smile since the midafternoon. He followed his mother to the door. "I guess we'll stay put for now. I want to keep an eye on the house. And it's an easier commute for the kids to school."

"Okay. The invitation's always open." Camille opened the door. "Right now I have to get to bed. I have a meeting at 7 in the morning. So, go home to your wife and kids."

Jesse stepped onto the porch. The porch light cast a glow on him against the darkness of the night. Gnats and mosquitoes flew about his head, appearing as tiny dancing points of light. "I don't know if I can do that right now. Jennifer's pretty upset."

Camille made her final words to him pointed and stern. "Respect your father. Love your father. But don't emulate him, whatever you do. Don't spend another minute away from your family."

Jesse turned toward his car. Camille shut the door behind him. As soon as Jesse got in the car, the porch lights turned off.

Jesse started the ignition and just sat in his car for a moment, replaying his mother's words in his mind. To him, the gist of it was *your wife's right. You're wrong. Go home and fall on your sword.* But that engaged his pride again. He had invested so much time and energy believing that he was right, only to be told he was wrong. He wasn't ready to face Jennifer with that admission. Besides, if he went home now, Jennifer would likely banish him to the couch for the rest of the night.

He thought to walk along the breezeway, past the garage, and check to see if the guest suite was unlocked, but he decided against it. The last thing he wanted to do was stay on his mother's property without her knowledge. A single woman living alone in such a huge house did not need those kinds of surprises.

He decided to check into a hotel, sleep until morning, then get up and head back home just before Jennifer normally awakened. He needed to be at the peak of his energy before dealing with her again.

Satisfied with his plan, he switched on the headlights and backed out of the driveway.

Adverse Possession

A Grisly message

* * *

After the kids had returned from their outing with Tabita, Jennifer put them to bed immediately, then tried to lay down to sleep herself. But her spirit was too heavy for sleep.

During previous arguments, he had stormed out of the house, but only for an hour or two. Never had he stayed away this long. It was 1 in the morning, and he had been gone for almost five hours.

The negative voices returned to visit Jennifer again, telling her in no uncertain terms that her husband had retreated into the comfort of another woman. Jennifer can see all the women at her church who would love an opportunity to console him after an argument with his wife. The thought nagged at her, ate her up inside. The only thing she could do was hope and pray that he would return home and return soon.

Jennifer pulled the blankets off her bed and walked into the family room. She turned on the TV and nestled under the blanket on the couch, hoping that watching some old late-night movies would settle her mind and make her drowsy enough to go to sleep.

Her plan worked. In about an hour she dozed off, but woke up again several times in the next three hours, each time hoping that her husband would be home. At 4 a.m., she decided to give up trying to sleep. She would borrow Lottie's car and search for Jesse's car at all the places she thought he might be, and hoped he was. This would save her from having to make phone calls and unnecessarily waking people up.

She planned her trip in her mind as she dressed. The church would be the first place she would look. Rodereck's house would be the second, and Camille Fairchild's house, the farthest away, would be third.

After dressing in blue jeans and a burgundy sweater, she checked in on the kids, saw that they were sleeping soundly, and walked up the basement stairs to the dining room. Lottie normally kept the keys to her car hanging on the wall next to the telephone. She used a notepad and pen next to the phone to jot a quick note for Lottie, in case she were to awaken and wonder what happened to her car. She taped the note to the inside of the front door, grabbed her coat from the coat rack, and opened the door.

Her scream split through the quietness of the night like a lightning bolt.

Lying on the stoop was a dead pit bull, its head almost completely severed, a kitchen knife piercing its stomach and attaching a note to its body.

Louis N. Jones

* * *

Sergeant Gwynn was just starting a two-week evening shift rotation, and he couldn't be happier. He loved working this shift, which started at 7 p.m. and ended at 7 a.m. Unlike most of the cops younger than his 40 years, he didn't crave excitement. The quieter his shift, the better. In his service area, consisting mostly of single-family homes, schools, churches, and parks, things got very quiet after 9 p.m., unlike some of the other service areas with heavy concentrations of apartment buildings, malls, and all-night convenience stores. With the exception of an occasional drunken-disorderly, or domestic dispute, or break-in, Sergeant Gwynn could expect to have plenty of time to park on a side street and catch up on paperwork.

The call came from dispatch at 4:03 a.m. on his police radio. Report of a dead dog placed on a resident's doorstep. 6612 Bynum Drive.

Gwynn remembered the street. He had answered a breaking-and-entering call there just last week. He acknowledged the call and headed for that address. He was only 10 minutes away.

When he arrived at the address, he noticed he was right across the street from the call he received last week. Gwynn hoped it was a coincidence, but had an itching feeling it was not.

Sergeant Gwynn approached the house, his flashlight in his hand. He walked in the grass, and used his flashlight to scan the walkway as he approached the stoop. He noticed that the bedroom and living room lights were on in the house, and the front door was closed. At the foot of the door lay a bloody mound of flesh with a knife sticking out of it.

Sergeant Gwynn pointed his flashlight at the dog. "Jesus," he exclaimed as he saw the extent of trauma to the dog's neck. He shined the flashlight on the body and noticed several scars etched in the dog's coal black coat. Gwynn nodded with recognition. As a rookie, he had spent several months shadowing the animal control unit in Alexandria. He had seen dogs with similar injuries that had been in dogfights staged by their owners. He was certain this dog was a loser in a similar dogfight.

Gwynn moved his flashlight around the circumference of the dog. There was not a lot of blood on the porch, although with the extent of injuries, the porch should have been covered in it. He concluded that the dog was killed elsewhere and brought here.

But why here? And why this house?

Sergeant Gwynn looked closely at the paper stuck to the dog's belly. There was some writing on the underside, but he couldn't tell what it was. As tempted as he was to do so, he could not pull off the note to read it. This was now an active crime scene, and he couldn't disturb it.

He got on his radio and called for a detective, crime scene, and animal control.

He stepped up to the living room window and rapped sharply on it. Lottie came to the window. Sergeant Gwynn motioned for her to come to the side door near the dining room. He walked around to the side door and holstered his flashlight just as Lottie and Jennifer opened the door. Lottie was still dressed in bedclothes and a robe, but Jennifer was fully dressed, looking distraught, her eyes damp and red from crying. She looked to be the most likely person to have discovered the dog and make the call to police.

Sergeant Gwynn remembered the details of the dispatch call and spoke to Lottie. "Mrs. Koch, two calls within a week's time? You're having a bad month."

Lottie pointed to Jennifer. "I made the call. But she found the dog."

Gwynn spoke to Jennifer. "And you are?"

"Jennifer Kane."

The name rang familiar to Gwynn. "You're Pastor Kane's wife?"

"I am."

"What's going on here?"

"Well, I woke up, saw my husband was not here. So, I was going to go out to look for him, and I saw the dog."

"When's the last time anyone used the front door?" Gwynn pulled a note pad and pen out of his shirt pocket.

"Probably last night, when my neighbor brought my kids home from the movies." Jennifer looked at Lottie for confirmation. Lottie nodded.

"What time was that?"

"Around 10."

"Was your husband at home then?"

"No. We had an argument, and he stormed out. He ain't been home all night." Jennifer looked sideways at Lottie. She had not yet told Lottie about the argument, or why she was heading out the door at 4 in the morning.

"Do you know anyone who would want to do something like this to you?" Sergeant Gwynn darted his eyes between the women, directing his question at either one.

"No," Jennifer answered.

Lottie emphatically shook her head.

Sergeant Gwynn flipped his notepad shut. "Okay. Where are the kids?"

"They're downstairs."

"Good. Keep them there. They don't need to be exposed to this." Sergeant Gwynn pulled a business card out of his shirt pocket. "I need you two to stay indoors. Don't go anywhere, and definitely do not use the front door. A detective is on the way, and he's going to want to speak with you. I called animal control, but their shift doesn't start until 6, so it may be a few hours before we are all out of here and you can go back to your business." He handed the card to Jennifer. "Call me on my cell if you need anything or think of anything else I need to know."

Jennifer looked down at the card, and then nodded.

Sergeant Gwynn took a step back, and then hesitated. "Mrs. Kane, do you think this has anything to do with your house across the street?"

Jennifer shook her head and said quietly, "I don't know."

"Well, there's some kind of note on the dog, so once a detective gets here, we'll be able to figure out what it says, and go from there." Sergeant Gwynn turned away. "Call me if you think of anything else."

Lottie shut the door, and then turned and took Jennifer into her arms. Lottie could feel fear radiating from Jennifer like a strong heat. "It's gonna be okay, honey."

With her head pressed against Lottie's shoulder, Jennifer said, muffled, "I need to find out where Jesse is."

"Did you call around to find out where he might be?" Lottie asked.

"No. I ain't want to wake anybody."

"Well, I think it's time." Lottie separated from the embrace. "This is an emergency. Losing a few minutes of sleep won't hurt 'em."

Jennifer went downstairs and used Jesse's cell phone to call almost every number that had been recorded in his phone the past few weeks. Pastor Rodereck, Joe Lippman, the men who had come to help Jesse move the belongings out of his house, most of his friends; all of them reported no signs of Jesse. She called the main number to the church, and the direct numbers to the offices of Jesse and Rodereck, but they all went to voice mail. She tried to call Tabita to see if he was there, even though she had no reason to believe he would be there. But Jennifer was desperate.

Jennifer tossed the phone on the couch and rubbed her head in frustration. Dead ends everywhere she turned. She had hoped to get in touch with him before the detective arrived and started asking more questions. She didn't want to go through this alone.

Suddenly she remembered. It was the call she should have made before any other call. *What was she thinking?* If there were any place her husband would retreat, it would be there.

With renewed hope, she grabbed the cell phone and dialed.

Camille Fairchild's dreary voice interrupted the ringing tones. "Hello?"

"Ma Camille, this is Jen."

Camille's voice brightened. "Jen. How are you?"

"Not so good. Is my husband over there?"

"No, dear. He was here last night, but he left around 11:30. I thought he was headed straight home."

"No. He never came home."

"Oh, my goodness. I hope he's okay."

Jennifer's voice slipped up a few decibels. "What'd you say to him?"

"Honey, I told him he was wrong for walking out on you, and that he should go home immediately. I said other things to him, but nothing that would make him stay away from home."

"Well, he did stay away. Why ain't you call me to tell me he was there?"

Camille sensed that Jennifer was blaming her for Jesse's not coming home, and she had no intention to travel on that road. "Jen, Jesse's an adult, not a child. He came to ask me for advice. I gave it to him. I thought he was coming home. Don't get in a snit with me."

Jennifer lowered her tone. "I'm sorry. I'm just goin' through so much right now, and I wanna make sure he's okay."

"Have you checked with his father? The church?"

"Yes. I can't find him."

"Well, if you haven't heard from him within the next three hours, call me."

"I will. Thanks."

Jennifer hung up the phone even more worried than before. Her husband had not come home as promised, and some nut had put a dead dog on the doorstep. What if the two were related? What if Jesse had come home and encountered whoever put the dog there?

Jennifer dropped her knees and bowed down until her forehead touched the seat of the couch. Her words to the Lord were strained and raw, but as earnest as anything she had ever said in her life.

"Lord, please bring my husband home to me. *Please.*"

* * *

Jesse did not put much thought into selecting a hotel for his night's stay, but he could have at least selected one with an alarm clock that actually *worked*.

He woke up the next morning with a splitting headache and his plans to be home by 7 a.m. completely dashed. It was only the noise of the housekeeping staff outside that stirred him from a fitful slumber.

When he looked at his watch and saw that it was 8:36 a.m., his headache became the last of his problems. He jumped out of bed, grabbed the room key and his car keys, and thought to call Joe Lippman to apologize for being later for their meeting and to let him know that he was on the way. However, he couldn't remember Joe's number. It was logged into his cell phone, which he had accidentally left at home.

Jesse slipped his shoes on, which was the only article of clothing he had removed for the night. He had no time to shower, shave, or brush. He flung open the door and rushed out, almost stumbling over a housekeeping cart on the way out.

He had 22 minutes to travel 12 miles from Potomac, through Washington metro area rush hour traffic, to Joe Lippmann's office in Tysons. If he were a betting man, he would not have wagered much on his chances.

* * *

Suddenly Jennifer felt like a prisoner in someone else's home.

It was 8:30 a.m., and the police were still outside working their investigation. Jennifer didn't think it took *this* long to investigate homicides, much less a killing of a dog.

Occasionally she peeked out her bedroom window to see what was going on. Sergeant Gwynn had long since departed, and a detective, a bulky black man wearing a rather fashionable black suit with soft-sole shoes, seemed to be in charge. Although they didn't seem to be doing much except for … waiting and talking. The bushes in front of the window obscured her view of the porch, so she couldn't tell if the dog had been removed. But when she saw a white van pull up about 10 minutes later, she figured the animal was still there, but was about to be removed shortly. It was about time. Likely every neighbor was wondering what was going on at 6612 Bynum Drive.

Per Sergeant Gwynn's instructions, she kept the kids downstairs, opting to serve them breakfast in the family room rather than have them go upstairs. Gwynn was right; the kids did not need to know anything about this. It was enough that she would soon have to explain where their father was, and she expected them to ask any minute. But adding a dead dog to the mix would just be too much.

Jennifer found it difficult to focus on anything; every move and every activity became infused with thoughts of Jesse, and where he could be, and how things might have been different if she were more understanding. There were moments where her kids would talk to her, and she would not respond or even hear them, due to being so caught up in her musings. The uncertainty, the mystery, was giving her palpitations. And then came the voices, the evil spirits, speaking into her mind, telling her that Jesse was gone forever, that he was dead, that he would never return to her. The voices churned the adrenaline within her; as it heightened her stress and increased her blood pressure. She could feel it taking effect on her body. She felt as if she could have a nervous breakdown at any minute.

The ringing of the doorbell upstairs distracted her from her thoughts.

Ashley turned momentarily away from *The Chronicles of Narnia* video and said, "Mom, someone's at the door."

"I know, honey." Jennifer picked up the remote and turned down the volume slightly on the TV so she could hear upstairs. "Lottie'll get it."

About a minute later, Lottie came halfway down the stairs and spoke to Jennifer. "Gentleman here to see you."

Jennifer nodded and walked to the stairs. As she started up, she said to the kids, "Stay here. I'll be right back." She shut the basement door behind her once she reached the top of the stairs.

The detective stood just to the right of the closed front door, eyeballing Jennifer as she approached. "Are you Mrs. Kane?"

"Yes," Jennifer said nervously. She drew strength from Lottie, who stood next to her and laid a comforting hand on her shoulder.

Adverse Possession

"I'm Detective Hartley." He handed her his card. "Animal control finally got that dog out of here. They had a few other calls, so they couldn't get here sooner. I apologize for the delay."

Jennifer nodded, keeping her eyes on him, eager to hear what he had to report.

"Are you certain you don't know of anyone who would do this?"

Jennifer answered meekly. "No, I don't."

"Sergeant Gwynn tells me you have some kind of dispute with the people living in your house across the street."

"Yes."

"Do you think they may have done it?"

"I don't know. Perhaps you should ask them."

"We tried." Detective Hartley scanned the living room while he was talking. "We knocked on the door. They didn't answer. I'm sure they were in there. They just didn't answer the door."

"Can't you force them to come to the door?" Lottie asked.

"Afraid not. Not without a warrant. I left my card in the door, with a note asking them to contact me." Hartley paused briefly before speaking again. "As you know, there was a note on the dog."

"What did it say?" Jennifer asked with a glumness of a person facing news they didn't want to hear.

"It's a little disturbing. You may want to prepare yourself."

Jennifer took in a deep breath, let it out, and then said, "Okay, I'm ready."

"The note said, 'If you don't back off, you and your entire family will be just as dead as this dog.'"

"Lord, have mercy," Lottie exclaimed. Jennifer sucked in a breath, and Lottie put her arm around her.

"Have any idea what that note is referring to?" Hartley basically restated his earlier question. He studied her eyes, noticing how they went up and to the side. Something just came to her mind. Death threats will do that sort of thing.

I risked my life for you and the kids.

The words came to Jennifer's memory suddenly, the words Jesse spoke the night before when describing his encounter in D.C. Maybe the dead dog calling card was connected to Jesse's confrontation of Perrin Houtin.

"Um, there might be somethin'."

Detective Hartley perked up. He was all ears.

"My husband tried to confront the people he thinks is responsible for the takeover of our house," Jennifer said. "He had some leverage on them, and he wanted to use it to get some money back from them they stole, and also get our house back."

"They stole money?"

"Yes. Ten thousand from my husband's account."

Detective Hartley pulled out his notepad and held it ready. "Who?"

"Some guy named Perrin Houtin and an organization he runs in D.C."

Detective Hartley asked her to spell Perrin Houtin's name, and also to give him the name of the organization. When Hartley pressed her for the backstory on Perrin, she told him everything she knew. When she was done, Hartley nodded. He had enough information for now.

"Okay. I'm going to check this out." Hartley slipped the

notepad in his inside jacket pocket and pointed to the card in Jennifer's hand. "If you think of anything, or you hear from your husband, call me. In the meantime, I wouldn't have any more contact with these people until I check things out."

"What about the court case?" Jennifer wondered.

"Tell your attorney to put it on hold for now. Let's not do anything to agitate these people until I find out who they are and if they had any connection with this."

Back home

* * *

Jesse arrived at Joe Lippman's office suite at 9:15 a.m. He pushed open the glass door and greeted the receptionist. There was a sheen of sweat on his face from having run most of the way from his car to the building.

He had been to the office several times, but this was the first time he had ever seen the receptionist. He looked down at her name tag. Chrysanthemum Atwell. He smiled inwardly. *Couldn't her parents have named her after a flower that was easier to spell?* No wonder Joe just called her Crissy.

The redhead looked up at Jesse through black-rimmed glasses that looked as if they could use a good cleaning. "May I help you?"

"Meeting with Joe for 9 o'clock. I apologize I'm a bit late."

A bit late? Crissy thought. *More like over an hour.* She pointed down the hall. "He said you can come straight back."

"Thanks." Jesse made his way down the hall until he arrived at Joe's office. He found Joe sitting at his desk reading a copy of *The National Law Journal*. When Jesse entered, Joe put the paper on his desk and looked at Jesse the way a parent looks at a child who is about to be punished.

Joe removed his glasses. "You're late."

"Yeah, I know. I overslept." Jesse was eager to get on with the reason he was here. "Where's Perrin Houtin?"

"Didn't show," Joe said without the slightest hint of surprise in his voice. "You still want to send those pictures to the police?"

Jesse said nothing, out of frustration that his plan had failed.

Joe didn't wait long for an answer. "Your wife called me this morning."

That got a response out of Jesse. "Really?"

"Yeah. Actually, she called twice. The first time was at around 4:30 this morning on my cell. She wanted to know if I had seen you or heard from you since last night."

Jesse planted himself in a chair. "What'd you tell her?"

"I told her I had spoken to you last evening, and that we had scheduled an appointment for 8 this morning. She called me again around 8:15, and asked if you had arrived. I told her no. She then told me about a situation that happened at your house this morning."

Jesse leaned forward. "What situation?"

Joe leaned back. "You need to find that out from your wife. But based on what she told me, I don't think Perrin is going to show."

"What was it?"

"You need to ask your wife."

"Joe, come on!"

"You need to go home, Jesse. And I mean now!"

Jesse examined the stoicism on Joe's face and knew that he would not be able to press Joe for more information. Her loudly sighed his annoyance and looked away from Joe toward a side wall.

Joe massaged his hands. "Jesse, you're not paying me $200 an hour just to let your marriage fall apart."

"Oh, come on, Joe." Jesse spoke without averting his gaze from the side wall. "My marriage is not falling apart. It's not even close."

"Maybe not now. But the seeds are being planted. The best way to keep weeds out of the garden is to not allow them to grow in the first place."

Jesse retreated back into silence.

Joe stood. "So, I'm going to do something that an attorney never does to a paying client."

"What's that?" Jesse asked.

"I'm going to put you out of my office. Fifteen minutes from now, I'm going to call your wife. I'm hoping you'll be home before I make that call."

Jesse looked at Joe and saw a seriousness that could not be challenged. Jesse stood and, without another word, walked out of Joe's office. He didn't even bother to say goodbye to Crissy as he stormed out the office suite door.

* * *

A 10-minute drive along Dolly Madison Drive, and Jesse was back at home. As he pulled up in the driveway, he noticed Lottie on the front porch, in an old down coat, on her hands and knees, scrubbing something on the concrete. He couldn't quite tell what it was from his vantage point in the vehicle, but thought it unusual that Lottie would be risking a cold by working with water in a 40-degree chill.

When Lottie saw him pull into the driveway, she stopped scrubbing and got to her feet. The scrub brush dripped soapy crimson water on the porch before she set the brush in a nearby bucket.

Jesse got out of the car and approached. He looked down at the reddened sudsy area on the porch and looked up at Lottie, his question etched in the confused frown on his face.

Lottie answered before he could speak. "Someone put a dead dog on my doorstep." The indignation in her voice was not so much because of the dog, but because Jesse had upset his wife by being away all night. "You need to talk to Jen."

Jesse's mind had not processed any words beyond *dead dog.* "A dead dog? Who would do that?"

"Your wife's inside. Go in through the basement door." Lottie returned to her scrubbing.

Jesse started jiggling his car keys in his hand, something he did whenever he was nervous. He walked around to the rear of the house and approached the basement door. Finding it unlocked, he opened it, walked inside, and then shut the door quietly and gently behind him. He could hear the kids further ahead in the family room, and he hoped that Jennifer was there as well, so that he could slip into the bedroom unnoticed and have a few minutes to gather his thoughts before he faced her. Jesse crept a few steps ahead to the open bedroom door and walked in, fully expecting Jennifer to be standing there waiting for him.

What he found was Jennifer, on her knees, her bare toes

Louis N. Jones

slightly curled, her arms stretched on the bed, her tear-streaked face almost touching the sheets. Her lips were moving slowly, passionately, framing an urgent appeal to God almighty. *Father, protect our marriage and our lives. Touch the heart of my husband, that he will act according to your will. Touch my heart, Lord, that I may know how to submit.*

Watching her there, praying earnestly, almost desperately, broke something within Jesse. This was the first time since they were married that she had ever said her morning prayer without him. Even when he was out of town, they always connected by phone and prayed together. Seeing her there, alone, struck him deep to the core. It was as if her connection to God was stronger than his own, and that embarrassed him. He was the one who had the title of preacher and pastor, and yet, his own prayer life was lacking. Despite his staying out all night, here was his wife interceding for him.

Joe had told him that the best way to avoid weeds in the garden was to never let them grow in the first place. At this moment, he had never felt so estranged from God and from his wife. He already felt the weeds, those troublesome growths, choking the life out of his garden.

But his pride was strong. He wanted to be right. He needed to be right. Everyone in his life—his mother, Joe, and now Lottie—seemed to have taken sides with Jennifer. But he could not bring himself to believe that he was wrong for trying to do everything he could to save their home.

Yet it was obvious his wife was unhappy. He could see it in her face. He could hear it in her prayers. What was confusing to Jesse was why she was not happy with what he was doing to save their home.

Adverse Possession

It's what you're doing. It's not what I'm doing.

The words came to Jesse's mind clearly, unfettered by confusion or ambiguity. He knew that voice, the voice of the Lord. Most of the time he obeyed it when he heard it, yet there were some instances where he did otherwise. Sometimes it was easier to ignore it, especially when it conflicted with his pride.

Jesse wanted to ignore it now.

Yet his wife was there, in their bedroom, praying for God to touch his heart and cause him to act according to His will. He knew, to his chagrin, that God was answering that prayer, touching his heart such that he couldn't stand to be disconnected from his adorable little country bumpkin any longer.

Jesse walked in the room and knelt next to her. She turned to him, her face registering both surprise and delight. She started to speak, but Jesse held up his finger, silencing her. He grabbed her left hand, squeezing it tenderly, and together, they found their way to the throne of God.

* * *

Fear and anger are frequent bedfellows. Now that Jennifer's fear had subsided, her indignation came to the surface like bubbles in boiling water. No sooner had they finished praying and got off their knees when Jennifer reached over, shut the bedroom door, and glared at Jesse with fire in her eyes. "Where have you been?"

This caught Jesse off guard. He had expected that after the prayer, she would fall into his arms, and they would have a quiet and productive discussion. Now it seemed as if Jennifer was poised for another argument. *Weren't we just praying?*

Jesse sat on the edge of the bed. "I was out clearing my head, thinking about a few things. I stopped in at Ma's for a bit."

"You were at Ma's for about a half an hour," Jennifer challenged. "You were gone for over 12 hours. You needed that much time to think?"

Jesse sighed. "I checked in at a hotel and spent the night there."

"You were at a hotel while your wife and children are being threatened with their lives?" Jennifer huffed.

Jesse turned to Jennifer, his concern registering amidst the shock. "Threatened? What do you mean?"

"Didn't Lottie tell you? Joe?"

"Lottie said something about a dead dog."

"Yeah. On our doorstep. With a note in it."

Jesse waited for an explanation.

"It said you and your family'll be dead like this dog if you don't back off." Jennifer's voice trembled slightly.

"What?" Jesse's face grew tense. "Are you sure?"

Jennifer couldn't believe he said that. "Why would I *not* be sure 'bout somethin' like that?"

"I didn't mean it like that." Jesse stood up and approached her. "I meant that—" Oh, he didn't know what he meant. It was one of those automatic reactionary statements people make when they don't know what else to say. He wrapped his arms around her. "I'm sorry, honey. I should have been here. I didn't know you were going through that."

Jennifer hugged him back. "I was so scared."

Jesse had a thought. "The kids?"

"No, they didn't see it. They don't have a clue what happened."

"Good. Did you call the police?"

"Lottie did. When I saw it, I screamed, and she ran downstairs with a baseball bat like she was ready to go to town on a burglar, or somethin'."

"What did the police say?"

"They're gonna check it out." Jennifer walked to the dresser and retrieved Hartley's card, handing it to Jesse.

"So what do we do?"

"We do nothing. Like I been telling you all along. Now I'm not even sure I wanna move back in the house."

Jesse broke from the embrace. "Why not?"

"You got these people all riled up," Jennifer explained, sitting on the bed. "You discovered secrets, stuff they ain't want nobody to know. Now you're a threat. Even if we win the court case and get the house back, they may be angry enough to follow through on their threat anyway. After all, they know everything about us, 'cause they got access to the stuff in our house. You exposed them. Now we've got to live with this looming over our heads."

"So, what do we do about that?" Jesse sat next to her. "Do we sell our house, move to some nondescript city near the mountains, change our names, enroll in witness protection? C'mon, Jen. I'm not running from these people. That house is ours, and we are going to get it back."

"Then do it God's way, and not yours."

Those were similar to the words Jesse heard in his spirit just moments before. They were difficult words to hear when his ego and pride demanded that he pick up his sword and slash his way to victory. But now, everyone dear to him was telling him to put his sword back in its place. He heard in his spirit the very words of Jesus in Matthew 26:52.

They were quiet for four minutes while temperatures returned to normal, neither looking at the other. Finally, Jennifer spoke up, her voice quiet and shrill. She grabbed his hand, and held it. "I know you're afraid that this Bernard is going to take everything you worked hard for. But it's possible for a man without riches to be a wonderful husband. Because it's not just about what's in your pocket. It's about the person you are. I didn't fall in love with your money, or your house. I fell in love with *you*."

"I bet the money didn't hurt."

"No, it didn't. But that's only 'cause I didn't let it. Money breaks up more relationships and sends more people to jail than anything." Jennifer started massaging Jesse's hand and spoke to him in bedroom tones. "Honey, you have almost 95,000 dollars in savings. We're not going to starve anytime soon. You are a wonderful provider, and you're a wonderful husband. But for me, please, just for me, let this thing go. Let God handle it."

Jesse watched as she laid his hand on her stomach and gradually moved it upward. "And you're good with me letting this go?"

"I've *been* good with it."

"Okay, I'll let it go. I promise. I'll just wait to see what happens with the court case."

Jennifer squeezed his hand. "That's all I ask."

"That's a lot to ask."

"I'm sure both of us will be the better for it." Jennifer placed three light kisses on his hand. "Thank you." She swung her feet around Jesse and lay down on the bed, turning on her side so that she faced away from Jesse.

Jesse gazed at her for a moment, then reached over and gently slapped her derriere.

Jennifer knew what that meant. "Not now. The kids are awake. Wait until they take their nap."

"When will that be?" Jesse walked to the closet to gather a change of clothes.

"It's up to you," Jennifer said. "I'm taking a nap. You're watching the kids."

Jennifer was fast asleep not five minutes later. Jesse watched her for a few minutes, then smiled and headed into the bathroom. He was dying for a shower.

* * *

This was David Hartley's first year as a detective, so his relative inexperience led to him being assigned low-priority cases. The high priority stuff—murders, sexual assaults, assaults with deadly weapons, homeland security stuff— those were assigned to the seasoned detectives. So his caseload consisted mostly of larcenies, domestic relations stuff. And dead dogs on a porch.

After talking with Jennifer that morning, he returned to the McLean district station and sat solemnly at his cubicle, decorated sparsely with photographs of his wife and two kids, and a photograph that a fellow cop had taken of him effecting his first arrest. That photo was taken 10 years and 20 pounds ago.

He looked down at all the notes on his desk and tried to piece together a logical chain of events. The animal control vet had told him that the wounds on the dog were inflicted by another animal and were likely the result of a dogfight. The trauma to the dog's neck was also caused by another animal. They placed the time of death at around 11 p.m., but noted that final lab results would not be available for a couple of weeks. But Hartley had enough to get started. He figured the dog had to be killed elsewhere and transported to the neighborhood, since Bynum Drive and its surrounding streets were not a likely location for a staged bloodsport.

Based on Sergeant Gwynn's report, Hartley checked out the perimeter of 6609 to see if there were obvious clues that Bernard MacNichol had anything to do with the dog. He checked the sidewalks and walkways for the presence of blood. He checked Bernard's beat-up pickup truck to see if there was a possibility the truck was used to bring the dog to the neighborhood. He checked for wet spots on the grass and on the concrete to see if anything had been washed off, as the dog was likely transported to Lottie's house in a container of some sort. He checked the drains for the presence of blood. He saw nothing conclusive, which meant that he could not prove that Bernard had anything to do with the dog. But he couldn't rule Bernard out, either.

Hartley had pulled traffic camera footage from the main road closest to Bynum Drive. Since the dog was killed on or around 11 p.m., he would review the camera footage to see what cars entered or exited the neighborhood between then and 4:30 p.m. The neighborhood was designed so that there were only two roads in or out. This made it easy for Hartley, since anyone coming in likely lived there or was visiting. He didn't have to deal with the cars that were just passing through.

He hated this part of his job, reviewing camera footage. Sitting there at his cubicle staring at roads for five hours was the part of this job they didn't show you on the TV cop shows. In addition, traffic camera footage wasn't the greatest, so he couldn't make out any license plates numbers or other identifying information. He could only note the model and color of the cars coming in, and watch to see if they came out. Between 11 p.m. and midnight, 10 vehicles came in, but none of those 10 came out. After midnight, only four cars came in, but none came out.

Detective Hartley checked the footage again, making sure he did not miss anything. After five hours of watching sped-up video footage, Hartley was certain. One of those 14 vehicles that entered the neighborhood carried the carcass of a dog. And whoever brought it in was likely still in the area when Jennifer had discovered it, and likely watching Hartley and animal control as they investigated.

His next step was to do a canvass of the neighborhood. But before that, he needed to check on this Perrin Houtin fellow. Maybe talking to him could shed some light on what happened and lead him in the right direction. Maybe information from Perrin would narrow his canvass from 25 houses to a number much lower. It was worth a try.

He would walk into his lieutenant's office to give him an update on the case. Then he would gear up for an early afternoon drive to the district.

Confessions

* * *

Perrin Houtin had just completed a telephone call with one of his other girlfriends and had arranged for her to meet him at a gym on Connecticut Avenue. He grabbed his gym bag, slipped on a North Face jacket, and then headed out the door.

The previous visit from Jesse Kane had made him paranoid. Before he stepped off the porch, he looked up and down the block to see if there was anyone watching.

His efforts paid off. Halfway down the block was a black sedan, parked far enough behind the car ahead of it so it could get out of its parking space quickly. He could vaguely make out the silhouette of a man in the driver's seat.

Perrin lingered on the porch to see if the black sedan would leave. After seven minutes, Perrin concluded that the sedan was not moving. At least not until he did.

Perrin decided to try to draw the sedan out of the foxhole. He walked to his Chevy Malibu situated further up the block. He started the engine, pulled out quickly, and drove to the traffic light, looking back to see if the sedan was following.

Just as the light turned green, the sedan pulled out of its parking space.

Perrin cursed and turned left. He drove to the next street, turned left again, and darted into the alley adjacent to his home. He carefully and quickly guided his car into his garage driveway, switched off the ignition, hopped out, and, keys at the ready, unlocked his basement door and ran inside, shutting the door behind him. He parted the basement door curtains slightly so that he could see outside.

About three minutes later, the black sedan rolled slowly down the alley, pausing in front of his car. Perrin could clearly see the driver, a stocky black man wearing a black suit. He was either a cop, or a minister. And Perrin didn't particularly want to speak with either.

After a few more minutes lingering in the alley, the black sedan pulled off. Perrin noticed it had Virginia tags. The blue and red lights barely visible behind a tinted rear window gave the car away. It was a police-issued vehicle. Some Virginia cop was watching him.

Perrin sighed, then pulled his cell phone out of his pocket. He had Lester Hampton on speed dial, although he had been advised not to do so. But right now, Perrin didn't care what Lester said.

He had to call three times before reaching Lester. At the third phone call, Lester finally picked up, dispensing with any greeting. "I thought I told you not to call me on this line unless it was an emergency."

"This is an emergency," Perrin retorted.

"Really? What kind?"

"I got a cop from Virginia watching my house. I guess that calling card you set up didn't work."

Lester played dumb, in case he was being listened to. "I don't know what you're talking about."

"You know exactly what I'm talking about. Look, man, I didn't get into this to be going to jail. Now I got Virginia police checking me out."

"Don't forget you're the one that's doing the teeny bopping."

"And that mess would never have been put on blast if it wasn't for us deciding to operate in Virginia." Perrin switched the phone on his ear. "I told you, don't fool around in Virginia. Stick with D.C. and Maryland."

"Why don't you calm down for a moment, get your head together." Lester's statement was not a request.

"Naw, man. I'm the one out there. If this thing blows up, you can just pack up and start over. I'm gonna wind up in upstate Florida doin' hard time. I gotta deal with this my way."

There was dead silence on the other end. That didn't deter Perrin one bit. "I quit, man. Take my name off this organization. I don't want anything else to do with it."

"Did you forget I own that house?"

"I don't care. I'll move out by tomorrow. Just don't contact me any more. I'm done."

Perrin hung up the phone, knowing as soon as he did, his life was in danger. Lester was not the type to let Perrin's resignation go unchallenged, and Perrin believed that Lester was now so paranoid, he would kill to keep his name from being exposed again. Perrin knew too much; he was a threat.

Perrin knew he had to leave this house immediately and never return.

Perrin's plan was to load all his clothes, small electronics, personal effects, and papers in his car. He would leave everything else. The girlfriend he was to meet at the gym would likely let him stay at her house for a few days until he regrouped and figured out what was next. But he had to make himself a ghost to Lester and anyone associated with him.

He shoved the phone into his pocket and turned to go upstairs. Before he could move, he noticed a business card lying on a side hall table. He picked up the card, reading Joe Lippman's office number.

He pulled his phone out of his pocket and dialed Joe's number. He now felt comfortable answering Joe's questions about Bernard. He hoped it wasn't too late.

* * *

Jesse looked at his watch. It was 10:55 a.m. the next morning. He and Joe Lippman sat together in Joe's conference room. Jesse looked across the table at Joe, who was giving him a look of uncertainty.

"You sure this guy's going to show?" Jesse asked.

"I don't know," Joe answered. "He told me he would be here by 10:45. He seemed genuine. A little scared."

"Maybe we'd better call Detective Hartley, get him in the loop on this."

"Wouldn't advise it. A cop might scare him off."

After three silent minutes, the intercom on Joe's desk beeped. "Showtime," he said to Jesse before picking up the phone to answer his receptionist. "Yeah, Crissy."

"Mr. Houtin here to see you."

"Show him in. And tell Raymond to come in. We're about to start video recording."

"You got it."

Seconds later, Crissy opened the door to Joe's office and allowed Perrin Houtin to enter. He wore a black suit, herringbone stitching, with a solid gray tie. Joe noted that it was definitely not a suit from the discount rack. He stood to his feet and walked over to greet Perrin. "Mr. Houtin. Joe Lippman."

"How's it going?" Perrin said to Joe. He looked at Jesse, but did not greet him.

"Have a seat right here." Joe pointed Perrin to a seat in front of his desk, across from Jesse. "Can I get you some coffee, some water, anything else to drink?"

"Naw, I'm good." Perrin looked to his right and saw a video camera on a tripod. "You recording this?"

"I'm representing Mr. Kane in a landlord and tenant dispute and I need to videotape this proceeding for evidence. Do you have a problem with that?"

Perrin hesitated. "What kind of questions are y'all gonna ask me?"

"Questions about Bernard and Amber MacNichol, who are defendants in our lawsuit. You are familiar with them, aren't you?" Joe said.

"Yeah, I know 'em."

"Great. So, do I have your permission to videotape?"

Perrin looked over at Jesse. Jesse gave him a blank stare. Perrin looked back at Joe. "Yeah. I'm cool."

Adverse Possession

Raymond, a short bespectacled middle-aged man who looked as if he were fresh out of high school, walked in the office and took his place behind the video camera.

"You got the money?" Jesse said to Perrin.

"No."

"Why not?"

"Just be glad I'm answering y'all's questions."

"The deal was, you bring money, *and* you answer our questions."

"Look, man, I ain't got nothing but the clothes on my back and the shoes on my feet. And 200 dollars in an account."

"Nice clothes, though. Is that a Hugo Boss? Probably set you back about a thousand dollars of my money."

Perrin looked directly at Joe. "Look, I didn't come here to get tongue lashed by your boy here."

Joe made a motion with his hand telling Jesse to back off. "Well, let's get started." He signaled Raymond to turn on the video camera. The red light on the front of the camera was Joe's signal to start. "It's 11:05 a.m. on the camera date in the offices of Joseph Lippman and Associates. Present in the room is myself, Joseph Lippman, representing Mr. Jesse Kane in a landlord and tenant matter against Bernard and Amber MacNichol. The premises in question are 6609 Bynum Drive, McLean, Virginia. The MacNichols are currently illegal occupants of these premises, and we have issued notice for them to leave the premises in 30 days.

"Also present in the room are Jesse Kane, the plaintiff in this matter, Mr. Perrin Houtin, and Mr. Raymond Scott, who is our video technician. Mr. Houtin, please state your full name, and then spell your full name, starting with your first name, then middle name, then last name."

"Uh, I'm Perrin Houtin. No middle name. P-E-R-R-I-N H-O-U-T-I-N."

"Is this your birth name?"

"Yeah."

"Do you have any aliases?"

"Naw."

"And are you here of your own free will, answering these questions willingly, and have not been paid, illegally forced, coerced, or threatened to answer these questions?"

Perrin stuttered, "That's correct."

"Are you familiar with Bernard MacNichol?"

"Yes, I am."

"How did you meet him?"

"One of the cats who is in our network works at a shelter off Route 1 in Alexandria. He introduced me to Bernard."

Joe started taking notes feverishly on a yellow notepad. "And how did he know Bernard?"

"Whatchoo mean?"

"Was Bernard working there?"

"Naw, he was staying there."

"He was living at the shelter?"

"Yeah. He and his wife."

"When did you meet him?"

"I don't know. Middle of January, I guess."

"How long had he been there when you met him?"

"Maybe about two or three months."

"What does your network do?"

"We do real estate consultation."

"Specifically what do you mean by that?"

"We help people in need of housing get into homes."

"And how do you do that, exactly?"

"Whatchoo mean?"

"I mean, do you help with loans? Do you hook them up with HUD? Do you have connections with low rent housing? How does a network like yours help a man like Bernard get into a home?"

"I don't know, man. Whatever information they feel they need to help get housing, we provide that."

"And is that information worth 10,000 dollars?"

"Whoa, hold up, man." Perrin vigorously waved his hand, signaling for them to turn the camera off. Joe nodded his permission to Raymond. Raymond switched off the camera. "Y'all told me I was gonna be answering questions about Bernard," Perrin said. "Now, it looks like y'all trying to get into my business. And I ain't willing to go there with y'all."

"We need to understand what you do in order to understand the extent of Bernard's relationship with you," Joe informed him.

"Naw, man. I ain't talking about what I do. That ain't none of y'all business. Y'all wanted to know about Bernard, I'll answer questions about Bernard."

Joe looked at Jesse, and then peered at Perrin over his glasses. "Mr. Houtin, you need to answer all of our questions."

"Naw, man. If I go down that road with y'all, I'm incriminating myself. So, no matter what y'all got over me, I'm gonna get locked up anyway."

Jesse leaned forward. "So, you're saying that you're committing criminal acts through this network?"

Perrin knew well that what he and Lester were doing was

not entirely legal, which was why Lester took great pains to keep himself at arm's length. But he could not implicate Lester without implicating himself, and his goal was to stay out of jail. Perrin scowled at Jesse. "I'm willing to bet, since you've been digging through my trash and spying on my house, that you know more than what you telling me. So, I don't need to humor you by answering these questions."

Jesse looked over at Joe. Joe twisted his mouth to one side and allowed his gaze to shift upward. After a few seconds, he said, "Okay. We'll stay away from the activities of the network."

Perrin nodded. "Fair enough."

Joe gave the signal to Raymond to turn the camera back on.

Joe started his questioning again. "So, Bernard was seeking real estate consultation through your network. Correct?"

"Yeah."

"Without revealing the activities that you did for Mr. MacNichol, what was it that he needed assistance with?"

"He needed help to get into a house in McLean. I think it's the one you mentioned when we first started."

"Get into? What do you mean *get into*?"

"Rent."

"Was he employed at the time?"

"Had a few odd jobs here and there. He was tryin' to get disability."

"Disability? Why?"

"Bernard is sick, man. Got cancer. Some long name I can't remember. Begins with *m*."

"Melanoma?" Jesse guessed.

"Naw. Something else. It's when you breathe in too much

asbestos."

"Mesothelioma?" Joe said.

"Yeah, that's it. He think he got it when he was working construction."

Jesse's face suddenly went blank.

"Why would Bernard, who is homeless at the time you met him, and presumably terminally ill, be suddenly interested in renting a 900,000-dollar house?" Joe asked.

"He said it was his parents' house."

"The house belongs to Mr. and Mrs. Kane. How can it be his parents' house?"

"Said it was his parents' house before Mr. and Mrs. Kane bought it," Perrin explained. "But they couldn't pay the note, and they got put out. About two months later, they died in a fire."

"Jesus," Jesse said under his breath.

Perrin heard Jesse's exclamation. "Yeah, man. Cat's got it bad. I don't normally do stuff in Virginia. I mainly focus on D.C. and Maryland. But I agreed to try to get this cat some legal help. And I was successful at finding an attorney for him."

"You have a name and address of the attorney?"

"Can't tell you that, man. Privileged information."

"What about your friend at the shelter?" Jesse asked.

"Same thing, man. Privileged."

"One more question, Mr. Houtin," Joe said. "Bernard MacNichol has a driver's license, a vehicle registration and utility bills, in his name, listing 6609 Bynum as the address. Do you have any idea why he would have those items listed at that address?"

Perrin paused for almost 15 seconds before he answered. "The attorney drew up a fake lease. Bernard used the lease to get the utilities changed in his name, and then used the utility bills to get his license changed. To make sure everything looked good, he had the Kanes' mail forwarded to another address, so it looked like they had moved. As for the vehicle, well, that truck belonged to Bernard's father. It's been registered at that address since his father lived there. They just never got the address changed."

Jesse had another question. "How did Bernard know where to send the mail?"

"That, I don't know."

"And how did he get in my house? The police said there was no forced entry."

"He had a key."

"How'd he get that?"

"Someone lives in your neighborhood. Bernard goes way back with him."

"Who?"

"Privileged."

Joe chimed in. "Mr. Houtin, you told me on the phone yesterday that you had left the Reclaim Network. If you are no longer connected with them, why are you being so hush-hush on names that we need?"

"'Cause these people can hurt me if I expose them. The less said about them, the better. I'm just here to save my own behind."

"Were they the ones that dropped off that dead dog?"

"I wouldn't worry about that. They was just tryin' to scare you. They ain't gonna go around killin' good white folk from

Virginia. You can believe that. But I'm different. They'll bump me off in a second."

"Who did it?"

"Did what?"

"The dog?"

"Somebody from the network. That's all I can tell you. But like I said, don't worry about it."

Joe and Jesse looked at each another to see if either of them wanted to ask any more questions. Satisfied that they had asked all the questions they needed to, Joe concluded his questioning with, "Is there anything else you think we need to know?"

"Naw. Y'all know enough as it is."

Joe signaled Raymond to turn off the camera. The red light on the camera slowly faded into oblivion.

"Thank you, Mr. Houtin, for coming in." Joe stood to his feet. "One more thing." Joe walked around to the front of his desk and Perrin stood up. "You are to keep this meeting completely confidential. Bernard, nor his wife, nor anyone else, needs to know about what occurred here today."

"No problem. I already told Bernard not to contact me for a while, and that was before I quit yesterday, so I ain't got no reason to talk to him again."

"Great." Joe shook Perrin's hand. Jesse stayed seated, seemingly immersed in thought.

Perrin glanced at both Jesse and Joe before he swaggered his way out the door.

Joe sat in the chair vacated by Perrin, while Raymond did some technical stuff with the camera. He noticed Jesse's sullen look. "Mr. Houtin said some good things. With his information, maybe try to get the records from the shelter, we can probably make a case with the police that Bernard is trespassing."

Joe's good news did not seem to faze Jesse.

Joe gave him a light and playful punch on the shoulder. "Cheer up, kid. You done good."

"Did I?" Jesse said doubtfully.

"What's the matter?" Joe asked.

"I need to talk to my wife."

* * *

Jesse walked into Lottie's house shortly after noon. Jennifer kept a careful watch on the kids as they made their own peanut butter and jelly sandwiches in the kitchen. Aiden greeted his father, and continued to slap peanut butter on a slice of wheat bread. Ashley greeted Jesse, and then offered his father a sandwich.

"Yeah, dear, I'd like a sandwich," Jesse said, not so much because he was hungry, but because he knew it gave his daughter pleasure to make one for him. He waited until she was finished, said "thank you" and pulled his daughter to him, kissing her on the cheek. Ashley grinned, then walked nonchalantly back to the table. Jesse walked over to his son, and patted him gently on the shoulder. He had hoped his bitterness and anger over the past few days had not affected his children, although he knew they missed their house just as much as he did. Almost every day, they asked if they would be moving back into their house. Every day, Jesse had to answer no. Telling that to his children increased his resolve to make the day happen where he would have a different answer. Now, his meeting with Perrin lessened his resolve, and that was something he needed to bounce off his wife.

Jesse looked at his wife, waited until she met his gaze, and nodded her toward the living room. They walked to the farthest corner of the living room and spoke in hushed tones.

"Kids are excited about goin' back to school next week," Jennifer said. "They miss a lot of their friends."

"Are they still asking about the house?" asked Jesse.

"Yeah. There's a lot about that they don't understand, so I try to talk them through it," said Jennifer. "So, how did it go today?"

"I went into that meeting expecting Houtin to give us something, a smoking gun, that I could use against Bernard," Jesse said.

"Didn't he give us that?"

"Yeah. He gave us some good stuff. Joe said he was going to contact Detective Hartley to see if the police can take any action."

"So, why so glum?"

"When you heard your parents could be kicked out of their house, how did that make you feel?"

The question seemed far out of left field and caught Jennifer off guard, but she answered nonetheless. "I felt betrayed. I felt angry. I felt that the church should be doing something for them rather than just kicking them out."

"So, you would sympathize with people whose parents are being kicked out of their homes?"

"Well, I guess it depends on the situation."

"Let's say this is the situation." Jesse starts to pace the

room. "A mother and father buy a house. Not even a year and a half later, the house is foreclosed, and the mom and dad have to move out. At some point during or before all this, their son contracts terminal cancer. He winds up homeless, which means he's probably unable to do anything to help his mom and dad. Two months after the parents move out, they die in a fire. Would you sympathize with the son?"

"I would. The son's goin' through a lot." Jennifer's eyes widened. "Are you tryin' to tell me that's what happened across the street?"

"Yep." Jesse stopped his pacing. "You know, up until that meeting, I thought Bernard was some scheming drug addict trying to take advantage of me. Now I realize that this has nothing to do with me. This guy is tortured beyond belief. With everything that has happened in his life, the pain he is going through must be incredible."

Jennifer nodded slightly, gazing at Jesse.

"I was so busy tending to my own pain, my own needs, that I was callous to Bernard's pain," Jesse confessed. "I didn't sense it. I didn't pick it up. I didn't even consider it. My goal was to make myself whole. And that's not the way for a man of God to be. That's not the way for any man to be."

Jesse paused for a minute, collecting his thoughts, looking at the floor. Jennifer drew next to him and held his hand in both of hers.

"I wanted so much to get that house back, for my family. But I completely neglected something. One of the most important things I can give my family is to let them see me maintain my holiness and my integrity. My kids needed to see my example of how God really wants his people to behave. And honey, I apologize to you for not being that example."

Jennifer gently patted his hand, giving him a wordless acceptance of his apology.

"I'd like to go over there, maybe invite Bernard and his wife to dinner tomorrow, if it's okay with you," Jesse said. "I'd like to just talk to him, find out where his head is at, and if there's anything we can do to help."

Jennifer nodded her approval. "I think that's a good idea."

"No guarantee he'll show up."

"Well, at least make the attempt," Jennifer said softly. "I'll be glad to cook. I'll call Lottie on her cell and see if it's okay with her."

"Okay." Jesse pulled his wife's hand up to his lips and kissed it. "I'm going to go downstairs and take a nap for a bit. Then I'll go see Bernard. His truck's not out there, so I assume he's gone."

"You know he parks his truck on Chester Street sometimes," Jennifer told him. "Lottie said she saw it over there yesterday. Why would he park it way over there?"

"Probably doesn't want anybody to see his comings and goings," Jesse guessed.

"Particularly *us*," Jennifer concluded.

"Yeah." Jesse headed for the basement. "Wake me up in an hour and let me know what Lottie says."

* * *

As requested, Jennifer woke Jesse up and told him Lottie's decision. While Lottie wanted to help any way she could, she drew the line with letting Bernard and Amber into her home, a sentiment that Jesse and Jennifer completely understood.

They decided to invite the MacNichols to a restaurant, somewhere that was neutral ground. They were aware that the MacNichols might be suspicious of their invitation and think something strange was afoot—perhaps an attempt to get them out of the house so the Kanes could reclaim it. Jesse decided there was no way they could make the MacNichols entirely comfortable with the invitation, so they prayed together and hoped that the MacNichols would accept.

At 3 p.m., Jesse and Jennifer walked out of Lottie's front door and headed across Bynum Drive to their house. As they stepped onto the property, Jennifer hesitated, as if she were a stranger on her own property. Jesse took her hand and led her to the front door, telling her it was legal for them to step onto their own property. All Jennifer could think of was the last time they were on the property, when they were held at gunpoint.

Once they stepped onto the porch, they noticed that the curtains at the living room window had been drawn, and there were sheets hanging across the glass in the front door, blocking their view inside. Someone had stuck two flyers from pizza joints between the door and jamb. Jesse pulled Jennifer behind him, and then knocked on the door.

He would knock for five minutes without an answer.

"Maybe they're not here," Jennifer said.

"They're here," Jesse said.

"How do you know?"

"I saw the curtains shift in the master bedroom. They know it's us. They're not answering. Is the phone still off the hook in there?"

"Yeah."

Jesse pulled out one of the pizza flyers, removed a pen from his pocket, and started writing. He then handed the flyer to Jennifer, who started reading:

Need to talk with you. This is not a trick. We heard some things about you, and we'd like to see what we can do to help. We are pastors with a local church. Please call us. 703-155-9856. Jesse and Jennifer, owners of 6609 Bynum Drive.

Jennifer nodded her approval, and handed the note back to Jesse. Jesse slid the note under the door. Together they walked until they were at the edge of the driveway.

"I hope they call," Jesse said.

"What if they don't?" Jennifer asked. "Are you still going to go through with your plan?"

"Jen, I know you might think I'm crazy, but I'm probably not."

"Why?"

"In Scripture, Luke 6:28, it says, 'bless those who curse you, pray for those who mistreat you. If someone strikes you on one cheek, turn to him the other also. If someone takes your cloak, don't stop him from taking your tunic.' That scripture says that we shouldn't retaliate or seek revenge. And that's exactly what I was doing. And I can't trust myself going in that direction without believing that retaliation is a part of what I am doing. I thought of Bernard as a criminal, a deadbeat, a low life. But in reality, he is in need of help. God is saying we should help them in any way we can, because they need it, and they need *Him*."

Jennifer looked at him and smiled in admiration. The husband that she had married, the compassionate, caring husband, the one that looked beyond her faults and the faults of her family, was *back*. She loved this about him, and would rarely argue when he would reach out to help *anyone*. Something had happened to him in that meeting with Joe and Perrin Houtin. Jesse had left home that morning determined to rip into Bernard with the force and fury of a tsunami, but returned home humble and wavering on his plan to evict Bernard. Jennifer believed the Holy Spirit touched Jesse during that meeting.

"I'm still going to go through with the legal eviction process," Jesse said. "I don't condone theft, and that house is ours. But the last thing I want to do is have the police put them out until we have an opportunity to know what is going on with them."

"What do we do in the meantime?" Jennifer asked.

Jesse sighed. "We get an apartment. We get the kids in school. We live our lives, as unaffected by this mess as we can possibly make it. And of course, we have to figure out what to do about your parents. But before we do, there's something I need to tell you."

"What?"

"It's about your father."

"What about my father?"

Adverse Possession

Delivering the news

* * *

The sun had just set on a particularly cold Thursday evening in Knoxville. Samantha and Harlan Trudeau had just finished a pork chop dinner. Samantha was cleaning the kitchen while Harlan enjoyed a Guinness at the dining room table while flipping through bills. He only half-listened to WNOX on the radio; it functioned primarily to kill the quiet in the room. He occasionally glanced at the volume-lowered TV in the living room.

"Honey, *Jeopardy's* coming on soon," Harlan yelled to his wife about her favorite game show. It was a pastime of theirs to see which of them could answer the most questions.

Alex Trebek had just walked onto the set when Samantha and Harlan heard a knock at their front door.

Harlan looked at Samantha. "You expectin' anybody?"

"No" was Samantha's response.

Harlan got up, went to the living room window, and peered out on the porch. "It's Jen."

"Jen?" Samantha stood in front of the recliner in the living room. "What's she doing here?"

Harlan opened the door and let his daughter in from the cold. "Hey, Pa," Jennifer said, hugging him at the door, enveloping him with the chill that hung on her like the stench of cigarettes. She then walked past him and removed her parka. Harlan looked out to see if anyone else was with her, briefly noticing only the shiny minivan in the driveway. Confused, he closed the door.

Once Jennifer had hung up her parka on the coat tree just inside the door, she hugged her mother, and then moved to the living room.

"Jen, is everything okay?" Samantha asked. "Where's Jesse?"

"He's at home with the kids."

"How did you get here?" Harlan wondered aloud.

"Caught a plane to McGhee Tyson, rented a van and came here." Jennifer removed her hat, tossed her hair, and placed the hat on the couch. "I need to talk to the both of you."

Harlan studied Jennifer's face. "You came all the way from D.C. just to talk? Must have been a heck of a plane fare."

"It's too important to talk about over the phone. I need to do this face to face."

"Honey, are you sure you and Jesse are okay?" Samantha asked, sitting on the couch.

"We're fine, Ma. This has nothing to do with us, but it has everything to do with you."

Harlan said down beside his wife while Jennifer remained standing. "Sweetheart, what's going on?"

Jennifer hesitated, then said, "First of all, I want you

to know that I had nothing to do with this. In fact, I'm just finding out—"

Harlan was abrupt. "Honey, don't butter the bread. Give it to us raw."

"Ma, Pa, the lease on this house is expiring in about seven weeks. The church is not going to renew the lease."

"Why not?" Samantha asked.

"Pastor Rodereck feels the church has helped you enough. They've been subsidizing your rent for 10 years."

"So, what does this mean?" Harlan asked. "Are we gonna get thrown out of our house?"

"In about 90 days, yes. Unless a new lease can be negotiated."

Harlan looked at his wife and saw that she had already dipped into a funk. Pressed to come up with a quick solution to their dilemma, Harlan took a shot in the dark. "So, we can pay the rent ourselves. We'll figure out a way."

"Pa, we're talking at least 1,200 dollars a month. The owners will likely raise the rent, so it'll be more than that. Can you really pay that much right now?"

"Like I said, we'll manage. Why hasn't Pastor Rodereck told us any of this?"

"He's plannin' to send you a letter. I found out about this through my husband."

"So, we'll call the owners. We'll work out a new lease directly with them."

Jennifer sat. "That's gonna be a problem, Pa."

"Why?"

"The owners don't want to lease directly to you."

"Why not?"

Jennifer's eyebrows narrowed, and the Lord had to give

her Holy Spirit boldness. "Maybe because of that gamblin' problem you have, that you never bothered telling me about."

Harlan and Samantha looked at each another, silently assuring each other that neither of them had told anyone about Harlan's gambling. He then turned to Jennifer and lowered his voice to a soft, non-confrontational tone. "Honey, how did you find out about that?"

"My husband."

That answer did not surprise Harlan. How else could she have known? "Honey, that was a long time ago. I didn't tell you about it, because I didn't want to diminish myself in your eyes. Sometimes a young, impressionable girl needs a father who is tough, strong, invincible, able to handle anything. Gamblin' was a weakness. I couldn't let you see that side of me. I didn't want you to see how imperfect I really was."

"You speak in past tense," Jennifer noted. "Jesse tells me you still have a problem."

"I don't."

"You play Powerball?"

"I do, but it's not somethin' that's out of control. I can handle my responsibilities."

"Pa, it's still gamblin'."

Harlan scoffed. "You sound just like your husband now. Tell me where it says in your Bible that gamblin' is wrong."

Jennifer hoped that Harlan was not about to test her Bible skills. Jesse played that game better, but she would at least try to hold her own. "It don't mention gamblin' specifically. But the Bible does talk about responsible stewardship, which, if you're gamblin', you can't be doing. And neither you nor me needs to go to the Bible to know that gamblin' can hurt you.

Pa, for Pete's sake, you lost this house to gamblin'."

"It was a problem. Not anymore."

"Well, the owners of this house don't think so. They don't want to rent to you, because they say y'all a risk."

"And where is this coming from?" Harlan voice started to escalate again. "Is this coming from Jesse? Or from Pastor Rodereck?"

"Jesse heard it from Pastor Rodereck."

"So, because he says that the owners don't want to rent to me, I'm supposed to believe it?" Harlan did not wait for an answer, but stood to his feet. "Pastor Rodereck never liked us. He never liked this family. He's a fool to think that the owners, who are almost a day's drive away, know anything about my personal life. It's probably a lie he told them just to get us out of this house. Well, I'm not gonna stand for it. Like I said, we'll contact the owners directly."

Rather than further upset himself, Harlan chose to leave the room.

Once Jennifer heard the bedroom door shut, she moved closer to her mother on the couch. "Ma, I know that Pa is a prideful man. He wants to do everything he can to support the two of you. But he can't afford 1,500 dollars a month, plus utilities. Not on his income."

Samantha drew back. "Is that what they'll charge us?"

"No. That's what they'll charge *us*."

"Huh?"

"Jesse and I are going to sign a two-year lease with the owners," Jennifer whispered. "I spoke with them yesterday. You can sub—"

Samantha interrupted her. "Harlan is gon' be madder than

a wet hen." Shaking her head, she continued. "It was hard for him to accept the church's help 10 years ago. But he did it, because he was desperate then. But now, he's got a job. Got a merit increase comin'. He's gonna figure somethin' out."

"You know what he's doin', Ma," Jennifer said softly, pointing down the hallway toward her father's bedroom. "He's in that room thinkin' very, very seriously about calling a bookie and bettin' on a horse. He knows that 1,500 dollars a month in rent is gonna eat up his whole paycheck, so he tryin' to figure out how to raise some money the only way he knows how. I need you to convince Pa that our leasin' the house is the best thing right now."

"And what's next?" Samantha said. "We continue to pay you the 400 dollars a month we pay?"

"Yes, to start. But we'll gradually increase the rent you pay until you can pay 1,500 dollars a month without a struggle. And Ma, I don't care what you have to do, as long as it's legal. You can go back to work. You can sell cookies, pies, or tin cans. Anything to make a little money. But in two years, I'd like to report to the owners that you and Pa have successfully paid your rent for two years, and maybe they'll reconsider rentin' to you after this new lease expires."

Samantha shook her head again. "Harlan ain't gonna like this."

"It doesn't matter what Pa likes," Jennifer said. "The truth is that the church is going to let the lease expire, and the owners are not going to give Pa a new lease. But, they'll give one to Jesse and me. So, me and my husband are the only way you're going to stay in this house."

Jennifer stood. "I don't want to force you to do anything

you don't want to do, so if you decide you don't want to sublease from me, I understand. But Ma, please talk to Pa. Let him know that he has only two options: either accept our help, or be put out by the Fourth of July."

Jennifer gathered her coat.

Samantha stood. "Where are you going?"

"To a hotel."

Jennifer, don't be silly. You can stay here."

"No, Ma, I don't think I should." Jennifer headed for the door, followed by Samantha. "Y'all got a lot to talk about and work out. I don't need to be around while y'all do that."

"Are you coming back?"

"I'll be back tomorrow morning to hear what you decided." Jennifer opened the door. The brisk air rushed in. Just before she left, she said, "Y'know, the Lord touched my husband, and he had to eat his pride. I'll be prayin' your husband does the same." Jennifer buttoned her coat and walked to the rented minivan. Samantha stood at the door and watched as Jennifer backed the van out of the driveway and headed east on Pelham Park Road.

Samantha shut the door. *Jeopardy* had ended, but in its place was a TV series about an obsessive compulsive detective. Samantha switched off the TV with the remote, and walked into the kitchen, thinking about what she would say to Harlan.

Samantha saw that the red light on the front of the cordless phone was steady, showing that someone was using the phone elsewhere in the house. Samantha hoped that Harlan was calling his boss, asking for extra hours or overtime.

Samantha smiled and tried to stay positive as she headed back to their bedroom. The fate of the house was now in her hands.

* * *

Jennifer returned to the Trudeau house at 7:30 a.m. the next morning, hoping to catch Harlan before he went off to work. While she arrived, there was Samantha, seated at the dining room table, still in her flannel pajamas, her elbows on the table and hands clasped in front of her mouth, a half-empty plate of scrambled eggs and bacon sitting two feet from another plate of eggs and bacon on which Harlan had only nibbled.

Jennifer removed her parka, thinking she was in for a lengthy, and perhaps contentious, conversation. "Where's Pa?"

"Off to work," Samantha said.

"His job doesn't start 'til 9."

"He wanted to go in early today."

"Did y'all have a talk?"

"Yes, we did."

"And I assume, since Pa barely ate his breakfast, that the conversation ain't go well."

Samantha exhaled hard. "He wanted to take care of this on his own. He don't want to depend on nobody anymore, includin' you and Jesse."

Jennifer parked herself in a chair next to Samantha. "Ma, you *know* what that means."

Samantha turned to her. "He said he wasn't gonna do that." She was trying to convince herself as much as Jennifer.

"Ma, I spoke with Jesse last night, and he told me that Pa would sometimes blow half his paycheck in one day playin' poker."

"Honey, he's not doin' that anymore."

"Ma, do you know what me and Jesse are goin' through right now in McLean?"

Samantha straightened in her chair. "What?"

"We've been stayin' in a neighbor's house since we got back to McLean. Somebody broke in our house and has been squattin' there. The police said there's nothin' they could do, that we would have to go through the courts. So, Jesse got a lawyer, and we are working on a case right now."

Samantha frowned her confusion. "How can they just stay in your house without your permission?"

"It's a bunch of legal stuff involved which I really don't want to get into," Jennifer said. "It's too complicated to explain."

"Oh, my! How long before you can get your house back?"

"Lawyer says it could be months."

"Oh, Jen," Samantha said sympathetically. "I had no idea."

"Well, the good news is that the kids are adjustin' fairly well to it, although they do miss the house. But I don't feel so good about it, and neither does Jesse. He's been working night and day tryin' to get the house back. He was feeling like he was less than a man because his family was livin' in someone else's basement."

"I imagine."

"Well, that's exactly what I'm hoping you do, Ma. If the Lord hadn't intervened, Jesse and I might've been in a heap of trouble in our marriage. We might have been in other trouble, too. And I reckon that eventually, we will get the house back. Now, imagine what it would be like for you and Pa if you were to lose your house, with no hope of getting it back. Imagine the stress, the hurt to his pride. Are you ready to deal with that?"

Samantha looked at Jennifer out the sides of her eyes. "You know, you really should have more faith in your father. I believe he can do it. Why can't you?"

"How can I have faith in someone that has faith in *no one*?"

"Jen, why does it always have to be about religion with you?"

Jennifer laughed at the ridiculousness of that statement. "Ma, you were born in Alabama. You can't walk three cracks in the sidewalk without finding someone that goes to church down there. Same here in Tennessee. I know you were raised in the church, Ma. Why did you walk away?"

"I realized I'd gotten all I could out of church."

"Yes, but has God gotten all He can out of *you*?"

Samantha stood, as good an indication as any that she did not want to continue the conversation anymore. "Honey, I'm glad you and Jesse are regular churchgoing folk. And I feel for your situation at home. But like I said, Harlan will figure it all out. You just wait and see."

Jennifer wished she could have the same level of faith in Harlan as Samantha did. But she knew her father, and knew that when he got like this, it was a hopeless case. He would try to take care of his own problem by himself until he was at the cliff and would teeter off without a rope. Even then, he might fall, hoping to catch a ledge on the way down. It was a perilous way to live, but no one could convince her father otherwise.

"I hope it all works out," Jennifer said as her mother left

the room. "I really, really do."

Adverse Possession

Waiting

* * *

Two months later

It was mid-April Thursday morning; spring had arrived, and the weather was milder. Lottie rose in the morning, gathered her paper from outside, and made breakfast, just as she normally did. She started to peel six potatoes, enough to feed a family of four plus herself. They would love her *Kartoffelpuffers*, potato pancakes, with her homemade applesauce.

Lottie insisted that the Kanes stay with her, despite their concern that they were an undue burden. Lottie found she enjoyed their company, and did everything she could to make them comfortable, including letting the kids stay in the upstairs bedrooms so that Jesse and Jennifer could enjoy the privacy of the basement. Since Perrin's disappearance, Detective Hartley was confident the death threat was only a bluff, even though he was no closer to figuring out who left the dead dog on the doorstep. Nonetheless, he arranged extra patrols along Bynum Drive and at the kids' school, just to be safe.

Every day Jesse awoke and, after he and his wife had prayed, walked to the small window in their bedroom and peered out at their house across the street. Each day, he looked for a sign that something had changed, that the MacNichols had decided to move on. The 30-day unlawful detainer notice had expired with no action by the MacNichols, and they were not responding to any of Jesse's requests to meet and talk. Jesse considered staking out Bernard MacNichol's car until Bernard came to drive it, hoping to have an opportunity to talk to him for only a few minutes. He decided against it after Jennifer told him he was getting dangerously close to self-correction again. *Let the Lord handle it* was her constant mantra to him over the past couple of months.

Nonetheless, Joe Lippman pressed forward with his case against the MacNichols. Just a few days after the unlawful detainer notice had expired, and the MacNichols had not moved out, Joe requested the court to issue a summons to the MacNichols. After several personal service attempts by a private process server, whom Joe had hired to serve the MacNichols, the process server posted the summons securely on the front door of 6609, where it remained to that day. The next day, Friday, was the date of the initial hearing, and there was no indication that the MacNichols had even seen the notice.

Joe invited the Kanes to his office to discuss last minute details of the next day's hearing.

Joe offered them coffee, but they refused. "So, no word from the MacNichols?" Joe asked, pouring coffee from a decanter into his "I ❤ Lawyers" mug.

"Nothing. Not a peep," Jesse said with exasperation.

"And you're sure they are still living there?"

"I see the lights go on and off in rooms on occasion. And Lottie says she sees their pickup truck parked on Chester Street when she drives by there to go to the supermarket. She says it's moved on a few occasions recently."

"Hmm." Joe sat behind his desk and stirred his coffee, the clanking of the spoon creating a cadence that permeated the silence of the office. "And no attorney has entered an appearance on their behalf, either." He lightly tapped his fingers on the desk. "Anything from Detective Hartley?"

"No. Trail's gone cold," Jesse reported. "Perrin's in the wind, and the police can't seem to figure out who brought the dog in the neighborhood. No witnesses, nothing."

Jesse and Jennifer waited silently to hear what conclusions Joe would draw. Joe only needed 15 seconds to twirl some things around in his mind before he spoke.

"This may bode well for you. Bernard and his wife might decide not to appear. That's usual in L&T cases. The defendant can't pay the rent, or won't pay the rent. They don't want to face the judge, so they skip the court date. If the MacNichols decide not to show, the judge will enter a default judgment in your favor, and the court will order the MacNichols to move within 10 days. If they do not move, the sheriff will come and put them out. If that happens, you'll be back in your own house within 20–30 days."

"What if they decide to come to court?" Jennifer asked.

"If they do, it's to contest the case," Joe explained.

Adverse Possession

"Otherwise, what's the purpose of them coming? If they contest, the judge will set a date for a trial, usually within 20 days. Now tomorrow, you don't have to come to court. But on the trial date, the judge *will* need you there."

"So, if they contest, when will we get our house back?" Jesse asked.

"Depends on the trial. If it were a simple unpaid rent matter, they could resolve it within one day. But for what you are claiming—trespassing and a fraudulent lease—it could take one or two continuances for the judge to sort it all out. So, best case, you're looking at two months before you get your house back. Worst case, considering any appeals, could be three or four months."

Jesse turned his head to look at Jennifer. "Do you think we can stand it in Lottie's basement for another four months?"

Jennifer rolled her eyes at him. Comments like that illustrated the fundamental difference between her and Jesse. In Tennessee, she had lived in worse conditions. A *lot* worse. In her quest to find love and independence after high school, she would move briefly into her boyfriends' apartments, which were usually squalid. In one instance, she and her boyfriend were evicted, and she found herself living in a rusty abandoned Impala in a driveway off Browning Avenue, at least until she could swallow her pride and ask to move back into her parents' house.

For Jennifer, it was enough to have a roof over her head. For Jesse, it had to be a $900,000 roof.

"We'll be okay," Jennifer said, a smile accompanying her good attitude. "If we put God first, we'll be fine."

Jesse smiled. *That was Jennifer. Always the voice of reason.*

* * *

At first, Amber MacNichol thought that Bernard's malaise and diminishing appetite were suddenly emerging symptoms of his cancer, or a side effect of his medications. Actually, Bernard had sunk into a deep depression. Most days, he did not bother getting out of bed. Just three weeks before, a process server had taped an unlawful detainer summons to the door of 6609, requesting Bernard and Amber's presence in court. Bernard had expected this, but he had also counted on having an attorney to guide him through this process. However, he had not heard from an attorney, or from Perrin Houtin. He violated Perrin's demand not to call him, but his calls went unanswered. Now, the court date was tomorrow. He had no attorney, nor any idea how to defend himself against a charge of trespassing. He felt ripped off, though the money he used to pay for Perrin's services was not his own.

Money was drying up quickly. They had eaten all of the canned goods and all of the dry goods in the Kanes' kitchen. All of the frozen food in the chest freezer was gone, too. Amber tried to keep food in the house by visiting free food pantries in the area, which normally distributed only produce and canned goods. Soon, that would no longer be an option, because the gas in the truck was almost on empty. There were only 10 minutes remaining on their prepaid cell phone, forcing them to use the Kanes' home phone for outgoing calls. Afterwards, they would promptly take the home phone back off the hook to avoid hearing it constantly ring. At least his cancer medication was holding up, but he would need a refill within two weeks, with no visible means to get more, even on the black market. He thought it ironic that he was living in a million-dollar home, but could not even afford to pay for a sandwich.

Nevertheless, Bernard's depression had brought Amber to the end of her rope. She loved Bernard deeply, and was dedicated to him despite his many problems. However, she had grown weary of the stress and embarrassment of this situation. Because Bernard did not want the house to be unoccupied, the two of them could never be out together. One of them always had to be home to defend the house in case the Kanes tried to reclaim it. Most of her friends no longer spoke to her since she became homeless. She did not know how long she could maintain the ruse of success for her parents and siblings in Westchester County, New York. She would avoid calling them, or even answering their calls, for fear of having to answer their probing questions such as "How are you doing?" and "How's work coming along?" She had lied for so long to her parents, who had no idea she and Bernard were homeless. If they even had an inkling of it, she knew her father would come down to D.C., whisk her back to New York to live in their palatial home just a stone's throw from the New Croton Reservoir, and likely beat Bernard to within an inch of his life.

The turning point for Amber came a few days before, when she paid a visit to the food pantry while Bernard remained in bed. She had always been an attractive woman, and was accustomed to men—both single and married—ogling her no matter where she went. However, this time, a volunteer, who was moneyed enough to give generously to the pantry, started to slip admiring glances her way. Amber did not know whether he was married or single, but she allowed herself to imagine life with a man whose only struggle was trying to stay out of a higher tax bracket. She was tempted to give the man her attentions, and eventually, her affections. With Bernard being in bed so much, and Amber now charged with keeping food in the house, Bernard would not notice an occasional tryst.

When she got home and thought the better of it, she realized how much her own thoughts sickened her. Although Amber did not relish her parents rescuing her from her difficult circumstances, the good values that they had instilled in her saved her from making a regrettable mistake.

She walked into the master bedroom. Bernard lay in the king-sized bed, on his back, the satin sets pulled up to his neck, a neck darkened by stubble. His eyes focused on the TV, tuned to a news program. He did not try to acknowledge that Amber had entered the room.

She sat on the bed next to him and looked at the cherry wood nightstand. The bowl of cereal she had prepared for him that morning was barely touched.

"What are we going to do?" Amber asked. "The court date is tomorrow."

"I don't know," Bernard said, his voice huskier than usual. "I don't know."

"I think we need help."

"That's what I tried to get. You see how that turned out."

"I don't mean Perrin's kind of help. I mean *real* help."

No response. Bernard's gaze was focused on the TV. Amber was certain he was not paying attention to it.

"I'm going to talk to the Kanes."

That statement made Bernard turn his head slowly in her direction. "Why?"

"They offered to help. They've been leaving notes and knocking on our door for the past two months. Maybe we should see what they can do."

"All they want to do is take back their house. That's all."

"Bernard, the court date is tomorrow. They're going to evict us soon. They're going to get the house back anyway. Maybe there is something they can do to help us."

"No, no." Bernard's gaze returned to the TV. "I don't trust them."

Amber did not go against his wishes often, but now was as good a time as any for an exception. "It's either that, or I call my dad and tell him what's going on. You know I don't want to do that. I love you so much. But I can't live like this anymore. We need help."

No response.

"I'm going to go and see them." Amber stood up.

No response.

"I sure wish you'd go with me."

Silence.

Amber grabbed the bowl of cereal and headed for the door. She took one final look at Bernard before she closed the door behind her. She loved him, but he was completely out of it right now. If the Kanes could not help, she was going to call her father. That much was guaranteed.

* * *

Lottie was taking a nap in her bedroom when the doorbell jarred her from her sleep. She rarely got visitors at 2 in the afternoon. She figured it was either a neighbor, or some sales person checking to see if she were satisfied with her cable service. She got out of bed and walked downstairs to see who had the audacity to interrupt her nap. She saw a pretty brunette, dressed in blue jeans and a red T-shirt, at the door. She assumed it was a neighbor. Until that moment, she had never seen Amber MacNichol.

"Hi," Lottie greeted, opening the door wide, as she often did for people who gave her no cause for alarm. "How can I help you?"

"Umm, I'm Amber MacNichol. I'm the woman from across the street."

Lottie stared at her. *This was the gun-wielding woman from across the street?* She looked more like a soccer mom than a pistol-packing gun moll.

Lottie became much less polite. "What do you want?"

"Well, Jesse and Jennifer Kane have been trying to get in touch with us. I wanted to talk with them."

"They're not here right now, but they should arrive shortly."

"Do you mind if I wait?"

Yeah. Somewhere else. This was the first thought that came to Lottie's mind. Still, she thought of the Kanes, and how much they wanted to talk with the MacNichols. Lottie did not want to do anything to ruin the opportunity, so she reluctantly agreed to allow Amber into her home.

Once Amber entered, Lottie directed her to the living room couch.

Adverse Possession

"This is a nice place you have," Amber said, sitting on the couch.

Yeah, and it's mine. Don't you even think about taking it. That was her thought. Instead, Lottie said, "Thank you. May I get you something to drink?"

"No thanks. I'm fine."

Lottie hoped she would say that. She was not sure if she wanted to go to the kitchen and take her eyes off Amber for any length of time. She sat in the chair across from the couch and wasted no time dealing with the elephant in the room.

"You know, the Kanes are good friends of mine," Lottie said. "They've been friends of mine ever since they moved in over there a year ago. They are good people, a great family. I don't know how long you plan to continue your *Extreme Home Takeover*, but I want you to know that you are hurting a very good family, a Christian family. I don't believe in God striking anybody down, but I do believe there may be some bad karma coming out of all this, for both you and your husband."

Amber nodded. Lottie had not expected her to be so receptive to her comments.

Amber felt the need to explain herself. "You know, my dad raised me and my younger brother and sister in church. Like some teenagers, I rebelled and wanted nothing to do with church. I graduated high school with honors, then went to Penn. After my first year there, I got more interested in a man than in my studies, and I dropped out to go live with him. My dad was furious that I dropped out, and he wanted me to come home, but I refused. Me and my boyfriend didn't work out, so I got a job and found an apartment. On the job was where I met Bernard."

Amber looked up at Lottie to see if she were listening, or even cared. When she saw that Lottie was seemingly engaged, she continued. "You know they say that many girls marry someone who is like their father. Well, I went out of my way to find someone that was not like my father. My father was strict and domineering, but Bernard was sensitive, caring, and compassionate. He's not jealous or clingy. He's a great man. He didn't deserve to get cancer."

Lottie looked down. She had heard about Bernard's illness from Jesse. "I don't know if anyone deserves that."

"I was angry with God because of that," Amber told her. "His sickness is most of the reason we're struggling. So, when you talk about karma, or about being punished by God, we were already there long before we moved into that house."

"You didn't move in, honey," Lottie said. "You *stole* the house. Let's call a thief a thief."

"You don't think I know that? You don't think I feel horrible for everything we have done? That's why I wanted to talk to the Kanes. If anything, we have to find a way to make this right."

Lottie winced. She could have kicked herself. She wished she had set a tape recorder to capture this conversation. It might have helped the Kanes' lawsuit. *Oh well, what's done is done*, she thought.

Lottie resisted the urge to give Amber a good verbal spanking. "Well, I'm sure the Kanes will appreciate that. In fact, let me call them."

Lottie got up, went to the phone, and dialed Jesse. She was only on the phone for a few seconds, and said very little other than "Amber MacNichol is sitting in my living room" before Jesse replied he would be right there and ended the call.

Ten minutes later, Jesse and Jennifer walked in the front door. Amber stood when they entered. Jesse was the first to greet her with a handshake, and could not resist the urge to toss a barb. "Nice to meet you without a gun pointing in my face."

"I'm sorry about that. I really am." Amber walked over to Jennifer, and shook her hand. Jennifer eyed her suspiciously.

The four of them sat in the living room. Jesse and Jennifer sat hip to hip on the couch.

"You mind me asking why your husband isn't here, too?" said Jesse.

"He doesn't trust you," Amber said. "The only reason I'm here is because I threatened to leave him if he didn't let me talk to you."

"Would you have really done that, honey?" Lottie asked.

"I don't know. I just know that I couldn't spend another day on the streets, or in a shelter."

"So, what can we do for you?" Jesse asked.

"Well, you said in your notes that you could help us," Amber said sheepishly. "I guess I'm interested in knowing how."

Amber went on to tell about her relationship with Bernard, his cancer diagnosis, and his subsequent lack of employment. She recounted the death of Bernard's parents, their time in the shelter, their relationship with Perrin Houtin and the Reclaim Network, and Bernard's determination to reclaim the house that his parents had once owned. She lied about nothing, and she held nothing back. When she had finished explaining,

Jesse still had more questions.

"How did you get into our house?" Jesse asked. "The police saw no signs of forced entry."

"When Bernard heard that his parents had died, he went to reclaim their belongings," Amber explained. "He found a key ring that contained the keys to his father's truck. He found another key that was to your basement door. The key had one of those plastic tags on it that said 'basement.' He thinks that the locks on the basement door were never changed when you moved in."

Jesse shot a confused look at Jennifer. He had tasked her with the responsibility of hiring a locksmith after they bought the house. "Don't they change the locks right after a foreclosure?" he asked her. "Didn't you have the locks changed?"

"Sure did." Jennifer shrugged. "No way could they have had a key."

Jesse turned back to Amber. "Are you sure Bernard had a key?"

"I'm sure. He showed me the key ring."

Jesse made a mental note to probe this further, but he decided to move on. "And the utility bills?"

"Bernard put them all in his name when we gained access. He used the lease that Perrin had drawn up for us. He changed the locks, and forwarded all the mail ... ," she looked at Jennifer, " ... to your parents' address."

"How did you know the address?" Jennifer had been anxious to know the answer to that question for months.

"Bernard found it in your email contact list. He knew you had taken your kids down there, because he read several of your emails to your parents dated shortly before you left."

Adverse Possession

"Did he also change the registration on the truck, too?" Jesse asked.

"No. The truck belonged to his parents. They never changed the address on the registration after the foreclosure and they were evicted. The police probably never bothered checking the names."

Jesse stood to his feet and gently paced the floor, trying to process all that he had heard. "So, you commit trespassing, theft, and fraud, just to gain access to a house that is not your own?"

Amber looked down before she answered. "I'd like to blame it all on the Reclaim Network, and what they were telling us. They were making it seem as if we could keep the house forever. But they weren't the only ones to blame. Bernard was angry and desperate. Mix those two together, and it's like a bomb ready to go off."

Jesse was quite impressed that Amber was not making excuses, which he fully expected her to do. However, Jesse still was not satisfied. "Something is still bothering me, Mrs. MacNichol, and —"

"Amber. Call me Amber."

Jesse nodded. "Amber, I'm confused about something. My wife and I go to Haiti for a couple of months. During that time, coincidentally, Bernard's anger and desperation lead him to break into my house, which he just happens to have the keys for, which just happens to be his parents' former house." Jesse looked at his wife, then at Lottie to see if they could see where he was going with this. "A series of events happening simultaneously, in Bernard's favor. My gut tells me something else is going on here. Amber, are you sure you're telling me the complete truth?"

"Yes, I am." Amber's voice was sure and confident.

"Pardon us for a minute, Mrs. MacNichol. My wife and I need to discuss this." Jennifer followed Jesse down the stairs to the basement.

Though they were out of earshot, Jennifer spoke quietly. "What did you mean when you said your gut was telling you something else was going on?"

"It's all too coincidental," Jesse told her. "Something's missing."

"What's missing?"

"I don't know, but it has something to do with that key."

"You think they didn't have a key?"

"How could they? The locks were changed twice since Bernard's parents got foreclosed on."

"You think they got in another way?"

"I don't know. But I think Bernard knows more than what he's telling his wife?"

"How do you figure that?"

"Just the look on Amber's face. Embarrassment. Disappointment. I know that look on a woman's face. I've seen it on yours."

Jennifer did not know how to respond to that other than to take him in her arms and hug him. After about a minute in the embrace, Jesse faced Jennifer and placed both his hands lightly on her shoulders. "Promise me you won't think I'm crazy for suggesting this."

"Suggesting what?"

"I'm thinking about dropping the court case?"

Jennifer frowned. "Why?"

"These people don't need to be sued. They need to be helped. I'm thinking, maybe they don't need to leave the house just yet."

"You're suggesting that they stay there?"

"In the basement, in the guest room. We can stay upstairs. The house is big enough for all of us."

Jennifer looked at him as if she had just seen something gross. "Jesse, I know you're a man of God, and I know you want to help, but you need to rethink this. We don't know these people, and you want to let them stay in our house? With our young uns? Why don't we just get the church to rent an apartment for them?"

"These people are down and out, and they need to be kept close," Jesse reasoned. "Besides, I don't think that my dad will approve the church getting into another lease. Not after the situation with your parents. I mean, we can pay the rent ourselves. But what about food, transportation, utilities, telephone? It's much cheaper to let them stay with us. That way we can hold them accountable to do the things they need to improve their situation."

"Jesse …"

"There's a bathroom with a shower downstairs. There's a fridge. There's a separate entrance from the outside to the guest room. Except to use the kitchen, there's no reason for them to come upstairs. If we need to, we can always lock the upstairs door to the basement."

"Jesse, I don't know."

"Honey, I feel the urging of the Lord on this. I need you to trust me."

Jennifer looked at her watch, finding a good reason to get

out of this conversation. "It's 2:45. I gotta go pick up the kids from school. Can we pray about this when I get home?"

"Absolutely."

"Whatever we do, I don't think we should drop the court case. Just to be safe."

"Certainly."

"You're a good man, Charlie Brown." Jennifer held out her hand. "Keys?"

"I left them upstairs on the table."

She puckered. "Sugar?"

Jesse pecked her on the lips.

Jennifer walked upstairs, with Jesse close behind. Jennifer grabbed the car keys off the coffee table and headed to the foyer, while Jesse remained in the living room with Amber and Lottie. Jesse was about to resume his conversation with Amber when he noticed Jennifer in the foyer, looking straight ahead at nothing, seemingly stuck in place.

Jesse called to her. "Honey, you okay?"

Jennifer snapped out of whatever stupor she was in. "Yeah, I'm fine. I'll be back shortly." She headed out the door.

Jesse attributed his wife's strange behavior to a final memory check to make sure she had not forgotten anything. He quickly dismissed it and turned his attention back to Amber. "Mrs. MacNichol, my wife and I need to discuss this further. Can we call you tomorrow and let you know how we would like to proceed?"

"Sure." Amber removed her cell phone from her pocket. "I can give you my cell number. But I won't be able to talk long. I don't have that many minutes left."

"Might I suggest you put our house phone back on the

hook, and you call us tomorrow around 7?"

"Okay. We can do that."

Jesse gave the number to their cell phone, which she promptly programmed into hers.

"What are your intentions with the hearing tomorrow?" Jesse asked.

"I don't know. I have to ask my husband," Amber said. "I guess I was kind of hoping that could … go away."

"No. We have to follow through with that," Jesse said. "You need to understand that whatever happens, we need to move back into our home."

"I understand."

"Good. You'll be in touch with us tomorrow, then?"

"Yes." Amber stood and shook Jesse's hand. "Thank you for whatever you can do." She shook Lottie's hand as Jesse escorted her to the door.

Jesse watched her as she walked across the street to 6609.

"Cute little charmer, isn't she?" Lottie said from behind him. "Too cute to be homeless."

"Yeah, well, poverty doesn't care how cute you are." Jesse watched Amber as she unlocked the front door and headed inside. A few seconds later, she came back out, ripped the summons off the front door, and went back inside.

"The point is: I know many men that would love a shot at taking care of her."

Jesse shut the door. "Maybe that's why she's reaching out. She knows it, too. Grass is greener."

"What are you going to do?" Lottie asked.

"Something very stupid," Jesse said. "But it's the right thing to do."

Jennifer had to pull over about three blocks away, before she reached the main road. Her thoughts were muddled, and it did not help that she had to concentrate on the road. She needed to focus, for just a few moments. In the foyer earlier, a flashback came to her, something shocking, yet feasible. She needed to think this through carefully, because to do otherwise could needlessly destroy a vital relationship of hers. What if these were the same voices as earlier, the whispers and shouts of the enemy, speaking against what she already knows in her spirit to be righteous?

She sat on the side of the road, praying, thinking, and praying again. She did not want to face her thoughts and her suspicions, but they made sense, and were impossible to ignore.

Five minutes on the side of the road, and she was convinced that she knew how Bernard had gained entry to her home.

And it crushed her deeply.

Adverse Possession

Prayer meeting

* * *

The Kane family Bible study and prayer night was usually Friday, but Jesse and Jennifer moved it up to Thursday in keeping with the urgency of the situation with Amber and Bernard. After dinner, Jesse, Jennifer, and the kids gathered in the basement. Since their decision would also affect Lottie, Jesse invited her to pray with them as well.

Jesse stood before them, opened his well-worn leather-bound Bible, and read a few verses.

"Romans Chapter 12, Verse 14 says, '*Bless those who persecute you; bless and do not curse.*' First Corinthians Chapter 4, Verses 12 and 13 read, '*We work hard with our own hands. When we are cursed, we bless; when we are persecuted, we endure it; when we are slandered, we answer kindly.*' Romans 12 and 21 says, '*Do not be overcome by evil, but overcome evil with good.*' And finally, Luke Chapter 6, Verse 28 reads, '*bless those who curse you, pray for those who mistreat you.*'"

Jesse closed the book and looked proudly at his family,

of which he had made Lottie an unofficial member. "What do these verses mean for us, for all Christians? I have always believed that God even brings enemies in your life for a reason. Anyone who would try to take your house away from you can definitely be considered as an enemy. But these verses show us how we should respond, how God wants us to respond. We ought to bless and not curse. We should overcome evil with good and pray for those who mistreat us. This isn't deep and theological. It's simple, clear instructions from God to us, those who want to love him and serve him."

Jesse looked down at Aiden and Ashley, who sat on the carpet, legs crossed, looking up at him, just as his father had done with him, just as his grandfather had taught his father. "Kids, when you are at school, and someone does something to you that you do not like, how does that make you feel?"

Aiden was the first to answer. "Bad."

"Do you ever feel like you want to do something bad to them?"

Both Aiden and Ashley reluctantly nodded. Afterwards, Ashley said, "But at Sunday school, they said you shouldn't do that."

"Exactly." Jesse stooped down to regard them. "And you know why? Because God wants his people to bless others. Do you know what a blessing is?"

"It's getting something you want from God, "Aiden guessed.

Jesse grinned. "In a way. It's really receiving the *favor* of God. His approval. His priority attention to you. Knowing that God is with you is better than anything in the world. When God says to bless our enemies, he wants us to help them to receive his favor. If they don't know God, God wants us to minister the gospel to them, and to help them in any way we can to encounter the goodness of God."

Jesse stood to his feet and tapped the Bible lightly in his hand. "I know that God wants us to bless that couple across the street. But we need clarity from God on how he wants us to bless them. And that's where we have to pray." Jesse lifted his right hand, gesturing them to their feet. "Can we all agree with that prayer?"

Everyone nodded and answered yes.

They gathered in a circle, symbiotically, without direction, joining hands, bowing heads. Jesse was the only one whose head was arched toward heaven.

"Father, in the mighty and matchless name of Jesus ... "

* * *

Jennifer awoke at 2:34 a.m. The thoughts running around in her mind were stressing her and causing her to lose sleep. She had decided not to tell her husband what she was thinking, at least not until they had prayed and some sense of clarity from God came to her. She recalled a statement that Jesse made to her shortly after they were married. *Sometimes when we pray to God, he gives us the answer right away. But because it isn't what we are looking for, or we don't like the answer, we reject it. And we go our entire lives waiting for an answer that we already have.* As she sat up in bed and perused her thoughts, she didn't know if what she was thinking was just her intuition, or if it was God speaking to her. She knew she had to talk to Jesse, but she didn't want to wake him now, especially since he was sleeping so soundly. She decided to get up and go to the kitchen for a drink of water to satiate her dry mouth.

Once she entered the kitchen and opened the refrigerator, the light from the fridge cut through the darkness and settled on the almost-motionless figure of her son Aiden standing by the living room window.

Jennifer had not expected anyone to be up at this hour, so she never bothered putting on a robe to cover up the bra and panties she was wearing. Not wanting to embarrass her son, she grabbed a kitchen towel, covered up, and walked over to him.

"Aiden, what are you doing up at this hour?" She placed her hand on his forehead, just in case he was feverish or sick. "Are you okay?"

Aiden turned his gaze to the house across the street. The street lights from outside passed through the window blinds and cast slivers of light onto his pajamas. "Don't put them out, Mom," he said quietly. "It can be their house, just as much as it is ours."

Jennifer nodded and drew her son into an embrace with the one free hand she was not using to hold up her towel. "Okay, son. But you need to get back to bed. You got school in the morning."

Aiden obeyed, dragging down the hallway toward his room. Jennifer watched him while she quietly said, "Bless his heart."

Jennifer turned toward the window and looked out at 6609.

For the first time since their crisis began, all of the lights in the house were off.

Louis N. Jones

* * *

Amber woke up the next day on edge. It was the date of the court hearing, and Bernard had told her he had no intent on going to court. Amber, who had never faced eviction before, had no idea what to expect. Would they come soon after the court hearing to put them out? Would it be the next Monday? Would it be 10 weeks from now? The uncertainty was tearing her apart, and she could not wait until she could call Jesse and find out what, if anything, he could do for them.

At least Bernard was occasionally out of bed now, and had bothered taking a shower for the first time in three days. He did not shave or dress. He walked around in his pajamas, venturing only to the kitchen to eat the occasional bowl of cereal with milk that was seven days past the expiration date, then to the basement to pour a glass of Scotch, then back to the master bedroom to sit in the wicker chair next to the bed and periodically nurse his Scotch. Amber tried to talk to him, but found he was not much interested in conversation. So, Amber let him be. At some point, she hoped he would snap out of this.

Meanwhile, it was sheer boredom. The Kanes had shut off the internet and the cable in the house weeks before. She had read almost every book and magazine she could find in their expansive library, except those requiring an advanced theology degree to understand, which were many. They had no friends, and no one, other than her family in Westchester, that cared whether they lived or died. On most days she could look forward to conversation with Bernard, or passing the time playing board games with him, or watching videos, or making love. Now, he was not much interested in anything.

Figuring she had a few hours before she could contact the Kanes, and needing something to occupy her mind, she decided to go domestic. She put on some sweatpants and a T-shirt, which were still packed in the suitcases full of stuff they had brought with them. She grabbed a few rags, a broom, and a dustpan from downstairs in the laundry room, pulled the vacuum from the entry closet, and gathered a few trash bags and some disinfectant from the kitchen.

Starting from the kitchen, she went around the house, tidying up, marveling at how much mess two adults could make in the course of a few months. She put away cleaned dishes that were still in the dishwasher, and loaded up dirty ones. She scrubbed around the stove, and threw away old Burger King bags and containers that were still sitting on the dining room table. She washed and put away the saucers that doubled as ashtrays, and the snifters that still had residual amounts of Scotch on the bottom. She put books in their proper places on the shelves, and laundered, dried, and put away all the linens they had used. She cleaned and disinfected all three of the bathrooms in the house, and vacuumed all the carpets. Using a Swiffer mop she found in an upstairs closet, she cleaned and polished the tigerwood floors in the living room, dining room, family room, and kitchen. Finally, she gathered all the trash and placed the bags downstairs in the garage to keep company with the three bags that were already there. She would later dump the bags in a green supercan for the municipal trash pickup Monday. When she was done at 4 p.m., the house was in as pristine a condition as when they moved in. It was three hours until the time to call the Kanes.

She walked into the bathroom next to the master bedroom, took a shower, and then, hoping to stoke his fires, pranced in front of Bernard partially damp and wearing only a loose-fitting towel. Bernard looked at her, grunted slightly, and then went back to watching TV. Dejected, Amber grabbed a change of clothes, dressed in the bathroom, and then went out to the family room to watch *Lord of the Rings* for the umpteenth time.

She barely made it through 15 minutes of the movie before sleep overcame her.

* * *

There was just no getting around it. Jennifer had tossed this thing around in her mind so often. She had to tell Jesse. He needed the information before Amber called him that evening.

She found her husband in the bedroom, laying in bed, fully dressed, his Bible open on the bed while he jotted notes on a writing pad. She hated to disturb him while he was studying, but this matter could no longer wait.

She sat on the edge of the bed. "Honey, could I bother you for a minute?"

Jesse spoke without looking up from his notes. "Sure you can."

"I need your undivided attention. This is important."

Their eyes met. Jesse saw concern in hers. He dropped the notepad on the bed and laid the pen on the bedside table. "What's going on, Jen?"

"First of all, have we made a decision about lettin' the MacNichols remain in the house?" By using the word *we*, she meant that it was largely Jesse's decision, but that she would support whatever he decided.

"I still feel as strongly as I did yesterday, Jen," Jesse told her. "I think it is the right move."

"Then I need to tell you something that may affect that decision."

Jesse raised his eyebrows. She had his attention.

"You remember the day we went over to the Beloos' for supper, shortly before we went to Haiti?"

"Yes, I do."

"And do you remember where you left your keys while we were there?"

Jesse searched his memory. As he recalled, they had arrived at the Beloos' home a little before 7 o'clock. The Beloos greeted them at the door. Simon, Tabita's husband, took Jennifer's coat, and Jaron, their son, took Jesse's coat. His keys were in his coat pocket. Jaron and Simon hung the coats in the coat closet just off the foyer.

Jennifer listened to this explanation, and then said, "After supper, we went down to the basement to watch a movie. What did Jaron do?"

"Jaron said he had a headache, and was going out to the convenience store to get some aspirin."

"How long was he gone?"

"I dunno. About 30 minutes."

"Hmm. Which would have given him enough time to go in the closet, get your keys, go across the street, try the keys to see which one fit to which door, take off the basement key, and then put the keys back in your pocket."

Jesse looked at her and chuckled for a second before his

chuckle migrated to a full-blown laugh. "Jen, you're really reaching here."

Undaunted, Jennifer asked, "When was the last time you used the basement key?"

"Only once, when I snuck Christmas gifts in the house through the basement, so the kids wouldn't see them."

Jennifer tossed the keys next to Jesse on the bed. "Check to see if the basement key is there."

Jesse examined the keys in the ring. There was the key to the Armada, their house front door key, the key to Lottie's house, the key to the side entrance of the church. The basement key, which he normally kept on the key ring, was not there.

Jesse looked up at Jennifer, puzzled.

"And given the strength of that key ring, there's no way the key could have just popped off," Jennifer noted. "Somebody removed that key."

"How do you know the kids didn't do it?"

"Honey, I know the kids are mischievous at times, but why would they remove a key from your key ring? They've never done it before."

Jesse tossed the keys back on the bed. "Honey, I'm a little uncomfortable with what you're implying. I mean, you think Jaron Beloo took that key?"

"That's what I think."

Jesse swung his legs off the left side of the bed and stood up. "Jen, I last used that basement key several months ago. That key could have gone missing anytime since then. There must have been dozens of occasions since then that that key was not in my hand. And you implicate Tabita Beloo's son? Our friends?"

"I have a hunch, Jesse. You have your hunches, and I have mine."

"Yeah, but Jen, your hunch has racial implications. The Beloos are the only black family within a five-minute drive of here. And you accuse them of stealing?"

Jennifer frowned. "I'm not a racist, Jesse."

"I'm not saying you are. But if you go to the Beloos with this, they'll think you *are*."

Jennifer looked at her watch. It was five minutes to 7. Amber MacNichol would be calling any minute. "We don't have to talk to the Beloos. Let's talk to Bernard. He knows the truth. And I would not extend any kind of offer to them until they tell us the truth."

Jesse had a better idea. "How about let's go through with the offer. Let's get possession of our house. Then, when we have the keys in hand and we are inside, we'll make them tell us the truth, or they cannot stay in our house."

Jennifer nodded. "I'm good with that."

* * *

When Amber woke up, it was 7:15 p.m. She ran to the kitchen counter, grabbed her cell phone, looked up the number, and dialed it on the house phone extension in the family room. The phone rang three times before a female voice answered and said, "Hello."

"Hi, I'm Amber MacNichol. Is this Jennifer?"

"It is. How are you?"

"I'm a wreck. Do you have any news for me?"

"I do. In fact, I have some news that may be very good."

After the 30-minute conversation, Amber hung up the phone, let out a loud yell, and then jumped so high she almost bumped her head on the rotating ceiling fan in the family room.

Even Bernard's funk could not stop him from coming out of the bedroom to see what the ruckus was about. His bare feet swished against the clean wood floors as he turned the corner, walked through the kitchen, and entered the family room.

"What is going on out here?"

Amber grabbed Bernard's hands and tugged him to a loveseat at the western end of the family room. "I just spoke with the Kanes, and guess what? We don't have to leave. Not for another year."

"What?"

"They're going to let us stay here for the next year," Amber said, her voice a few decibels above normal. "They said we can stay in the guest room in the basement, where we have our own bathroom, entrance, and exit. They will live upstairs. We'll share the kitchen and the laundry room."

"No." Bernard shook his head. "We'll just be in the way."

"Bernard, have you taken a good look at this house?" Amber screeched. "There's four big bedrooms up here, and two bathrooms. This house was designed for a family twice their size. We will *not* get in the way."

"And why would they do that?" Bernard asked. "Why would they let two total strangers live in their home?"

"I asked them that same question. They told me to look in the Bible. Luke 10:29–37, I think they said."

"So, what's the catch? Do we pay rent? What do they want

in return?"

"No rent, but we do have to participate in the church's programs. And we have to work off the money we took from them. Mowing the lawn here. Working at the church there."

"No." Bernard got up to leave. "We can make it on our own."

"And how will we do that?"

Amber's tone was so sharp and biting it froze Bernard in his tracks. He turned toward her, the look on his face suggesting that he was not in the mood for an argument.

Amber stood, undaunted, confronting him. "How, huh? Stealing stuff that belongs to others? Relying on a D.C. con artist to help us get a house we were never going to get anyway? Bernard, the judge in court today issued a default judgment. Jennifer told me we have three weeks, at most, before the sheriff comes to put us out. Three weeks, verses one year. Which makes better sense to you?"

"Amber ... "

"The church will help us, Bernard," Amber continued. "We can participate in their group health insurance plan. You can get treatment. You can get your medicines without having to go through drug dealers. They can help you get a job. This is a chance for us, honey. The best we've had in a long time."

Bernard elevated his head and scowled down his nose at her. "So, if I don't agree to this, does that mean you're going to leave me?"

"No. It means you're going to leave *me*."

Bernard's scowl turned to bafflement. "What are you talking about?"

Amber's voice was full of defiance and conviction. "I'm

going to stay here no matter what. Whether you chose to stay with me is up to you."

"You can always go live with your dad. Why would you stay here?"'

"I guess I'm kinda hoping you would think the better of it and agree to stay with me."

Bernard's eyes remained pinned on Amber for several minutes, enough to cause Amber to avert her gaze to a nondescript corner of the room. They stood there, in silence, while Bernard's thoughts rumbled in his head like an unbalanced washing machine. He was angry, not so much because his wife was dishonoring his authority, but more because his wife trusted two strangers more than him. For the first time since their marriage, he felt his wife slip farther away from him, and he wished a magic solution could fix it.

He should have seen it coming. Ever since his wife pulled the gun on Jesse, she had not been the same. The possibility that she could have taken a life — maybe more than one life — weighed heavily on her. She had become more interested in reading the Christian books from the Kanes' bookshelves, and several times, he thought he saw her in a corner of the bedroom praying. When he asked her what she was doing, she responded that she was looking for some change on the floor, or some other flimsy excuse.

Yet Bernard was not ready to lose Amber. He doubted he would ever be. She was a doting wife. She was absolutely gorgeous. He had many problems, yet Amber remained by his side, tooth and nail. She could have snared some rich sugar daddy with barely a bat of her eyelashes and been gone a long time ago. She had given much, sacrificed much, and endured much. No wife could be as dedicated as she could. The least he could do was to support her now.

"You know, if I had known you were this good at arm-twisting, I would never have married you," Bernard said.

Amber brightened. "So, does that mean you'll stay with me?"

"If they make us get up at 4 in the morning and pray, I'm out of here."

Amber smiled. That was about as close to an agreement as he would get. She was willing to settle for that. She ran to him and wrapped her arms around him so tight he almost lost his balance.

For the first time in months, a tear formed in the corner of his eye.

Ground Rules

* * *

For Jesse and Jennifer, moving back into their home the next morning seemed surreal, as if they would wake up at any minute and find themselves back in Lottie's basement. The sun was bright, the temperature was warm, but not too hot, and there was a not a cloud in sight, a perfect Saturday. A few of the neighbors were outside, one fertilizing his front yard, another tending to something under the hood of his '60s-era Studebaker, another walking a tiny fur ball of a dog tied on the end of a leash. Most of them were seemingly oblivious to the drama that the Kanes had experienced over the last few months. Those who kept their ears tuned to neighborhood gossip had heard rumors, and took great steps to ensure that their homes were unattended for no more than a few hours. Some had heard about the dead dog and had become more vigilant concerning strangers in their neighborhood. Others, the grand majority of them, were too busy with their own lives to be concerned with their neighbors' problems. A few of them did not even know their neighbors' names.

So, there was no grand fanfare from the neighborhood, and no gathering of curious onlookers, when Jesse and Jennifer walked across the street at 8 a.m. to meet Amber and Bernard on their front stoop to receive the new keys to their home. Amber greeted them with a smile and dropped the keys, attached to a paper clip, into Jesse's hand. Jesse clasped the keys in his fist as if it were a precious stone.

"Thank you," Jesse said, with Jennifer nodding her agreement over Jesse's right shoulder. "You have no idea how blessed a day this is."

"We're sorry for putting you through so much." Bernard could not look them in the eyes, instead looking off to the side. Jesse could not tell whether it was shame or half-heartedness.

"Well, you're going to have to repay us," Jesse said. "And the best way to do that is by getting your lives together."

"We're ready!" Amber chimed in, looking the polar opposite of the frightened woman who, weeks before, had pulled a gun on Jesse. She looked at Bernard, whose face was blank, with no discernable emotion.

Jesse nodded toward the front door. Amber and Bernard caught Jesse's cue and stepped to the side so that the Kanes could enter. Jesse and Jennifer took a deep breath before they entered, expecting to see their house completely wrecked. Instead, they found a house that looked just as pristine and tidy as it was when they had left for vacation. As the Kanes walked around the house, inspecting every room, they were grateful that the MacNichols did not trash the place. But they were annoyed that the place smelled faintly of cigarette smoke mixed with disinfectant, and that most of the food in the cabinets and freezer was gone.

Once Jesse and Jennifer inspected the premises and gave each other thumbs up, Amber, who stood in the living room with Bernard, spoke up.

"Well, we moved all our things downstairs, so we'll leave you folks to it."

Before Amber and Bernard could get beyond the living room, Jesse called out to them. They turned toward him.

"We're going to have to set some ground rules for living here," Jesse told them. "Nothing outrageous, but we are going to insist that you do not smoke or drink in my home."

"Not a problem," Amber said.

"And we will not allow visitors without my permission."

Amber nodded. That was not an issue. They had no friends anyway, and she was likely not going to extend an invitation to her family to come see her room in a basement of a stranger's home.

"And the gun, if it is still in this house, it needs to leave."

"No worries. I already got rid of it."

This news surprised Bernard. "When did you do that?"

"A few weeks ago, when you started getting depressed," Amber said. "The last thing I wanted was a depressed man having access to a gun."

"So, what did you do with the gun?"

"Threw it in the Potomac River."

"There's probably enough guns in that river to arm the entire U.S. Marines," Jesse quipped. "But, other rules, we can talk about over breakfast."

Bernard finally smiled, realizing he had not had a home-cooked breakfast in a while, but discovering quickly that it would not happen that day.

"My kids would be highly upset if I did not take them to the Pancake House this morning, like I promised" Jesse said. "We'd like you to come along. Give you a chance to meet the kids."

Bernard nodded, while Amber verbalized his response. "We'd love to come along."

"Great. Meet us at the edge of the driveway in about 15 minutes. We'll get the kids, and then pick you up."

Jennifer watched as Amber and Bernard walked down the hallway to the basement door.

She looked at Jesse. "After the kids finish breakfast, I'll announce that I am takin' them across the street to the Kids Corral. You stay, and find out how they got in our house."

Jesse gave her a silent nod before she walked out the door and headed across the street to Lottie's house.

* * *

As was typical for a Saturday morning, the Pancake House was crowded, and Jesse, Jennifer, Bernard, Amber, and the kids had to wait about 15 minutes for a table. After a hostess seated them at a booth, Ashley and Aiden quickly reminded their parents that they had promised to let them order whatever they wanted. This resulted in Ashley and Aiden ordering the most sugar-laden, syrup-drenched pancakes on the menu, and the presence of a few strawberries did not help much.

Once the kids had finished eating, Jennifer waved the kids out of the booth and then slid out behind them. "Going over to the Kids Corral," she announced, barely audible over the din of the crowd. "Be back in a few."

Jesse watched her as she left, thinking how grateful he was to have her. He then turned back to Amber and Bernard, who were a little suspicious of Jennifer and the kids' sudden exit.

"There is one more rule I want to tell you about," Jesse said, his half-drank cup of coffee in his hand and getting colder by the minute. "I need you to be 100 percent truthful with me about everything, starting with the question I'm about to ask you, and continuing throughout your stay. Agreed?"

"Agreed," Amber responded before Bernard had a moment to think about the question.

"I need to know how you got into my house."

Both Amber and Bernard were silent initially, and then looked at each other. Finally, Amber spoke up. "I told you. My husband got the key from his parents' apartment, and ... "

"No, that's not true." Jesse looked pointedly at Bernard, whom he knew possessed the whole truth of the matter. "Your parents would not have had the key to my home. The locks were changed twice before we moved in. All of my doors have deadbolts. There was no sign of a door being kicked in. So, you had to have used a key, and you got that key from somewhere. I need to know where."

Amber looked at Bernard just long enough to let Jesse know that she was deferring any responses to him, and then quickly looked away in disgust.

Bernard looked at Jesse with a half-smile, an admiration of sorts for having been smart enough to peep his game. He then cast his gaze down to the table, collected his thoughts, and said, "Jaron Beloo gave me the key."

At the mere mention of Jaron Beloo, Jesse knew he would have to eat crow later. *My Lord, Jennifer was right.*

"How do you know Jaron Beloo?"

"Actually, my mother and father knew him. They became friends as soon as the Beloos moved in the neighborhood. Jaron was actually fond of my parents, because they were the first ones really to show him any type of friendship, and they were always in his corner. My dad gave him summer jobs when he was a teen. My Mom helped him pick out birthday gifts for his girlfriend. So naturally, he was upset when he heard that my parents were getting put out of their home."

Jesse tried to tune out the noise in the restaurant. "So, what happened?"

"Jaron tried to get help for them. He couldn't keep them from getting foreclosed, but he could help them get back in once they were put out. So, he did some looking around, and he stumbled on the Reclaim Network."

"Jaron was a member of the Reclaim Network?"

"Yeah." Bernard decided to cast off all inhibition. Perrin had let him down, and so did Jaron. There was no sense in protecting them now. "Perrin charged 150 dollars a year to be a member. In exchange for that, he gave the members resources and guidance on how to reclaim foreclosed homes. He says the banks are making billions on giving loans to people who they know can't pay. The banks know they can get their money back by reselling the foreclosed house. In the meantime, folks are paying interest like crazy for houses they will never own any part of. He thinks it is unfair, and this is his way of fighting that system."

"So, what did Perrin tell Jaron to do?"

"Give him a detailed plan, A to Z, beginning to end. The first step was to get the key to the house. This way, there'd be no breaking and entering, and if any neighbor saw you enter the house, they'd see you enter legit, with a key. Once you got in, they'd send one of their crooked locksmiths to change the locks."

"So, how did you get involved?"

"My parents passed on before Jaron got to execute the plan. So, Jaron came to the funeral. After it was over, he pulled me aside, after the burial, and told me what he was doing for my parents. He asked me if I wanted to continue the effort. I said yes, because I was also upset that my parents got kicked out of their home, and I blamed that situation for my parents' death. But Jaron still needed to get the key to the house, so he took my cell number and told me he'd call me when he got the key. Of course, a few weeks later, you and your family moved in."

Jesse took a sip of his coffee, barely noticing it was cold. "He finally got the key, but it wasn't until several months after we had moved in."

"Yeah. Jaron worked at a shelter in Alexandria, and he got me and my wife in the shelter. Then, he introduced me to Perrin, and we started pow-wowing about how to get in the house. He said he got the key from you when you and your wife came over to their house for dinner, around the beginning of December. He told me he knew you and your wife were going to be out of the house for a couple of months, and that would be the perfect time to reclaim the house. He said he got the basement key because you likely wouldn't notice it was gone right away. And by the time you did, there was no way you would trace it back to him."

"He was wrong," Jesse said proudly.

"Yeah, so I got the key, and the rest, as they say, is history." Bernard had already come clean, so he figured he might as well throw in one more tidbit. "Jaron was the one who put that dog on the porch."

"Jaron did that?" Jennifer looked at Jesse, and he looked back with one unspoken thought: how could Jaron have been so intricately involved with Reclaim's plot, and the elder Beloos knew nothing?"

"Yeah. Jaron's into dogfighting. Big. That's what they did a lot on the streets of Cape Town before Jaron and his mom came over to this country. He goes to a dogfight at least once a week, in an abandoned store nor far from the shelter where he works."

Jesse scoffed. "Jaron Beloo." He shook his head and looked at Jennifer. "Y'know, Jaron never really liked us. We never could figure out why."

"Now you know why," Bernard offered. "Jaron loved my parents, and he was very angry that they got kicked out of that house. Naturally, he's not gonna be too fond of the people that bought it."

"So, why did you have to lie about all that?" Amber said.

Bernard looked at her, but she continued to look away. "One of the rules of the Reclaim Network is you cannot expose another member of the network, not even to your spouse. That's why I said I had gotten the keys from my parents' apartment. I didn't want to include Jaron's involvement at all."

"A network that encourages you to lie to your wife." Amber shook her head in disbelief.

"Their philosophy is that spouses leave their husbands and reveal all their secrets, including the members of the network. Therefore, don't share any info about members with them. Perrin doesn't want anyone to know what they do, either. They have some people in that organization that don't want anyone to know about it. Lawyers. Locksmiths. Real estate agents. He's got like 250 people paying dues."

"That's a lot of crooks," Amber retorted.

"Yeah, well, a lot of them are people who, like us, have fallen on hard times and just need a fair shot." Bernard's eyes trailed to a corner of the room. "These people are so desperate, so beaten down, that they'll buy any hope that anyone offers. For that 150 dollars, Perrin sells hope. It may be false hope, but it's hope anyhow."

Jesse leaned forward so that Amber and Bernard could hear him over the noise in the room. "Y'know, in First Timothy, it says that Jesus Christ is our hope. In fact, he is our only hope. There are times when money is gone. Houses are gone. Spouses are gone. Even our health is gone. But Jesus Christ remains. He is everlasting. And those who put their hope in him will never be disappointed. I'm praying that as you stay with us, you will experience that."

For the first time since Jennifer and the kids had left, Amber managed a smile. "That's my prayer, too, pastor."

Jesse smiled back at her, and then looked at Bernard. His face was stoic, unwavering. He had seen the same face on Harlan Trudeau whenever he spoke about Christ.

Jesse knew he had a challenge. Nevertheless, it was a

challenge to which he would look forward.

* * *

The Woody Allen saying, "If you want to make God laugh, tell him your plans," came prominently to Jesse's mind when he and Jennifer got home and started to discuss what Bernard had told them.

Jesse had planned not to have another argument with his wife for at least several months.

God was laughing.

"Are you kiddin' me?" Jennifer was oblivious to the fact that it was the first few moments they had spent in their own bedroom in months. And they were spending it arguing. "You wanna press charges on Jaron?"

"Oh, you bet." Jesse was not backing down from his wife's fire. "Jaron stole our house key and gave it to a stranger. He killed a defenseless creature, and then used it to make a death threat. If it weren't for him, this whole mess would never have started. This guy needs to go to jail."

"Are you forgettin' that Tabita and Simon are our friends? And you want to send their son to jail?"

"If he had hurt one of us, one of our children, would that have made a difference?"

"But he didn't."

"But he could have."

"I think that's a decision that we should make together with the Beloos."

"And I agree."

"But if they don't want us to file charges ... "

"I'll do it anyway. And if they don't want us to file, maybe they aren't the type of people that should be our friends."

"Then we ain't gonna have many friends, 'cause you ain't gonna find many people, Christian or not, who are gonna be okay with their son goin' to jail."

"I realize that. But they also have to realize what he's done."

"And what has he done?" Jennifer threw up her hands as she started pacing about the room. "Stole your keys? Animal cruelty? Is that any worse than what the MacNichols have done? They stole your house. They stole your money. You saw Bernard buy illegal drugs. And poor, sweet lil' Amber almost shot us. But *they* get the blessings to stay in our home, with no jail time. And let's not even talk about Perrin, who you allowed to get away with statutory rape. But you send our friends' son to jail. That ain't right."

Jesse gritted his teeth and tried to find a good come-back to that remark, but it eluded him. He sat on the bed and looked blankly at a corner of the nightstand.

Jennifer managed a smile. "Honey, you wanted to tear the MacNichols apart, but the Holy Spirit got into you and gave you compassion for 'em. Now you want to redirect your anger to Jaron. You can't do that. Either all of 'em have to go to jail, or all of 'em have to go free."

She was right. Jaron had become Jesse's new whipping boy, and it seemed as if he was becoming God's. *What was God trying to do with him, anyway?* It had dawned on him that God was using the events of the past few months to do something in him. God was using his wife so powerfully to instill humility and submission in him. Yes, he had become proud and haughty like his father. He wanted his wife to be wrong, and he to be right, just because he bore the responsibility of caring for her. It was painful to realize that, as much as he liked to deny it.

Jesse had never believed in the inferiority of women, and he practiced it by making his wife an equal partner in almost everything. But when Jennifer stepped up to challenge him, as she had done frequently over the past few months, haughtiness would rise up within him. *He was the man.* It was his responsibility to take care of this. He needed to have the answers, the solutions. It was just he and God tasked with handling this problem.

But God had jumped ship and landed in Jennifer's boat. For that reason, he once again had to admit she was right. That voice of reason prevails again.

But that didn't make things easier for Jesse. If he showed compassion to Bernard and Amber, then he had to show compassion to Jaron as well. What made him think that Jaron was any less deserving?

He turned to his wife. "Tell you what. Let's talk with the Beloos. Maybe after speaking with them, God will reveal what direction we should take."

"Fair enough." Jennifer nodded and walked to the telephone in their bedroom.

Confrontation Again

* * *

When Jennifer made the call to Tabita and told her she and Jesse wanted to have a talk with her and her husband, Simon, Tabita readily agreed. They would gladly interrupt their Saturday chores to spend a few moments with their next-door neighbors.

Jesse and Jennifer dropped off the kids at Lottie's, then walked across the street to the Beloos' home. Simon Beloo, his bald head glistening in the high noon sunshine, greeted them on the porch with a smile and a hug, and then showed them inside. Tabita was waiting in the foyer wearing an apron. She had been cooking. Jennifer hoped she was not cooking for them.

After Tabita had hugged them both, she said, "Care for some grilled chicken wings. I just made them."

Jennifer shook her head and spoke for her and her husband. "We just had a big breakfast not long ago. We're still full."

Translation. Jennifer didn't want to accept their hospitality, as this would likely be an unpleasant visit.

"Okay." Tabita's smile was undaunted. "You can take some home. Have them if you get hungry later." She returned to the kitchen.

Simon led Jesse and Jennifer into a room adjacent to the living room. It was their sitting room, a smaller, cozier, more intimate room with soft fabric furniture arranged in close quarters. For a few visitors, the Beloos preferred this room to the cavernous living room, which they normally used only for parties.

Simon and the Kanes made small talk for a few minutes until Tabita returned, her apron removed, her hands filled with a wooden tray filled with canned soft drinks. She sat the drinks down on a table in the center of the room and sat next to her husband on a couch. "Please help yourself," Tabita offered.

Jesse did not look down at the drinks, but instead kept his eyes on the Beloos. Tabita, who knew the Kanes better than her husband did, sensed a vibe that discomforted her, and her smile faded somewhat.

"Is everything okay?" Tabita said.

Jesse was the one to break the ice. "We've received some news that, uh, you're not going to like."

"Okay." Tabita leaned forward. "Tell us."

Jesse paused for a few seconds, not because he needed to think, but because he didn't want to sound abrupt with his news. "Your son is responsible for a lot of what we have been going through over the past few months."

Simon and Tabita gave each other the same confused look at the same moment, then Simon leaned forward. "What do you mean? What is this about my son?"

Jennifer sensed a need for diplomacy and decided to take over the conversation. "We received some information, which may or may not be true, that Jaron was involved with an organization that helped Bernard and Amber take over our house." She told the Beloos everything that Bernard had explained, from his bitterness over Bernard's parents' foreclosure, to the dead dog and the death threat. By the time she had finished, the smiles on the Beloos' faces had given way to anger and distress.

Tabita was the first to speak after a long uncomfortable silence. "I don't understand this. How can you accuse my son based on the words of someone who tried to steal your house from you?"

"This is not just based on what Bernard said, "Jennifer shot back." The fact is, my husband's key is missing. And the police detective said that whoever dropped off that dead dog was likely someone who lived in the neighborhood."

"It could have been anyone." Tabita's voice was sharp. "My son would not do something like this. And the police talked to us the same day it happened. If he did that, why haven't they arrested him?"

"Then let us talk to him, get it cleared up," Jesse suggested. "And to be honest, I hope you're right." But Jesse knew that he wasn't.

Tabita looked at her husband. "Get him."

Simon obeyed immediately, rising up and walking out of the room. Jesse and Jennifer were left in the room with Tabita, who did not look at them, her scowl becoming more prominent by the minute. Jennifer could feel their friendship slowly slipping away.

After a few minutes, Simon returned with Jaron. Jaron was a tall young man, with his braids hanging down the back of his neck like tentacles. His face looked curious; Simon had not briefed him before they walked in the room.

Simon returned to his seat beside his wife, while Simon stood near the doorway. He did not plan to stay long.

"Son," Simon started, "our neighbors … "

Our neighbors? Jesse thought. *No longer calling us Jesse and Jen? We're like mud to them now.*

" … say you are involved with the plot to take over their house."

Jesse and Jennifer studied his reaction carefully.

Jaron furrowed his brow, sucked his teeth, and said, "I ain't had nothing to do with that."

Jesse expected that response. He had some questions ready. "Why does Bernard say he got the key to my house from you?"

"I dunno. He's lying."

"Really? He's lying? He just *happens* to know about the Christmas dinner party. He also *happens* to know that you took our coats that night, and that you took my keys out of the coat pocket and removed the basement key. And that is the key that just *happens* to be missing from my key ring."

Jaron could see he was being backed into a corner, so he conceded, if only to give himself another escape route. "Yeah, I talk to Bernard. His mother and father and I were good friends. I told him about the party. That's how he knew enough about it to lie on me."

"And what about the key that's missing from my key ring,

which he said you stole."

"He's lying. He probably stole it from you, or maybe somebody else did."

"Like who?"

"Maybe Lottie did it. She comes over your house all the time. Maybe she stole your key. Or maybe it was too easy for you to believe *I* did it, since I'm one of the only black men in this neighborhood."

Jennifer fired back in Jesse's defense. "Don't make this about race. My husband doesn't have a racist bone in his body."

Tabita stood. "I don't want this to become an argument. My son says he didn't do it."

Jaron determined this was as good a time as any to make his exit. "Can I leave now?"

Tabita glared at Jesse. "Do you have any more questions for him?"

Jesse never took his eyes off Jaron. "No, I don't."

Jaron turned and started to leave.

"Jaron, wait."

Jaron turned back at the sound of Jesse's voice. Jesse stood, positioning himself so that Jaron could see his eyes, the sincerity on them, and know that he was not bluffing. "In about five minutes, my wife and I are going back to our house. Then I'm going to call Detective Hartley and tell him everything that I learned from Bernard, and everything that Perrin told me."

The mention of Perrin's name made Jaron's face twitch. He hadn't thought that Jesse had spoken to Perrin.

"It may not happen right away, but you will eventually be

arrested on at least three charges. Enough to send you to jail well past your 30th birthday."

Jaron kept a straight face, barely revealed that his jaw was clenched so tight it could have crushed walnuts. He looked briefly at his parents hoping they had something to say in his defense, but they only sat there bewildered.

"Another option is, you could tell me the truth." Jesse managed a slight smile, indicating that this was his preferred option. "If you confess, then that's the beginning of remorse. And that's a good step. And my wife and I will be vindicated in the eyes of your parents. And the only people who will know about this are the five people in this room."

Jaron dropped his gaze to the floor.

Jesse continued. "You tell me a lie, and you have a lot to lose. Tell me the truth, and you have a lot to gain."

Jaron moved his eyes in the direction of his parents. Simon and Tabita were watching him, then watching Jesse, then watching him, almost as if they were viewing a tennis match. Jaron finally lifted his eyes to meet Jesse's and struck a prideful posture. "I ain't have nothing to do with this." He turned and left.

The four that remained were silent for a moment as they searched for something to say, neither looking at any of the others, except Jennifer, who had her eyes on her husband. When it had reached the point where the silence would have been just as awkward as any attempt at conversation, Jesse met his wife's eyes and tilted his head, alerting her that it was time to leave. "Well, I guess this conversation is over," Jesse finally announced.

Jennifer stayed put, urging Jesse with her eyes not to

leave yet, not this way. A hard sigh from Tabita momentarily distracted Jesse.

"Are you really going to have my son arrested?" Tabita's question was not so much a question as it was a plea.

Knowing that his wife would be whole-heartedly in favor of forbearance, Jesse relented. "I give Jaron 24 hours. If he does not confess the truth by the time I get out of church tomorrow, I *will* call Detective Hartley."

Simon and Tabita sat quietly, looking like scorned lovers. Jesse, with another tilt of his head, finally got Jennifer to her feet.

"I guess we shouldn't expect invitations to this year's Christmas party," Jesse said. "We'll show ourselves out."

Simon and Tabita waited until Jesse and Jennifer had left before they looked at one another, wondering what in the world had just happened.

* * *

"Jesse, why did we leave so quickly?" The question came as soon as they were out of the Beloos' door and were halfway across the lawn to their own home. "We shoulda tried to smooth things over with 'em. They're friends of ours."

"They'll still be our friends."

"How so?"

"They didn't want to confess it, but they knew I was right. Simon and Tabita may love their son, but they are not stupid people," Jesse said. "They are going to go back to their son with this. They are going to question him more directly than I could. And whether they get the truth out of him or not, they know he's guilty."

They reached the driveway of their home and stood, facing each other, in the middle of it. "I'm surprised Jaron didn't go for your offer," Jennifer noted. "It would keep him out of jail."

"He doesn't trust me. He figures if he tells the truth, I would get him arrested anyway."

"Is that true?" Jennifer wasn't sure if Jesse's offer to keep him out if jail was legit, or if he was just bluffing to get Jaron to confess.

"I wasn't lying to him," Jesse explained. "If he'd told me the truth, I would have kept my promise. And it's still not too late."

Special Guests

* * *

The next day there were bright sunny skies with barely a hint of clouds. Local meteorologists had been predicting an arid, summer-like day, and local residents were taking the news in stride. Convertibles whizzed by on open roads with the tops down. Shorts and tank tops appeared to be the necessary fashion choice for the day, and parks and playgrounds were teeming with kids playing, burgers grilling, and joggers and bicyclists trying to melt off those winter pounds. On a day like today, Harvest of Righteousness Fellowship was usually light in volume, as some people would ordinarily skip church and spend the day outside.

But today, as Jesse peeked out into the sanctuary after the morning ministers' prayer, every available chair in the 200-seat sanctuary was filled, a feat that could only be attributable to the Holy Spirit. It was one of those days Jesse wished he were preaching, but his father was on the preaching schedule, and Jesse knew that Rodereck, a man of protocol, would likely not make any changes.

Jesse admired his wife, sitting in the front row wearing a pretty peach sleeveless dress with white polka-dots. Though he would have loved to focus on her more, he shifted his eyes to the right, where Bernard and Amber sat next to his wife. Amber seemed excited to be there, while Bernard looked as if he were expecting birds to attack him at any second. His eyes turned left and saw his kids, sitting next to Jennifer, fidgeting as they waited for service to start.

This was a proud moment for Jesse. Over the past few weeks, he had been giving regular reports to the congregation about his housing situation and how he wanted to reach Bernard and Amber. He asked the congregation to pray for his family and for the MacNichols. And pray, they did. Now, here was Bernard and Amber in church for the first time. Maybe that was why the church was packed. The Lord didn't want anyone to miss this.

The service started normally, with worship and praise for about 30 minutes, followed by the offering. Then came the announcements. Elena Ruiz took to the podium, looked out over the crowd with a smile, and said, "I would like all of the visitors to remain seated. Harvest, let's all give a great Harvest Fellowship welcome to all of our visitors!"

All of the members of the church stood and applauded. Many of them reached out and shook hands or hugged anyone who was seated. The usher handed them special acknowledgement cards.

Elena continued. "As special as all of our visitors are, we have some very special guests with us this morning. Sister Jennifer, would you please introduce your special guests."

Jennifer stood, her white wedge sandals giving her an extra two inches of height above the rest of the congregation. "Most of you know about the challenges we have had with our house over the past few months. And I want to thank you so much for your prayers, because God has heard them. Yesterday morning, we moved back into our house."

Her statement prompted a standing ovation and an eruption of praise and worship. Jesse, on the stage with Rodereck and five other ministers, stood and joined in the ovation. He looked back at his father, who was applauding, but seemed nonplussed.

Once the applause had died down, Jennifer continued. "Now, you may be wondering what happened to the couple who had taken over our home. Well, my husband and I did not want to see them homeless, so once they agreed to give us back the house, we agreed to let them continue to live there until they found a place of their own."

Amens and nods of agreement came from the congregation. Rodereck shifted in his seat.

"And I want you know, they are here with me today and will be coming to church with us *every* Sunday." With an upward motion of Jennifer's hand, Bernard and Amber stood. "Please welcome Bernard and Amber MacNichol."

Once again the crowd stood to its feet, faced Bernard and Amber, and applauded. Some of them let out whoops of praise. Others expressed their approval with loud whistles and shouts. The outpouring of love touched Amber and somewhat embarrassed Bernard, but he enjoyed it nonetheless.

Rodereck studied his congregation, the 150 members, the 25 or so regular attendees who had not yet become members, and the rest visitors. All of them were joyful and excited and thanking God, some with smiles, others with fist pumps of victory. Some of the members stepped across the aisle to hug Bernard and Amber. This was as good an outcome as they could have hoped to have.

But this was not the outcome that Rodereck would have engineered. And as he observed the approbation from his congregation and the ministers on his platform, Rodereck felt, for the first time in many years, deeply ashamed.

* * *

After church, as Jesse headed to his car with his family and the MacNichols in tow, he didn't think the day could have gone any better. As they drove home, he prayed that he would find a message from Jaron Beloo on his answering service, agreeing to confess his indiscretions.

As he pulled in the driveway, the kids noticed a grey sedan in Lottie's driveway. To them, that was good news.

Aiden was the first to ask. "Mom, Dad, can we go over to Lottie's house? Carrie and Kaitlyn are there." Carrie was Lottie's daughter, and Kaitlyn was Carrie's 10-year-old daughter.

"Sure," Jennifer answered.

"But not until you change out of your church clothes," Jesse added, turning off the ignition. Aiden and Ashley pulled open the car doors and jumped out, running up to the front door to await their parents.

Amber stepped out next, followed by Bernard. She looked up at the kids bobbing on the front porch and said to Bernard,

"I'd be nice to have our own kids some day."

"Lord willing, you will." Jesse stepped out of the car, followed by Jennifer. Jennifer stayed back to chat with Bernard and Amber, while Jesse went up to the porch to unlock the front door. Once he did, the kids scurried inside like mice and headed to their rooms. Jesse was only a little less excited to go to his. It was where they kept the answering machine.

Jesse walked into the bedroom and checked the number of messages on the machine. There were three. Still hope. Jaron could be one of the three.

He listened to the first one. It was Lottie, telling them she had just returned from Mass and that her daughter and granddaughter were visiting. Bring the kids and come say hello.

Jesse erased that one.

The next one was a hearty congratulations from a member of the church in getting his house back. He saved that one, desiring Jennifer to hear it once she came in the house.

There was one message left. It was from Tabita Beloo. Jesse let out a sigh of relief.

But as he listened, it became clear that his relief was premature. Tabita's voice explained that Jaron had packed his things sometime during the night and moved out. Then she hung up the phone, without a goodbye.

Just then, Jesse had a harrowing thought. What if Jaron felt just as threatened by the Reclaim Network as Perrin did? Perrin had already confessed that the Reclaim Network was not above hurting people to protect its interests. He wondered if Jaron was simply afraid to tell the truth.

Jesse sat down and buried his head in his hands. Giving

Jaron an ultimatum was a serious miscalculation. Instead of giving him a choice between jail and freedom, it was actually a choice between jail and a contract on his head. No wonder Jaron decided to run.

Jennifer walked in shortly after.

"Got a message from Tabita," Jesse said.

"I know. I just talked to her." Jennifer's sullen look was enough to convince Jesse that the conversation did not go well. "She told me that Jaron ran away last night. And she blames us for that."

"Figured as much."

"How can we make it up to her?"

"I assume flowers and candy won't cut it?" Jesse stood and shut the door to their bedroom, in case the kids could hear them. "Jaron ran because he's guilty. The Beloos have to know that by now."

"But why?" Jennifer asked, confused. "So he doesn't trust you. Would that cause him to run away?"

"I think Jaron and Perrin were both tied in to a higher level at the Reclaim Network. That's why they both were so tight-lipped about what was going on. There's some higher-ups that would likely hurt them if they gave up too much."

"So, why ain't Bernard and Amber in danger?"

"They weren't in that deep. They dealt with Perrin and Jaron, and that's it. Jaron and Perrin dealt with somebody higher up. Somebody we don't know about."

"So, what do we do now?"

Jesse walked over to the answering machine. "We give Tabita and Simon a little time. Until then, we cut our losses and move on with our lives."

Louis N. Jones

Jesse erased Tabita's message on the answering machine.

Adverse Possession

Amends, Amens and Loose Ends

* * *

For the next five weeks, Amber and Bernard kept their commitments and followed through with everything the Kanes required of them. Bernard started working a janitorial job at the church, and started slowly coming out of his depression. Amber worked in the kitchen to help prepare meals for special events and for the church social every third Sunday after service. The Kanes required them to attend counseling sessions with a minister from the church. Although they were not obligated to attend services, Amber enjoyed her exposure to the church and would attend anyway, dragging her husband along. She became the chief driver behind their efforts to improve their lives, mostly because Amber was tired of living life beneath her purpose, also because she wanted to call her family in Westchester, and tell them she was doing well, without lying. She looked forward to the day they could have their own house and invite her family down for visits.

Amber also became a capable babysitter for Aiden and

Adverse Possession

Ashley, drawing on her experience babysitting her younger siblings in New York. Aiden had developed a crush on Amber, and wanted to spend most of his time around her when she was at home. Jesse and Jennifer did not discourage the crush, but knew they would have to have some pointed conversations with him about his feelings and how to deal with them as a Christian. Bernard, on the other hand, thought it was cute, commenting that he might have been jealous if Aiden were 15 years older.

It was a beautiful arrangement to both the Kanes and the MacNichols, but for some reason, Rodereck was silent about it. For several weeks after, Jesse waited for the day that Rodereck would approach him and tell him his true opinions about the arrangement, but that day never came.

Until now.

It was a warm Sunday in May. After church that day, Rodereck invited Jesse and Jennifer to dinner, something that he rarely did. So, Jesse guessed that this would be the day he would finally hear how his father felt about the MacNichols living with him.

Rodereck had made reservations at McCormick & Schmicks, a popular seafood restaurant. Jesse and Jennifer left their car at the church and rode with Rodereck to Fort Washington, Maryland, about a 30-minute drive. The restaurant was nestled at the banks of the Potomac River, and surrounded by acres of retail, office space, hotels, and restaurants in a waterfront development called National Harbor. Once they arrived, the hostess led them to seats outside, just yards away from the river and a boat pier. People milled around near the banks of the river, and children played on *the Awakening*, a huge aluminum sculpture of a giant trying to free itself from the golden sand near the river's edge. The edges of a green umbrella shade above their table flapped in a light breeze.

After they had placed their orders, Rodereck looked out at the harbor, clearly uncomfortable with the subject he had come here to discuss. After a few minutes, during which all three of them gazed out upon the river, Rodereck finally broke the silence. "So, how's the MacNichols working out?"

Jesse twirled his straw in his glass of ice water. "They're working out good, Dad. They've been a real blessing for us, as well as the church. I'm not sure Bernard is totally on board with all this, but at least he's not fighting it."

Rodereck nodded. "Yeah. He's likely going along just because he's living in your house, and he doesn't want to upset his wife."

"Well, what does the scripture say? *'That they may be won over by the behavior of their wives?'* Amber's really been into this thing, and I hope she can influence her husband."

"And you're confident the Lord told you to shelter the MacNichols in this way?"

"Yes."

"Not many people would have done what the two of you have done." Rodereck stopped when the waiter brought an appetizer of coconut shrimp to the table. Once the waiter had left, Rodereck continued. "I mean, I wouldn't have done it."

"That wasn't the call of God on your life," Jesse noted, talking between bites of shrimp. "You weren't in agreement with us going to Haiti, but we did it, and it was a wonderful trip. Sometimes, when God calls us, others that did not get that call reject it, say it is a mistake. But at some point, they get the revelation. God was really working in that situation."

"Well, I have to admit, the church is really speaking positively about what you have done. I wish you had told me about it before you announced it to the church."

"Dad, I didn't want to tell you at the time because, frankly, you can be very negative sometimes, and I didn't need to hear that coming from you."

Rodereck cast his gaze down at the half-empty shrimp plate, a look of hurt yet understanding coming over his face. "Yes, I can be negative sometimes. But with all the church members talking about the wonderful Jesse and Jennifer Kane and how they took under their wing the people who tried to steal their home, I've done some reevaluating."

Rodereck devoured a few pieces of shrimp while waiting for Jesse to give him the cue to continue.

"Reevaluating what?" Jesse asked.

Rodereck continued. "Myself, and my competence as far as being compassionate and merciful. You know me. I'm a business man. In business you have to be tough. You can't afford unbridled compassion. You can't wear your heart on your sleeve. So, when there's a conflict between human interest and business, business will always win out."

"Which means you'll have a lot of money," Jesse said. "But not one person who can say, 'Pastor Rodereck truly cared for me.'"

Rodereck turned to Jennifer. "I don't know how much Jesse has told you about my history, how I started my church."

"He's told me quite a bit," Jennifer responded, darting her eyes to Jesse, seeking silent validation of her words. "I know you were an assistant pastor at one church, but you left it and started your own."

"Well, I didn't leave on friendly terms. Pastor Seagraves thought I was trying to take over the church, and he resisted that. So, I left and started my own church, and I took half his congregation with me. Most of those people have since moved on."

"Why?" Jesse asked a question he already knew the answer to.

"I guess my prosperity and faith message was exciting for a while, but it began to get old." Rodereck averted his gaze down to the table while he spoke. "People needed more substance in their ministry, and I wasn't providing that."

Jesse was stunned silent. He couldn't believe his father was being this vulnerable and transparent. What brought this on?

"Anyway, when I saw how the congregation responded when you told them about your victory with Bernard and Amber, I got a little jealous." Rodereck pulled his glass of water closer to him and almost seemed to hold on to it for comfort. "Well, a lot jealous. I hadn't seen the congregation that gleeful in a while. And I thought, this was exactly how Pastor Seagraves felt when my popularity began to rise in his church. He felt threatened. And when I saw how that crowd responded to both of you, I felt the same way."

What goes around comes around, Jesse thought. But he dared not share his thought. He didn't want to antagonize his father while he was in the middle of a rare moment of spilling his guts. Jesse remained silent, nodding his head slightly, looking empathetic.

"So, I figured I could respond by either going to war with you, which is what Pastor Seagraves did with me. Or, I could find out what juice you are serving to the congregation and serve it up myself. And we know how the first option turned out for Pastor Seagraves. He lost half his members. So I thought, instead of trying to beat 'em, why not join 'em?"

"And what does that look like for you?" Jennifer asked.

"Not sure. Maybe it means toning down the business rhetoric in my messages and preaching to the real needs of people. And I'm not sure I've been doing a good job of that."

"It's good that you recognize that," Jesse stated.

"Maybe there's a lot I could learn from you in that area," Rodereck said. "If you could stomach the idea of teaching your old man a thing or two."

Jesse nodded and smiled. "By all means, Dad."

Rodereck continued, speaking to Jesse. "You and I? We need to work together as partners to lead the congregation to what God is calling them into. I'm 55 years old. I'm too old for petty battles that go nowhere."

Jesse nodded. He was heartened by Rodereck's words, and felt as if he was going to float straight out of the restaurant. He felt Jennifer's hand under the table on his knee. "I got you, Dad. No problem."

Rodereck then turned to Jennifer. "Jen, my understanding is that your parents have been issued a writ of possession. Is that correct?"

Jennifer looked shocked. "I hadn't heard that." She looked briefly at Jesse, then back at Rodereck. "I spoke with them a few days ago, and they never mentioned it to me."

"I think it happened within the last couple of days. It's only a matter of a few days before the Knox County Sheriff puts them out."

"Oh, dear." Sadness came across Jennifer's face. "I didn't know they were this far along. And my Pa is so stubborn. He doesn't want us to help."

Rodereck decided to let the tense mood linger in the air for a few minutes before he smiled and said, "Well, there's good news."

Jesse and Jennifer leaned forward slightly.

"I have instructed our attorney in Knoxville to cancel the writ." Rodereck saw the beginnings of a wider smile on Jesse. "The owner is willing to enter into a one-year lease with us, so your parents can stay for another year, if they want."

Jesse nodded. "Dad, that's great news."

Jennifer, however, was not as impressed. "I appreciate that, sir, but my Pa was very insistent on not accepting any more help from me or the church. When he hears about this, he's gonna think I was involved."

"I spoke with your dad this morning." Rodereck pulled his glass of iced tea close to him. "Looks like receiving the writ has humbled him a bit. He has no other options, and he has only a few days, if that many, so he was willing to listen. Bottom line is, your dad's going to accept the deal."

Jennifer brightened. "Are you serious?"

"It's done." Rodereck took a sip of his tea. "Now, this is the last time the church will do this. After a year, we're done. Your parents know that, and they understand that. There will be no further extensions."

"That's more than fair." Jennifer looked at Jesse and saw the agreement in his face. "This is really exciting." Turning back to Rodereck, she said, "Pastor, thank you so much."

"No, I'm doing this to thank *you*." Rodereck noticed

Jennifer's questioning face. "I've been really hard on you the past few years. I'm sure it's no secret that I didn't think you were a suitable wife for my son."

Jennifer nodded, finding his words both truthful and unsurprising.

"Over the years, however, looking at you, and how you showed yourself to be a virtuous woman to my son, and raised two wonderful children, I can honestly say that he's blessed to have you."

Jennifer felt her eyes getting misty. Rodereck had rarely said anything kind about her, but those words had made up for the 10-year drought.

"You hung in there with my son through all this, and demonstrated just how beautiful a woman you really are. You remind me of Jesse's mother. Back then, I was too stupid to realize that's the kind of woman she was."

Jesse handed her a tissue out of her purse. Jennifer started to dab her eyes with it.

"So, I guess this dinner is also my way of saying that I'm sorry for not believing in you. For treating you like a distant acquaintance instead of my daughter-in-law."

Rodereck looked across the room, his eyes meeting the waiter who was serving their table. Rodereck gave a small nod, and the waiter disappeared into another room. Moments later, the waiter emerged with 12 long-stem roses in a box wrapped with a red ribbon, and handed them to Jennifer.

Jennifer gasped as she received them, her mouth wide open, her gaze focused intently on the box of flowers. "Pastor Rodereck, this is so nice." She left her chair and went over to hug Rodereck. Rodereck stood and took her in his embrace.

The hug lasted for almost 20 seconds before Jennifer returned to her seat. She grabbed Jesse's hand under the table and squeezed it gently, while Jesse dabbed away at moisture in his own eyes.

Jesse looked at her father admiringly. Rodereck had blessed his wife so sweetly that Jesse believed that his father had gone through a metamorphosis, or a catharsis spurred by Jesse and Jennifer's selfless kindness toward the MacNichols. It was a side of his father that he had seen all too rarely.

Rodereck raised his glass to toast. "So I say we eat, be merry, and celebrate new beginnings. For the MacNichols. For the Trudeaus. And for the Kanes."

Jesse and Jennifer raised their glasses, and the three of them clinked them together.

"Hear, hear," said Jesse.

While Rodereck went to do some window shopping at the mall, Jesse and Jennifer went to a boat pier and sat on the edge, looking out over the Potomac River, their legs dangling over the churning water. Jennifer held the box of flowers in her hand as if she were cradling a baby.

"Good day, huh?" Jesse remarked.

"Good day indeed," Jennifer said, smiling at him.

"Can you believe my father?"

"I'm still checking to make sure I'm not dreaming."

"Well, that's God for you. He makes dreams come true."

"Yes, He does."

"At least my dad's getting clean. I wish I could."

Jennifer turned to him. "What do you mean?"

"I still got some guilt."

"The Beloos? Honey, I'm sure they'll come around at some point."

"Not just that."

"What else?"

"The picture."

"Picture?"

"Yeah. The photo. The one I used as a bargaining chip to get Perrin to talk to us. The guy was a pedophile. And I just let him go free. I don't feel good about that."

"Well, you can still take action," Jennifer noted. "You can turn the photos in to the police. You won't be breakin' any agreement by doin' that, 'cause Perrin never kept his end of the bargain by bringing you the money."

"No. The police will wonder why I took so long to turn in the photos," Jesse explained. "But I got another idea."

* * *

The sun hung low in the Western sky, and the streetlights along Morgan Place had just started to flicker to life. Jesse pulled the Armada into a parking space as far from 456 Morgan as possible. He did not want Perrin Houtin to notice him inadvertently, in case he was still living in the house.

He got out of the vehicle and followed the sidewalk to a house across from 456 Morgan Place. He walked up the steps, dropped a kraft file folder on the stoop, and rang the doorbell once. He then scrambled down the steps and hurried up the street, hoping that he could get back in his car before anyone answered the door.

He was not successful. The woman came to the door and

saw Jesse just as he was halfway up the block.

The woman called out to him. "Hello? Excuse me!"

Jesse ignored her, climbing into his vehicle.

The woman picked up the envelope on her stoop. Opening it quickly, she gasped as she saw the photos of her daughter, along with a note written on Joe Lippman's letterhead:

Hi:

I took these photographs a few months ago of your daughter and Perrin Houtin, the man who lives at 456 Morgan Place. I used them initially to force Perrin to give me some information, but now I realize I cannot keep them to myself. I trust you will use these as an opportunity to counsel your daughter, and protect her, and hopefully many other young girls, from a person like Perrin Houtin.

If you have questions about these photographs, you may contact my attorney, Joe Lippman, at the number in the letterhead. God bless you.

The note was unsigned.

Jesse started the Armada and pulled out of the parking space. As he waited for the traffic light at Porter Street, he looked in his rearview mirror and saw the woman, with flaring nostrils and tense muscles, walking up the street, hoping to catch his car before the light changed.

Jesse smiled as the light changed, and he turned the Armada left on Porter. He was okay with letting squatters stay in his home for a year. He was also okay with not pressing charges on the young man who had stolen his house keys. Yet he could not—and would not—allow a child molester to continue to ply his trade unabatedly.

Confident that an angry mother would see justice done more effectively than he ever could, Jesse continued to drive toward Connecticut Avenue on his way to his house.

And to home.

Louis N. Jones

Did you enjoy this book? You may also enjoy the following selected books by Louis N Jones

Prodigal in the City

The Colors Will Change

Wallflowers in the Kingdom

For more books by Louis N Jones, go to:

www.louisnjones.com

CPSIA information can be obtained at www.ICGtesting.com
Printed in the USA
LVOW08s2131260715

447743LV00003B/137/P

9 780988 380974